Coming Home to Cariad Cove

Darcie Boleyn has a huge heart and is a real softy. She never fails to cry at books and movies, whether the ending is happy or not. Darcie is in possession of an overactive imagination that often keeps her awake at night. Her childhood dream was to become a Jedi but she hasn't yet found suitable transport to take her to a galaxy far, far away. She also has reservations about how she'd look in a gold bikini, as she rather enjoys red wine, cheese and loves anything with ginger or cherries in it – especially chocolate. Darcie fell in love in New York, got married in the snow, rescues uncoordinated greyhounds and can usually be found reading or typing away on her laptop.

Also by Darcie Boleyn

A Very Merry Manhattan Christmas
Love at the Italian Lake
Love at the Northern Lights

Conwenna Cove

Summer at Conwenna Cove
Christmas at Conwenna Cove
Forever at Conwenna Cove

Cornish Hearts

The House at Greenacres
The Cottage at Plum Tree Bay
The Christmas Tea Shop

DARCIE BOLEYN

Coming Home to Cariad Cove

CANELO

First published in the United Kingdom in 2022 by

Canelo
Unit 9, 5th Floor
Cargo Works, 1–2 Hatfields
London, SE1 9PG
United Kingdom

A CIP catalogue record for this book is available from the British Library.

Print ISBN 978 1 80032 379 7
Ebook ISBN 978 1 80032 378 0

Look for more great books at www.canelo.co

Printed and bound in Great Britain by Clays Ltd, Elcograf S.p.A.

For my husband, children and dogs, with love always.

Chapter One

This wasn't how it was supposed to be…

Ffion Campbell's gaze roamed over the dark amber sand, the slate-grey expanse of wintery sea, and the rugged cliffs studded with trees and bushes. Everything looked shutdown, sparse, uninviting.

I should be here with him, with children, to celebrate good times.

The place where she'd grown up had never looked less appealing, although a small voice at the back of her mind whispered that it was because of her pain and not the location itself. She gave a wry laugh at the name Cariad Cove because for her, love meant loss and pain. Cariad was the Welsh word for love, and the cove was originally named Cildraeth Cariad, but over the years the English and Welsh had merged and it had become known as Cariad Cove.

Her eyes stopped when they locked on the hotel nestled in the Welsh cove. Its white façade had always reminded her of a face because of the two arched windows on the first floor that overlooked the beach, the French doors beneath like a wide mouth and the black roof tiles resembling hair or a hat. At night, when the lights glowed in the windows, the comparison was even more striking. The sight of the hotel had made her happy all her life but now, it felt almost as if it was mocking her. She had gone away, built a life elsewhere, glimpsed the joys of being married to a man she loved, but the hotel had remained: smiling and unchanged, whereas she was changed beyond all recognition and would never be the same again.

Cariad Cove had been home for twenty-one years, then Ffion had left, heading to Perthshire in Scotland where she'd lived happily until thirteen months ago when the sky had fallen in on her world.

And now she was back in Wales.

Alone. Heartbroken. Lost. Floundering.

Instead of visiting with a brood of children and a loving Scottish husband at her side, she was widowed at thirty-two, childless and unemployed.

She had no idea what to do and so she had come to her former home, needing to rest, to find comfort from her family and, hopefully, to heal. Although how she could possibly do that, she had no idea.

—

Ffion grabbed her handbag, locked her car and walked around the back of the hotel to the kitchen entrance. She paused outside the door, aware that at this time of the afternoon preparations for the evening meal would be underway and she'd likely encounter some of the staff. But then she'd have to face them all at some point, so better to fake a smile and hurry through than to delay the inevitable. Like ripping off a plaster, this would be best done quickly.

She sucked in a deep breath and pushed open the door. The warmth hit her immediately like a welcoming hug after the chill of the February wind outside. Aromas of roasting meat, frying fish, rich tomato sauces and chopped herbs greeted her nostrils and her stomach growled. After the long drive, she realised she was hungry, something she hadn't felt too often lately, which explained why her belt was on the tightest hole and she'd layered up with a vest, long-sleeved T-shirt and baggy jumper underneath her duck down jacket. She was used to wearing lots of layers after living through so many Scottish winters but knew that it could get pretty cold here on the Gower Peninsula too.

'Ffion, bach? Is that you?'

She pulled off her beanie and smoothed her hair back. So Nerys was still calling her *bach* after all these years? Even though she wasn't so *small* these days. But then, it had been more a term of endearment than a physical reference after she'd reached adulthood.

'Hi Nerys.'

Ffion moved her lips into a smile as the duty manager hurried across the kitchen and placed her hands on Ffion's shoulders.

'Oh, bach, look at you. So good to see you but...' Nerys pressed her lips together, evidently controlling herself. 'Yes, it's good to see you. Your mam and dad will be glad you're home.'

'Thank you.' Ffion looked behind Nerys at the staff in the kitchen and gave a small wave which they returned.

'Lots of changes here over recent years but I'll introduce you properly to everyone once you've settled in.'

Nerys's green eyes were shining and Ffion knew she wanted to say more, but the duty manager was ever the professional, used to controlling her emotions even with irate guests and grumpy delivery people.

'You go on through, Ffion, and if you give me your car key, I'll get your things taken to the cottage.'

Ffion was about to argue that there was no need, but knew that organising was Nerys's way of showing she cared, so she got the key from her bag and handed it to the older woman.

'Thank you. There's not much really… just two suit-cases and a few boxes.'

'Is the rest of it following?' Nerys frowned.

Ffion shook her head. 'I… didn't want to bring much with me. Travelling light.' She gave a small laugh even though inside, her heart was aching.

'Go and find your mam. She's desperate to see you.'

Ffion nodded then passed through the kitchen and into the restaurant. She hadn't been back in two years because life in Scotland had been so busy, then Graeme had become unwell and leaving Scotland – and his side – had seemed impossible. Rounds of tests had followed their initial attempts to ignore his condition (*if we ignore it, perhaps it'll go away*), then treatments, more tests and hushed conversations with specialists that never seemed to provide the answers Ffion had wanted to hear. However, being back in the hotel now, passing through rooms she'd walked through so many times before, she could almost pretend that none of it had ever happened. She was eighteen years old again, embarking upon an exciting degree in PR and Media at Swansea University while working evenings and weekends at her family's hotel; happy, healthy, enthusiastic about life. She closed her eyes for a moment, keen to grab on to that feeling if only to escape the pain for a moment.

'Ffion.'

The voice snapped Ffion's eyes open and there she was.

Petite. Brunette. Arms open wide.

It had been so long. Too long.

Ffion staggered forwards into the woman's embrace.

'Oh Mam…'

Chapter Two

Settled in front of the log burner at her parents' cottage on the hotel grounds, Ffion cradled a mug of tea between her hands. She'd gone to the hotel because she'd known her mam would be working but had hoped she would be able to find some time to have a cup of tea and a chat.

After her mam had hugged her in the hotel restaurant, she'd told Ffion to go over to the cottage and get the kettle on and she'd be right behind her. That had been half an hour ago and Ffion was still alone and on her second mug of tea. It was what Ffion and her older sister Mari had come to expect, growing up with both parents owning and running a popular hotel. Their parents were warm and loving, had given them everything they could want, but they both worked hard and the family business had to be prioritised unless there was a major emergency.

It was one of the reasons why Ffion had stayed in Scotland in the time immediately after Graeme's passing – as well as the all-consuming numbness and shock, of course. She hadn't wanted to get in the way for her parents, had known that her presence would have taken their attention from the hotel, made them feel that they had to be there for Ffion rather than work, and she'd have hated to be a burden to them. She had also remained in Perth because she still had her job and home and was clinging to her memories of her time with Graeme. Unfortunately, returning to work too soon after losing Graeme had led to a breakdown of sorts. It had all simply become too much and Ffion had been overwhelmed.

During that time, she had quit her beloved job as a communications and engagement officer for Dundee Council, despite her caring line manager's attempts to get her to take some time off instead. Unemployed, she'd spent days cooped up inside the home she'd bought with Graeme, hours lying in bed trying to sleep away the time, ignoring the finances that needed attention, the phone that rang constantly, and the knocks at the door. Eventually, her in-laws had let themselves in with their key, taken one look at Ffion and made her an appointment with the doctor. Never particularly affectionate towards her, they had been cool and practical, managing their own grief at the loss of their son while trying to help the daughter-in-law they'd never really seemed to care for. It had hurt Ffion even then, even after losing Graeme, that despite her attempts over the years to prove that she was good enough for their son, that she did make Graeme happy, his parents couldn't seem to thaw towards her.

Medication, counselling and Netflix had got her through the next few months and her mother-in-law, Bonnie Campbell, an experienced bookkeeper who'd run the family estate with a keen eye throughout the years of her marriage, had sorted out Ffion's finances. It had, Ffion supposed, been her way of showing that she cared what happened to Graeme's wife – or at least his estate – although there were times when Ffion yearned for a hug and a chat far more than financial security. If Bonnie had just put her arms around Ffion, cried with her about their loss, then Ffion had felt sure it would have helped, but instead, Bonnie had been unemotional, aloof. As the medication had kicked in, Ffion had been able to enjoy the detachment it offered, and soon she'd displayed a form of outward control herself, and that had seemed to gain more approval from Bonnie than her distress had ever done.

Ffion's mam and dad had come to Perth several times over the past year but she knew it was difficult for them in more ways than one, and so she'd insisted that she was fine, and had hidden from them her distress, her weight loss and the insomnia that had started to plague her, vowing to herself that she would only come back to Wales when she'd regained some of her strength. Thirteen months on from losing Graeme, Ffion's world was unrecognisable. The house had been sold, furniture and more – including most of Graeme's clothes – given to charity shops. Graeme's life insurance had been squirrelled away in an ISA and some bonds that Bonnie had told her were a good investment, and Ffion finally felt ready to make the journey to Wales. She couldn't bear to touch the money Graeme's death had brought her, feeling that it was soiled by his loss and glad it was tucked away. She had the proceeds from the house in her current account and had settled all her bills and debts. Some might think she had a clean slate, another chance at life, though she'd have given her right arm to have her husband and her life in Perth back again.

'Hello, lovely, so sorry about that.' Her mam plonked herself down in the chair opposite Ffion, bringing with her the scent of violets from the perfume she'd used all her life, and placed a mug of tea on the small table at her side. 'It's always the bloody same, isn't it? I tell them all I'm off to spend some time with my girl and someone has a huge problem they can't possibly deal with alone.'

Her mam blew upwards in exasperation and her thick brown fringe lifted for a moment revealing heavy frown lines before settling again.

'It's fine, Mam.' Ffion smiled.

'Your dad will be over in a bit. He was handling a booking and it's taking him far longer than it should. We got one of those fancy new computer systems before Christmas and he's still getting to grips with it.'

'Poor Dad.'

'I know.' Her mam sighed. 'At some point we'll have to step back and let someone else manage the hotel, but even through the winter, we've been busy. It's like people are very keen to get away at the moment, desperate for a change of scenery. Good for business, obviously, but also exhausting.'

'Dad OK apart from his technology phobia?'

'Fine, love, yes. Still watching his cholesterol while sneaking chocolate brownies from the kitchen.' She laughed. 'But he gets in a good walk every day and does eat a lot of fish, so I cross my fingers and hope that the one cancels out the other.'

She sipped her tea and Ffion watched her, aware that something was different between them. Her mam had always been bubbly, effervescent, a whirlwind around the hotel and their home. As a parent, she'd been firm but fair, loving and supportive, warm and caring. Ffion had felt more relaxed with her than with anyone else except for her sister, Mari, but today, there was tension in the air. It was palpable but also signalled by her mam's avoidance of eye contact and in the way she picked absently at the jagged end of a nail until it came away in her fingers.

And Ffion knew what it was. Since she'd lost Graeme, everyone she'd known had been awkward around her, treating her like a china doll that might break at any moment. The fact that her mam felt the same way made her throat scratch and her head heavy. If the woman who gave birth to Ffion was struggling around her then how would she ever get back to any sense of normality? Would she ever be simply Ffion again, or would she forever carry the epithet *The Widow*?

'It's OK, Mam,' she said softly. 'Please treat me normally.'

'Normally?' Her mam's eyebrows rose. 'What do you mean, Ffion?'

'You seem... edgy, like you're walking on eggshells, and you don't need to be. I'm still me, Mam.' She blinked hard as her vision blurred and her throat tightened. 'I'm still me.'

'Oh love, I know. I know.' Her mam got up then crouched down at Ffion's side and took her hand. 'It's just been so hard. We've been terribly concerned about you. Your dad was beside himself with worry, walking the floorboards so often at night that he wore a groove in them, I swear. We tried to plan out how we could take turns being there for you, but you said not to come and time went on and... and...'

Ffion met her mam's pain-filled gaze and the lump in her throat expanded.

'It's bloody terrible knowing your baby girl is struggling and that you can't be there for her. There were nights when your dad and I would sit up in bed and talk about getting in the car and driving to you. We almost did a few times. Then we'd wonder if it would be what you wanted. You were so happy heading off to your life in Scotland and... we did wonder, now and then, if you went all that way to get away from us… some children do that, you know, and—'

'It was never that, Mam. I just fell in love with Graeme and our life was there. I missed you all the time.'

'I hoped it was that, love, but as a parent you never know for sure. We were torn between giving you space and coming to get you and bringing you home. I spoke to Bonnie about it but she insisted that you had to deal with… things in your own way. *Process them*, she said. Bit of a cold one she is, I think, at times, but then I feel dreadful because who am I to judge that poor woman? Losing a child is beyond comprehension and who knows how they'd cope if they were in that situation. I could never…' She shook her head and crossed herself, something she'd always done despite never being particularly religious, but Ffion knew it went back to her childhood and her own chapel upbringing.

'I know, Mam.'

Graeme's death had not just been hard on her, it had affected all of their family and friends too. Losing a young man in his prime was too much for most people to bear. Everyone had coped in their own way. Some cried, some baked cakes and lasagnes and some drifted away as if they could avoid the shadow of death by doing so.

'But I feel like I failed you, Ffion.'

'You didn't, Mam. I think I did need that time to come to terms with things. To clear my head a bit. The early days were just a haze, they blurred together, and then you did come and stay and I knew you were there. I was so grateful for that. But if you'd stayed longer, I might not have dragged myself out of the depths of it all, and I guess I had to do that.' She had learnt that the hard way; no one else could go through grief for her because no one else was feeling it exactly the way she was. It was her burden and a very heavy one indeed.

Her mam patted her hand then stood up. 'Time carries us forwards even if we don't feel like going.'

'That's true,' Ffion agreed.

'Have you been down to the beach?'

'Not yet.'

'A brisk walk will do you good.'

'You coming?'

'I would, love, but I have to see to a few things.'

'Of course.'

'You take your time and we'll have some supper together later. I'm so glad you've come home at last, Ffion. You can't understand how much peace of mind it gives me knowing that I can take care of you again.' Her mam pressed a kiss to the top of Ffion's head then left the room.

Ffion finished her lukewarm tea then pushed herself up out of the chair. Her mam was right; a walk along the beach would be good.

—

Ffion pulled on her hat and stuffed her feet into her walking boots. She checked the clock in the hallway and saw it was four forty-five, so she'd have about an hour before darkness fell, enveloping the beach in velvety blackness that could seem impenetrable.

Outside, the temperature seemed to have dropped significantly since she'd arrived, but then she had been sitting in front of a warm fire so would likely notice the difference more. She tugged gloves from her pockets and slid her hands into them, finding comfort from their softness next to her skin.

Ffion walked past the hotel and down the rough stone ramp to the beach. The tide was on the way out and the sand glistened in the weak late-afternoon light, a dun canvas ready to be decorated with boot imprints. Off to her right were the cliffs and the narrow tree-lined road that led to the coastal path, while to her left was the expanse of the beach, all 4 km of it. In the summer, the beach swarmed with tourists and locals, while in the colder months, locals had it mostly to themselves and could walk there to blow off the cobwebs and exercise their dogs along the sand. At the eastern end of the beach were more cliffs but at low tide, it was possible to walk around them and on to the connecting sands of Barddoniaeth Bay.

At the end of the stone ramp, Ffion stepped onto the coarse sand. Seagulls squawked overhead and the air was heavy with the tang of brine and the sulphurous aroma of green seaweed that lay in clumps, some of it tangled up with driftwood. She breathed deeply, dragging the cold air inside her and holding it there, finding reassurance in the familiarity of scents.

As she walked, droplets of water kicked up and landed on her jeans then sat like beads on the tops of her waterproof boots. Shells and shingle crunched beneath her soles while the water lapped at the shore with its perpetual push-pull motion. She walked closer to the sea and the sand sucked at her boots, making walking more of an effort.

She passed a few people, some walking alone or with dogs, couples with arms linked, eyes only for each other. Her heart squeezed. She'd walked along this beach with Graeme many times, since the early days of their relationship when they were both students at Swansea University, then later when they visited from Scotland. Their visits hadn't been that frequent because of her husband's fear of flying and because finding the time to drive all the way back to West Wales was difficult. Their weekends had been precious and the idea of sacrificing their alone time, the mornings of snuggling under the duvet, eating brunch at their favourite cafe on Saturdays and a lazy Sunday lunch in front of the TV, was something they hadn't been keen to do. Looking back, she wondered if it had been selfish of her, if she should have made more of an effort to come back, but then she wouldn't want to change a moment of her life with Graeme, a life she had loved and missed so deeply she felt like part of her had dropped off, leaving a gaping hole.

She stopped walking and gazed out to sea. The horizon was grey, the water dark and hostile in the cold air. She huddled deeper in her coat, tugged her hat lower over her ears. What would Graeme have done if the situation had been reversed? How would he have coped with losing her? Would he have been able to rebuild his life?

A tear trickled down her cheek and she brushed the back of her hand over it, wiping it away, exhausted by it all.

Suddenly, she was hit by a force that knocked her flying. She screamed as she landed on the sand with a thump and water flew up around her. Dazed, she shook her head as she tried to push herself up, aware as she did so that she was soaking wet and winded. She sucked in air, wheezing, the pain in her stomach now caused by an external force.

'Oh my god! I'm so sorry!'

A tall figure towered over her and she blinked as the shock of being thrown to the ground seeped away and the reality of being cold and wet sunk in.

She took the large hand that reached towards her and was gently lifted to her feet.

'I can't apologise enough. Are you OK? Please, please tell me you're OK.'

Blue eyes peered at her from underneath a black beanie. The lower half of the man's face was hidden by a scarf and he wore a navy wax jacket, waterproof trousers and wellington boots.

Ffion straightened her hat, found her breath, muttered, 'I'm fine.'

'I did call to you… to look out… but you seemed miles away. I thought perhaps you had earphones in or something and couldn't hear me.'

Ffion touched a hand to her right ear as if to check. 'No. I'm not wearing earphones. I was looking at the sea. Thinking.'

'I was playing Frisbee with Odin as we walked and when his focus is on the Frisbee, nothing gets in his way. I got distracted by a shell… and my throw was slightly off. The Frisbee went in your direction and before I knew it, he was heading straight for you.'

He gestured at the beach behind Ffion where a large black and brown dog was rooting around in the sand trying to get hold of a red Frisbee with his teeth. The dog's fur was wet and sandy but he seemed oblivious to everything other than his desire to dig the Frisbee out of the sand.

'I'd better help him or he'll eat half the beach.'

The man held up a hand as if to touch her arm then seemed to think better of it and dropped it to his side again. 'I really am sorry. And you're sure you're OK?'

'Yes.' *Not at all…*

'You'll be OK to get home?'

'Of course.' Ffion snapped now, keen to get away from this man and his giant sandy dog, to get back to the cottage and change into dry clothes. 'You should be more careful, though.'

He tugged at his collar with both hands as if it had suddenly become too tight. 'I should.'

He walked away, then leant over and prised the Frisbee from the sand. Ffion sighed. She was wet and cold and her arm was aching from where she'd fallen on it but apart from that, she was all right. It could have been worse, she reasoned. Might have been funny if it was a scene in a movie. She could just imagine the stage directions on the script: *Small Welsh woman knocked off her feet by large, excitable canine.*

She glanced once more at the tall man and his dog then turned back the way she'd come and headed for her parents' home. A bath and some dinner were in order, simple things that would help her to feel normal – or as close to normal as it was possible for her to feel these days; simple things that kept her going, even if they didn't ease the ache inside.

The grief counsellor had told her: *Keep moving. Keep breathing. Keep going through the motions. Most importantly, keep trying. And one day the pain will ease.*

Being knocked over by a giant dog might not be the best way to begin that process but she couldn't deny that it had shaken her from her melancholy and given her something else to worry about. It was hard to ignore the physical sensations of being wet and cold, of having the breath knocked from her body, of dealing with an apologetic stranger when she just wanted to get away. So even though she did feel mildly irritated at the dog walker, she also felt something else, even if it was just a desire to get dry and warm again.

Chapter Three

'Bore da!' Joe Thomas called as he opened the door to his aunt's Swansea home and let himself and Odin inside. 'It's only us.' He often used the Welsh greeting for 'good morning' when he arrived at his aunt's home, as if in preparation for his day at school where teachers were encouraged to use incidental Welsh with pupils.

Odin raced off through the large house, his claws pattering on the floors, and Joe smiled. It was the same every weekday when he brought Odin to spend the day here. The detached house in the Mumbles area of Swansea was two streets away from the seafront. It was set within a large garden that ran right around the house and surrounded by well-established hedges that afforded the property privacy from streets that became busy in the summer months.

In the kitchen, Joe found his aunt sitting at the old pine table, her iPad and a mug of steaming coffee in front of her. Odin was already sitting at her side as she rubbed at his ears and smoothed his giant head.

'Morning, Joe.' She looked up and smiled at her nephew. 'There's fresh coffee in the pot.'

'Thanks.' He set down the backpack containing Odin's things, went to the counter and poured coffee into a mug then sat opposite his aunt.

'What've you got today, then?' She pushed her reading glasses back into her blonde bobbed hair and looked at him.

'It's Wednesday so I have a double lesson with my year tens first, followed by PPA, early lunch, year seven then PPA.'

'Not a bad one, then?'

'It's always nice having PPA last.' PPA was time for planning and preparation and he appreciated having that time at the end of a day as it gave him a chance to catch his breath. Teaching was such a busy job, involving jumping from one task to the next and though Joe loved it, he'd be lying if he said he didn't find some days tiring. 'No meetings today either, so early finish.'

'Do you want to eat with us this evening?'

'What's on the menu?' He grinned.

'Spag bol.'

'You know I can't say no to that. Is Darryl making his garlic dough balls?'

'Of course.'

'Where is he this morning?'

'Gone for a run.' Caryn rolled her eyes. 'Doing that Couch to 5k that's all the rage. He has the time since he retired.'

'It's a good programme,' Joe said. 'We encourage the pupils to use it if they want to start running and I know a lot of the staff have done it too.'

'He wants me to go with him.' She pursed her lips.

'You should.'

'Joe, I am a fifty-nine-year-old retired nurse. I spent years pacing the wards, lifting patients of all shapes and sizes and battling to stay awake through night shifts. I had plenty of exercise throughout my career and it kept me in good health. However, I'm on the verge of turning sixty so do you really think I'm up to starting to run now?' She laughed, then sipped her coffee. 'Besides which, I get a walk with Odin at least five days a week so I'm doing all right.'

'Walking is brilliant exercise and I'm not denying that you're fit and healthy but if you wanted to start running, you could. Couch to 5k is a really good way to start... at any age.'

'I'll bear it in mind.'

She gave him the look he knew well, the one that told him that she was listening to him and did think he had a valid point, but she would do what she wanted as she always had done. Caryn was his mother's older sister. She was kind and witty but called a spade a spade and didn't let anyone walk over her. Joe loved her and she had been his rock over the years; there for him before and after he'd lost his mum, and not a day went by when he didn't feel that he owed her a great deal. When he'd said as much to her though, she'd shaken her head and told him not to be so daft. She said she loved him, he was her sister's boy and of course she'd always look out for him.

'I need to tell you about what Odin did yesterday.' He shook his head at the memory.

'Has he been misbehaving again?' Caryn raised her eyebrows.

'Not deliberately. We went for our usual evening walk along the beach and I was throwing the Frisbee for him...'

Odin's ears pricked up as he gazed at Joe.

'Not now, Odin. After work.' Joe held the dog's gaze as if to communicate that now was not the time for Frisbee.

'Was your daddy trying to wear you out, Odin?' Caryn leant over and kissed the dog's head.

'He loves that Fri… I mean, that *thing*.'

'Best not to name it.' Caryn's lips twitched in obvious amusement. 'He'll be nagging all day otherwise.'

'It's in the bag just in case you do want to take it with you to the park today.'

'Thanks for that.' Caryn smirked. 'So what happened?'

'I threw it, but I was a bit distracted and didn't spot the woman standing on the shore.'

Caryn's hand flew to her mouth. 'Oh no.'

'It was awful. With him being so big and running full pelt, he knocked the poor woman over.'

'Was she all right?' Caryn's eyes were wide now.

Joe frowned. 'I think so. I helped her up and initially she seemed a bit dazed but she'd been staring out to sea, like she was lost in her own world, so I think she was as surprised as Odin was.'

'Poor woman. That must have been a shock. Was it anyone you knew?'

'Never seen her before. Could be that she's a tourist or just someone taking a walk on the beach after work. I don't think she lives in Cariad Cove, but then I don't know everyone who lives there so…' He shrugged.

'Perhaps she's staying at the hotel?'

'It's possible. Then again, lots of people use that beach.' He sipped his coffee, his mind straying back to the moment when he'd rushed over to the woman and helped her up. In the late afternoon light, he'd seen dark eyes set in a pale face. A few strands of long brown hair that had escaped from her hat. A small straight nose. Nothing really and yet…

'What is it?' Caryn asked.

'What?'

'You look thoughtful.'

'Do I?'

'Now you're blushing.'

'Am I?'

'Stop answering me with questions, Joe. Don't forget I've known you since you were a tiny baby and I've been with you as you've grown into a man. You can try and hide things from me, but I can tell when there's something on your mind.'

'Can you?' He sniggered. 'Sorry, couldn't help that one.'

'Well if you don't want to talk about it, that's fine, but if you do, you know where I am.'

'Thanks.' He drained his coffee. 'I'd better get going if I'm going to make morning briefing.'

He swilled his mug in the sink, rubbed Odin's head, kissed Caryn's cheek then let himself out of her house.

But as he drove to school, it wasn't work on his mind. Instead, he was thinking about the woman from the beach again, wondering how she was, hoping that she hadn't hurt herself as she fell. There had been something about her, something in her deep dark eyes that had stirred something inside him. She'd seemed lost, vulnerable, sad. Joe hated to see anyone sad. He'd been there himself, knew how difficult life could be, but even in the dark moments, he was able to keep the faith that there would always be better days ahead. It was something Caryn had taught him after his mum died when he was sixteen. She'd encouraged him to grieve, to feel the sadness and not to try to shut it out. And she'd promised him that while he would always love his mum and always miss her, he'd wake up one day and find that the pain of his loss wasn't so sharp and that he could enjoy the good memories without feeling so sad. She'd been right.

He wondered if he'd ever see the woman from the beach again and find out exactly what he had seen in those brown eyes of hers, or if the memory of her would soon fade and become as indistinguishable as a grain of sand on the beach.

Chapter Four

Ffion unzipped her suitcase and stared at the contents. She'd brought two suitcases with her, along with some plastic storage boxes, and yesterday, after her arrival, Nerys had the porter bring them over to the cottage.

After her walk along the beach, she'd been soaked and shivering. As she'd trudged back to the cottage, her jeans and coat had been heavy with water and by the time she'd let herself in through the front door, her teeth had been chattering. She'd stuffed her clothes in the washer and headed upstairs to run a bubble bath. In her old room, she'd found her belongings parked in the corner but had been too exhausted to even consider unpacking. However, a pair of fleecy red pyjamas and a fluffy white dressing gown had been on the bed waiting for her, all smelling of the floral fabric softener her mam used. She guessed that her mam had bought them and washed them ready for Ffion's return.

Bathed and dressed in the pyjamas and dressing gown, Ffion had flopped onto the bed. Her parents hadn't yet returned and she knew they'd be late working at the hotel, so she'd closed her eyes, meaning to rest for half an hour or so. Stirring only when her dad had come in to say hello, she'd been so tired that she could hardly reply to him when he'd asked if she was hungry. Instead, he'd tucked the duck down duvet around her, kissed her forehead then crept from her room. She'd tried to drag herself to consciousness, but the comfortable bed, the gentle murmuring of her parents' voices in the lounge below and the knowledge that tonight she wasn't alone in the house had sent her back off to sleep.

For the first time in about two years, Ffion had slept soundly through the night. When she'd woken, the room had been grey with the dawn light that crept through the gap in the curtains. Having climbed out of bed and gone to the window, she'd pushed aside the curtains and her heart had lifted to see Cariad Cove. It had seemed different to when she'd arrived the previous day, as if she were seeing it anew after a good night's rest.

Ffion had loved her home in Scotland, had enjoyed walking in the glorious countryside and snuggling in front of the fire with Graeme as snow fell outside, but after Graeme had gone, none of it had felt right. Her surroundings hadn't changed, neither had the home that they'd bought, decorated and furnished together, and yet none if it had been the same. Graeme had been the centre of her world in Scotland, and without him, she'd felt lost, lonely, adrift. The idea of returning to the Gower Peninsula hadn't appealed at first because it seemed like a backwards step to return to the point where she'd begun. Wasn't a person meant to keep moving, growing, seeing new places and meeting new people? She'd possessed that thirst for life and adventure when Graeme had been there but without him, it was as if a core part of her had disappeared.

And so she had struggled on until her mother-in-law had taken her to the doctor and medication and counselling had ensued. The counselling had been slow, difficult and painful. The meds had helped to dull some of the ache but it had been like the ebb and flow of the tide; at times the undertow had been stronger than at others; at times the medication had been more effective than at others. The counselling, with a kindly fifty-something woman named Helga, had dug deep and exposed the rawness beneath. Helga had told Ffion to cry, to let go, to release the feelings into the room because otherwise they would swallow her up and eat her whole. Ffion had seen the sense in what Helga was saying and at times she did let go, did expose her grief, but at others she felt resentful of the whole process and furious at the universe for making her go through it. There had been a few dreadful times when Ffion had believed that she didn't want to go on. But they hadn't lasted. She knew that Graeme would have wanted her to keep going, would have wanted her to live and to laugh again because it was who he had been. Graeme had been funny, outgoing, loud (so loud) and always laughing; he had been sweet, tender and gentle in ways Ffion hadn't known a man could be. He had held her and kissed her and cherished her, and together they had enjoyed life.

She gasped and pressed her hands to her chest as the enormity of his loss hit her once again. Only this time she was in the room where she had slept as a child, a teenager and as a young woman. She was not in their Scottish home, not able to go to Graeme's wardrobe, slide open the door and pull out one of his shirts as she had done so many times – pressing them to her face, wrapping them around herself and sobbing as she tried to will him to come back.

How could someone so full of life be gone?

She needed to get busy or she'd sink to the floor and curl up, lie there for hours until her limbs were stiff, her head ached and goosebumps covered her skin. It was a new day, her parents had already gone off to the hotel – she'd heard them leaving – and she had the chance to begin again.

Start over. Try again.

Even if she didn't fully want to; she owed it to Graeme and to her family and to the girl she'd once been who would hate to see the broken woman she was right now.

She peeled off the dressing gown, rolled up her pyjama sleeves and started to unpack. Clothes went on hangers in the wardrobe, socks and underwear into drawers, and soon she'd emptied the first suitcase. She went downstairs and made a coffee, grabbed a Welsh cake from the cake stand on the kitchen dresser – her mam always kept cakes handy – then she went back to her room and carried on. The plastic storage boxes contained things that she might need, including paperwork, and the few things of Graeme's that she'd allowed herself to keep. Those, she slid under the bed and on top of the wardrobe, then she sat on the bed and allowed herself to rest.

She straightened her back and closed her eyes, settled her hands in her lap and followed her breaths in and out, feeling her heart rate slowing down, her body settling. The cottage creaked and groaned familiarly; some things didn't change at all. Pipes clanged as the heating kicked in, the air in her room warmed slowly and her head cleared as she focused on the sounds around her. Helga had recommended meditation and mindfulness and so Ffion had downloaded several apps for her phone to practise both. Sometimes, they helped.

Returning her awareness to the room, she blinked then stood up and went to the window. Off to the left was the hotel, to the right was the view of the cliffs and beyond the hotel lay the beach. The wind was up today and white horses rode in on the waves and crashed against the shore. She opened the sash window and the cold air washed over her, salty and fresh, tangy and bracing. The sound of the waves carried to the cottage and she listened for a moment to the lullaby of her youth. Ffion had lost the person she loved more than any other in the world and yet the tides still ebbed and flowed, the sun still rose, set, and rose again.

Life went on…

Being near the sea was the best place to accept this fact. Ffion couldn't escape it here, nor would she want to, because if she couldn't heal in Cariad Cove, then she really was lost.

–

Joe placed his mug on the draining board in the staffroom. The final bell of the day had just rung, and the corridors were busy with pupils heading to after-school clubs or hurrying to catch buses, grab lifts or to walk home. The inner-city school ran plenty of extra-curricular activities for its pupils and Joe was involved in some of the PE ones, but today he was free to leave when he was ready.

He'd packed up his things before the bell and gone to the staffroom so he could avoid the corridor chaos. It was amazing how quickly pupils could move at the end of the day because getting them from one lesson to another often took a lot longer than it should do. He liked working at the school. The pupils were a good bunch – there were a few who liked to cause trouble, but they were in the minority – and he liked his colleagues. He'd done his sports science degree in Cardiff followed by a secondary PGCE, got his first job at a valleys school, his second at a Cardiff school then moved to the Swansea comprehensive three years ago. The only thing he wasn't sure of was what he wanted to do next. He liked teaching his subject, liked the salary and holidays, but didn't know if he wanted to climb the ladder. Thirteen years in, he thought he probably should know, but time had flown and he was so busy out of school – renovating the house he'd bought in Cariad Cove just under a year ago, walking and running with Odin, and visiting his aunt – that he didn't have time for much else.

There had been another reason for his lack of focus on his career too, but he seldom admitted it to himself. However, when he received texts like he had this afternoon, it was hard to deny the impact that his one major romantic relationship had had on his life. As soon as his mobile had buzzed in his pocket at lunchtime, he'd checked the screen, expecting it to be his aunt. She sometimes messaged him during the day to tell him stories about Odin that made him laugh, like the dog chewing one of her slippers then hiding it under the sofa or taking a poo in the garage against the tyre of Darryl's prized vintage Jaguar E-Type. But when Joe had seen Demi's name on the screen, his stomach had clenched. She didn't text often these days so when she did, Joe felt the world spinning around him.

He hadn't replied yet because he wasn't quite sure what to say. How did you respond when the woman you'd once loved with all your heart sent you a message telling you she was feeling low and she needed to see you?

Joe knew he needed to think about it before replying, so for now he'd head to his aunt's, eat dinner with her and Darryl then take Odin home and probably head to the cove for a long walk. A blast of sea air always helped to clear his mind, which he needed, because while his head was telling him that seeing her wasn't a good idea, his heart was already donning rose-tinted spectacles and remembering how good it had felt to be in love. His head told him that it could never be that way again, that Demi had changed and so had he, but his heart was treacherous and liked security, longing – sometimes – for the way things had been. And even though some people might think he was weak after what she had done to him, he hated to think of Demi feeling low.

Chapter Five

Ffion hooked her small handbag across her body and pulled her hat on. She was meeting her sister, Mari, at the hotel and they were going for a walk along the coastal path. She'd been back in Cariad Cove for two nights but hadn't seen Mari yet. Her older sister was a teacher at a primary school in Swansea and had two young children of her own, Anwen aged six and Seren aged two, so was always busy. Whenever Ffion had seen her in recent years, she'd been harried, exhausted and distracted. Ffion had put it down to Mari being a wife and mum, as well as holding down a full-time job outside of the home, something that was bound to be a challenge. Mari's husband, Bryn, was nice enough but Ffion had never thought that he was as good a partner as he could have been, and knew that Mari did the lion's share of the chores in their home. Although she also knew what her sister could be like — a bit of a control freak at times — and so Mari might have engineered a domestic situation that meant her life wasn't running as smoothly as it could be. Sometimes Mari was her own worst enemy and wanting control over every aspect of her life had meant that she'd probably stopped Bryn contributing around the house because he wasn't doing things her way. Growing up, Mari's need for control had worsened if she was anxious about something, and Ffion had often worried about her sister because of this.

Since Ffion had moved to Scotland eleven years ago, she hadn't seen that much of her sister. In fact, they hadn't had much contact at all, apart from the times when Ffion came back to Wales and when they spoke on the phone at birthdays and Christmases. Mari had phoned, FaceTimed and Zoomed since Graeme's passing, but it had been awkward, the conversations stilted and brief, and neither Mari nor Ffion had really known what to say.

Ffion let herself out of the cottage and made her way to the hotel. It was just after three thirty, so they wouldn't have that long before dusk fell, but she was glad her sister had been able to sort childcare and come to see her. She hoped that they could speak more easily face to face.

Outside the front of the hotel, she spotted her mam standing in the beer garden with another woman who was wearing a bright pink bobble hat. Ffion's mam waved then the other woman turned and Ffion recognised the face that was the same shape as her own.

'Ffion!' Mari trotted down the path and embraced her. 'Hello, love.'

'Hi, Mari.' Ffion hugged her sister back, although with all the layers they were both wearing it felt a bit like sumo wrestling.

'My beautiful girls back together again.' Their mam was smiling as she watched them, a dish towel in one hand, the other holding her hair back from her eyes to stop the breeze sweeping it over her face. The tip of her nose was pink from the cold. 'Are you two sure you want to go for a walk? It's bloody freezing out here. Why don't you go and have a coffee at the cottage?'

Ffion looked at Mari, keen to let her take the lead as had always been their way. Mari was the elder sister by a year and growing up, she had been the one to take charge and make their decisions. Their parents had often laughed about it, teasing Mari for being bossy and Ffion for being so compliant, but it was how their dynamic had worked and it had never bothered Ffion.

'You want to walk, Ffi?' Mari asked. 'I've been cooped up with twenty-eight nine- and ten-year-olds all day, so I'd love some fresh air, but if you'd prefer not to…'

Ffion shook her head. 'I'm up for a walk.'

'Hold on then!' Their mam held up a finger. 'I'll grab you some takeaways.'

Five minutes later, Ffion and Mari held reusable coffee mugs from the hotel.

'It's hot chocolate to keep you warm. Now, you take care because it's breezy and that coastal path can be treacherous.'

Mari rolled her eyes. 'Mam, we're both in our thirties now so I think we can manage.'

'I'll always worry about you both. That's my job as your mam. You wait and see, Mari, when your little ones are grown up, you'll still worry about them.'

'I'm sure I will.' Mari smiled.

'See you in a bit.' Ffion kissed her mam then they headed off along the road that wound around the hotel and up to the start of the coastal path.

'So, Ffion.' Mari glanced at her. 'How're you doing?'

Ffion shrugged. 'I've been better, I guess.' Such an understatement but these conversations were always going to be tough.

'I'm sorry I didn't get here when you arrived but things are just… mad at home.'

'It's all right. I know how busy you are, Mari. I don't know how you juggle it all.'

'I did want to come to see you straight away but some evenings, by the time I've fed and bathed the children then read them a bedtime story, I'm dropping off myself. I had the imprint of one of the elephants in a pop-up book in my forehead for two days last week because I passed out reading a story to Seren.'

'Nightmare!' Ffion laughed, picturing the image clearly. 'Are the children all right?'

'They're good. It's hard at times being a mum but it's also incredible. I feel very lucky.'

Mari's voice wavered on *lucky* and Ffion slid a look at her but Mari kept walking.

'I'm glad all's going well for you.'

They walked in step along the narrow gravel path as they had always done as children. To their right, there was a steep bank, dotted with trees and shrubs, that rose up to a flattened-out area with an old church and graveyard. To their left were trees, brown branches exposed in winter, spindly limbs entwined like a basket weave. But beyond the trees lay the beach and the sea, stretching out to the cliffs of Barddoniaeth Bay. The horizon was pewter-grey but seemed almost silver where it met the water, as if the fusion there had created a glow.

They kept walking along the path until they emerged in a clearing at the top of the cliff. Ffion was surprised to find herself out of breath and when she looked at Mari, she could see that her sister was the same. They stopped for a moment in silent agreement and looked out across the cove. The breeze coming in off the water was chilly and damp, bringing scents of the deep, and the harsh aroma of engine oil from a boat making Ffion wrinkle her nose.

'We're more like a pair of eighty-year-olds than thirty-somethings,' Ffion said.

Mari snorted. 'Tell me about it. I feel tired all the time, though. If it wasn't for the fact that I work and have young children I'd think there was something seriously wrong with me.' She laughed then froze, the sound dying in her throat, and turned to Ffion. 'Oh god, Fi, I'm so sorry.'

'What? Why?'

'That was so insensitive of me.'

Ffion shook her head. 'It's fine. I didn't even think anything of it, to be honest.'

Mari's brown eyes were wide and she was worrying her bottom lip with her teeth. 'Shall we sit down?'

They sat on the bench and huddled together instinctively. Ffion wrapped her gloved hands around her hot chocolate, keen to glean any heat from it that she could.

'Ffion… Now that we're here, alone, tell me honestly… How are you?'

Ffion swallowed hard. 'Do you really want to go there?'

Mari touched a hand to Ffion's knee. 'I'm a bad sister, I know I am. I haven't been there for you… and I should have been.'

'Mari, I could have come back to the cove a long time ago but I didn't. I stayed in Scotland because I was trying to hold on to what I had there… but bit by bit, it slipped away from me.'

Mari slouched over. 'I'm so sorry about everything.'

'Me too.' Ffion peeled the lid from her mug and took a sip. The chocolate was sweet and frothy, comforting as a hug.

Out at sea, a horn sounded like a solitary wail that was carried on the breeze. Ffion could just about make out the bulk of a ship against the grey.

'I think my eyes need testing,' she said. 'I can't see as far as I used to.'

'You and me both.' Mari huffed. 'I have to wear reading specs now. I always had twenty-twenty vision but once I hit thirty... it started to deteriorate.'

'Things do.'

'Everything goes downhill.'

They both sniggered.

'The optician told me it's usually at forty that you notice a change but it can happen sooner. I blame all the screen time with reading, report-writing and making resources. But then, it could be using my phone and iPad too.' Mari sipped her drink. 'This is gorgeous but Mam always puts too much sugar in. I'm getting so fat.' She patted her middle and Ffion turned to look at her.

'No you're not.'

'I bloody am. I've had two babies now, Ffion, and my body is not what it was. I have stretch marks and saggy bits and... don't tell anyone, but when I cough a tiny bit of pee leaks out.'

'Mari!' Ffion laughed. 'It does not.'

'I try to do those pelvic floor exercises but it's just another thing to fit into the day. The health visitor was all like... *Do them when you're on the bus or brushing your teeth or eating your dinner. It's an exercise you can do and no one will know.* She said it was easy to fit them in, but what does she know?'

'It's not that bad, is it?'

'Only when I really need to pee and then I dare not cough, sneeze or laugh.'

'It sounds awful.'

'Don't get me wrong, the children are worth it, but sometimes I do miss my pre-pregnancy body. It's partic-ularly challenging when I'm at work because I can't go to the toilet when I want, and I have to wait for break time.

I dread getting a cold because coughing is like Russian roulette for my knickers.'

Ffion snorted with laughter. She'd forgotten how funny her sister could be. 'Try to do the exercises if you can, then. It sounds like you should make it a priority.'

Mari's face turned suddenly serious, and Ffion mentally braced herself. 'Ffi… I need to tell you something.'

'OK?'

'After I had Seren… I had a bit of a difficult time. For a while, actually.'

'What do you mean?'

Ffion thought back to when Seren was born, struggling to remember if Mari had had any health complications with the birth, but she couldn't recollect anything having been mentioned.

'I wasn't going to say anything but I can't stand to think of you believing I let you down and… it wasn't something I could say in a text or a Zoom call… but I was constantly exhausted and could barely drag myself out of bed. I eventually went to the doctor and she said I had post-natal depression. It's why I wasn't there for you as I should have been.'

'Oh Mari.' Ffion shook her head. 'I had no idea.'

'You were deep into dealing with your own… devastating issue by the time I started to get some normality back.' Mari sipped her chocolate and licked her lips. 'When Graeme got ill then… passed away… Seren was only eleven months old and I wasn't very well at all. I was struggling to cope with her and Anwen, so I took some extra time off work, but my maternity pay had stopped and so we were struggling financially. There was so much pressure. It was a tough time, although not as tough as what you were going through, obviously.'

'Everyone has their own battles, Mari. It sounds like you had a dreadful time and I'm sorry I didn't know and couldn't be there for you.'

'There was no way Mam or Dad would have told you, not that I think either of them really understood what it was, mind. They kept hoping it was just tiredness and that it would pass once Seren started sleeping better. It's only in the past few months that I've started to feel more like myself again.'

Ffion unzipped her bag to find a tissue because her nose was running. She pulled at the packet but as it came out of her bag, a small, squashed box came with it and fell on the ground at their feet. Mari leant over and picked it up.

'What's this?'

Ffion reached for it. 'Nothing.'

'Yes it is. Zopiclone. Isn't that for—'

'Helping you sleep.'

'You're not sleeping?'

'Not well, no, but the past two nights being back in Cariad Cove has helped. I think it's the sea air.'

'That magical sea air, eh?' Mari smiled but her eyes were wary.

'I only take the tablets when it's really bad. I've been trying not to but sometimes… I need a bit of help and that's when I use them.'

'Are you taking anything else?'

'An antidepressant. But I'm on a low dose now and the aim is to wean myself off it completely. I just need to find something else to help me, I guess. But first things first; I need to settle in.'

'Are you going to stay?' A hopeful look flitted across Mari's face.

'For now, yes. Long-term, I don't know, and yet… where else would I go? Scotland was my home for over a decade but without Graeme… it just wasn't the same. Everywhere I went I was reminded of him and of what I'd lost. His parents weren't exactly—'

'The warmest?'

'Yes.'

They smiled sadly at each other.

'They meant well but they were dealing with losing their son and they're quite old-fashioned in that they don't believe in showing emotion. They think you should swallow it down, lift your chin and keep on going.'

'Easier said than done.'

'Exactly. I mean… I tried to do it. I thought that if I pretended everything was OK with me, then it might be. Then I went back to work, had too much wine at a pub lunch with colleagues and… it didn't mix well with my medication. I told my boss to grow a pair because he was dithering over a contract.' Ffion winced at the memory.

'You didn't?'

'I did.'

'God, Ffion.'

'I wasn't fired but I left voluntarily. They wanted me to get some help and to take more time off but I just knew I couldn't work there again. I'd snapped for a reason and I knew I needed to make some changes.'

'I can't imagine telling the head teacher to grow a pair. Mind you, the head is a woman so there's that, but even so… the thought makes me cringe.'

Mari's eyes had changed now and there was something different in them. She looked more like the Mari that Ffion had known growing up. There was a sparkle there, possibly one of admiration. Didn't a lot of people want to be brutally honest with their boss? It seemed that the idea appealed to Mari, although if she ever did tell her head teacher to grow a pair, there would be terrible repercussions.

Mari took Ffion's hand and squeezed it.

'I've missed this.'

'Me too.'

And Ffion had. Growing up, they'd been close until Mari had started dating Bryn in year eleven, and suddenly, her sister hadn't had as much time for Ffion. She'd been jealous of the time Mari spent with Bryn and even resented him for a while. But then Mari had gone to college followed by university, and Ffion had made new friends and had her own relationships, the most serious one being with Graeme. Only then had she understood why Mari had been so keen to spend time with Bryn. Falling in love was powerful and all-consuming and though Ffion had striven to maintain friendships and a life away from her marriage, Graeme had been her focus and her whole world.

And now he was gone.

She sighed and closed her eyes.

'Ffion.' Mari shuffled closer and wrapped an arm around Ffion's back. 'You're home now and we can work through this together. Nothing's perfect in life. We lost our way for a while there but I'm here for you now and I'll help however I can.'

Ffion opened her eyes and gazed at her sister.

'Thank you so much. I'm here for you too.'

She was grateful to be there with Mari and to have her sister's support, but she knew Mari needed to lean on her too. She could tell that there was more to what was going on with Mari than her sister had told her, and she hoped she'd be able to help in return.

As for her own grief, it would be good to have some support, but she knew that no one could take her pain away. It was something that only she could deal with, suffer through and process, and only time would help. At least, she *hoped* time would help.

'One day at a time, Ffion.'

'That's all I can do. All anyone can do.'

They finished their drinks gazing out to sea, watching gulls swoop and soar like white kites carried on the breeze, listening to the waves as they crashed against the rocks below, and breathing in the salty air. Ffion's pain was still there, sitting like a lead weight in her chest, clouding her vision like fog, squeezing her stomach with every breath she took, and yet being back where she had grown up was comforting because she had always felt safe here. She could go through the motions and know that she was around people who cared, people who would ensure that she ate and washed her hair and clothes, who would give her a hug or accompany her on walks.

Her recovery wasn't over – it wasn't anywhere *near* over – but that was OK. Graeme had been everything to Ffion and losing everything was going to take a while to digest. But she felt that she'd be able to start to do that here, in the bosom of her family, in a place of love.

–

Joe threw the Frisbee again and Odin raced after it, splashing through the sea, oblivious to everything other than his mission. His fur would be soaking and sandy, and Joe would need to bath him when they got home, but he didn't mind. Seeing Odin enjoying himself, his pure unadulterated joy in the game, was worth it.

The walk was also giving him some much-needed time to think. Since he'd received the text message from Demi yesterday, he'd been churned up inside. It wasn't that he still loved her, because he was quite sure that he didn't; it was more that every time she came back into his life, he felt wobbly. Demi was beautiful, determined, intelligent and funny but she had also broken his heart and he didn't want to go through that ever again. She'd been his first proper love and dealing with the hurt after she'd left him for someone else had been hard. But he'd got through it and come out stronger. And yet, whenever she came back to Swansea, he felt vulnerable again, almost raw, as if she had the power to turn him inside out all over again. He'd been weak the last time he'd seen her at a mutual friend's wedding about a year ago. Demi had come to the wedding alone, telling him that her husband was away on business – and, after a few drinks, he had *almost* ended up kissing her. She'd asked him if he thought there was still a spark between them, had sidled up to him and taken his hand, and he had faltered in his resolve to remain impervious to her charms. *Stupid. Reckless. Irresponsible.* But in a moment of weakness, as the bride and groom had taken to the dancefloor and the marquee had seemed to be filled with couples in love, he'd wanted to remember what it was like to be loved by her. They had a history and for a moment that history clouded his judgement. Thankfully, he'd stopped himself from kissing her, but it had been a wake-up call for him. Demi was not a goddess; she was a normal human being and she had flaws just like everybody else. One of her flaws being her need to know that Joe still fancied her, even if she had no real romantic interest in him at all anymore. In the cold light of day, Joe suspected that he'd always care about her, but that the love he'd felt had long gone.

So perhaps it would be OK to meet her for a drink while she was back. Besides which, he was worried about her after the text she'd sent telling him that she was feeling low. He knew deep down that the reason Demi needed to believe that all men found her attractive was because of a confidence issue. She'd been through some tough times and it had impacted upon her. Even so, he wished she could be confident enough not to feel the need to try to prove that she was attractive.

He resolved to reply to Demi's message when he got home. If he didn't agree to meet her, he'd worry about what was wrong and lose the peace of mind he'd battled to find.

Odin lolloped back to him and dropped the Frisbee at his feet so he picked it up and threw it again, strolling farther along the beach. As he watched the dog chasing after it, movement from outside the Cariad Cove Hotel caught his eye. Two women, bundled up in hats and coats, were hugging in the doorway. As they broke apart, something about one of them – her height, the way she held herself like she worried she would break if she moved too quickly – made him think of the woman Odin had knocked over at the beach. It could be her, but he couldn't tell from this distance.

As she turned away and walked around the side of the hotel then disappeared, a sense of regret filled him. He was still curious about what he'd seen in the woman's eyes and now he was curious about whether that was her and if she was staying at the hotel or nearby. Would he see her again, have the chance to apologise properly and perhaps to find out more about her?

But as Odin dropped the Frisbee at his feet again, he laughed. There was nothing like a dog to keep you firmly in the present. He'd always been a bit of a romantic but letting himself wonder about some woman he'd bumped into on a beach was taking it too far.

Better to play with Odin and to focus on the joy the dog gleaned from playing his game than to wonder about strange women and their troubles.

Chapter Six

Ffion checked her reflection in the bedroom mirror. In a black skirt, tights, pumps and white blouse, with her long hair in a neat low bun, she looked like she was eighteen again and getting ready for work at the family hotel. That was, if she squinted a bit, because at thirty-two, she had a few more lines around her eyes and her skin wasn't as clear as it used to be. Grief had etched itself onto her features, making her cheekbones sharper, her mouth less likely to smile. Beneath her eyes, purple shadows stained the skin and her eyes themselves held something that hadn't been there before, a heaviness that seemed likely to remain. She'd seen people who'd been through pain, in real life and on TV, the internet and in magazines, and they all bore physical evidence of what they'd suffered. Ffion believed that grief had aged her, dimmed her complexion and darkened her gaze.

She'd been back in Cariad Cove for five days and was already fed up of sitting around. Her parents worked from dawn until well after dusk and apart from snatched cups of tea and hurried meals, she wasn't getting much time with them. She understood, of course she did; it had always been this way. Running a business was hard and it meant that they never really got a day off. They had an excellent staff at the hotel but it was popular and busy throughout the year, and so they needed all hands on deck. That was another reason why Ffion had offered to help out this evening. She'd never been one to sit on her hands waiting for things to happen and even though she was still drained and felt like lying in bed for most of the day, she knew she had to get up and get moving. One of the waitresses from the hotel restaurant had called in sick and Ffion had been there at lunchtime when her mam had told her dad they'd be short-staffed this evening. That had pushed Ffion from the sofa and into the shower. She'd dug around in the wardrobe for some simple clothes to wear and luckily found that some of her Scottish work wardrobe would be fine, even if the garments were a bit loose now.

And so here she was, ready to wait on tables and to put her own troubles aside for a while. She knew from experience that by the end of the night she'd be bone-weary, that her feet would throb, her back would hurt and her face would ache from plastering on a hospitality smile, but it would get her out of the cottage and into human company. Plus, she'd be doing a good deed in assisting her parents and, according to all the self-help websites, helping others was meant to be good for you.

She grabbed her coat and gloves then set off across the car park in the direction of the hotel, getting her best smile ready and hoping that waitressing would be just like riding a bike, because she hadn't done this in quite some time.

—

Joe checked his mobile as he walked. It was fine; he still had time.

He'd agreed to meet Demi this evening at the Cariad Cove Hotel for a drink because she said she'd be back in

Swansea for the weekend. She'd asked him to book a table for dinner but he wasn't sure that he was quite ready for that, or if it was a good idea. At least with a drink, he could make a hasty retreat if it wasn't going well, whereas with a meal in front of him, he'd feel that he had to stay and finish before making an excuse to leave.

He was curious about why Demi was feeling low and why she was turning to him. They'd had a bond for many years and been through some difficult times, but then she'd decided that Joe wasn't enough for her and left him for another man. It had taken him time to come to terms with and he'd been through a whole range of feelings, including anger, numbness and grief, but three years on he felt stronger and believed in his own resilience. He would help Demi if he could because of the love they had once shared and because he still believed she was a good person, in spite of everything.

Curiosity killed the cat… Caryn had said to him when he dropped Odin off and she asked where he was going. When he'd laughed nervously at her comment, she'd raised her eyebrows, staring hard at him before asking if he knew what he was doing. He'd shrugged, blushed a bit and she'd sighed and told him to be careful. Odin was spending the night at hers because Joe wasn't sure what time he'd get home and didn't like to leave his canine companion alone for long periods of time. Odin was delighted though because Caryn and Darryl were having steak and chips and he knew he'd get his fair share of both.

Joe reached the hotel then paused at the bottom of the steps that led to the beer garden, and turned to look at the beach. The sky was clear and stars twinkled in the black canvas that stretched for as far as he could see. The water was dark too and he thought of the times he'd plunged into the sea at night, unable to see a thing other than the silver reflection of the moonlight on the water, enjoying that feeling of uncertainty because it made him aware that he was just a small part of something bigger. As one being, he was insignificant, in some ways powerless, but he had a part to play in the grander scheme of things, though as yet he was still unsure about what that part would be.

The wind coming in off the sea was icy and he shivered as it tugged at his hat and slid under his collar like chilly prying fingers. Cold as it was, Joe liked how refreshed it made him feel, as if it had the power to restore order to his thoughts. He needed to be able to think clearly this evening and the brisk sea air would help him to do that.

–

Ffion had slipped back into waitressing as easily as she'd hoped and found that she was quite enjoying being so busy. As she led people to their tables, took orders for drinks and meals and went between the kitchen and the restaurant, she was able to work on autopilot. She'd been raised to do this, trained at an early age, and it gave her a strange form of comfort going through the familiar actions and routines. Many of the staff were people who'd worked there for years, and though they were initially a bit cautious around her – clearly wondering if she was OK or if she'd break down at a customer's frown or a returned order – they quickly realised that she had this, she was a professional, and she wasn't made of glass.

Soon, Ffion was as much a part of the well-oiled machine as everyone else there. Surrounded by her parents, Nerys and other people she knew, she felt safe, calm and warm – not just because she was rushing around with orders or because of the log fires that burned in the restaurant and bar. It was more an easing of the loneliness and isolation that had dominated her life since she'd lost Graeme. She knew she'd needed to take that time out to be alone so she could process what had happened but she wondered if she'd been that way for a bit too long; if she could have lifted her spirits sooner by returning to Cariad Cove.

As Ffion walked back into the bar, she spotted a couple standing there looking expectant so she went over to them.

'Good evening and welcome to the Cariad Cove Hotel. My name's Ffion and I'm one of the waitresses here. Have you booked a table?' The restaurant was filling up and she didn't fancy their chances of getting one in there if they hadn't.

The man shook his head. 'We're just here for a drink.'

'I was hoping to have something to eat,' the woman said, twisting her mouth as if in irritation at her companion's remark. She was taller than Ffion in her high black leather boots, and her tight purple dress accentuated an athletic frame. Her shiny afro hair was full and beautiful and Ffion thought she was probably one of the most attractive women she'd ever seen.

Ffion followed the woman's gaze to the man. His blue eyes met Ffion's, and something shot between them, a spark of recognition or possibly something else. She couldn't be sure, but she was already racking her brain to try to remember if and when she'd seen him before. Perhaps she'd gone to school with him or had served him here in the past, or he could have been a friend of a friend who she recognised from a Facebook photo. There were so many possibilities. She shrugged the thought away.

After all, what did it matter? But when she looked up again, he was staring at her as if he was thinking the same things.

'Do I know you?' he asked, a line appearing between his brows. '*Ffion*. The name isn't ringing a bell but somehow… I think I've seen you before. Yes, in fact I know I have.'

Heat bloomed in Ffion's cheeks. What was happening? It wasn't like she was fifteen and the handsome head boy had just walked into the classroom and asked for her, for goodness' sake.

'I don't think so.' Ffion shook her head. 'I just have one of those faces.'

'Oh.' He raised his eyebrows a fraction. 'OK.'

'Would you like a table here in the bar?' Ffion asked, assuming her professional air.

'What do you think?' he asked his companion.

'I really would like to eat. You know me, Joe, I'm always *hungry*.'

The way she said the words made Ffion cringe inwardly. It was clear that it was some kind of 'in' joke.

'If you take that corner table near the fire, I'll bring you some bar menus.'

Ffion watched as they wandered over to the table then she grabbed two menus and carried them over to the couple.

'I'll be back in five minutes to take your order.'

'Thank you.' Joe flashed her a smile and the blush crawled into her cheeks again, unwelcome as a cockroach in a hotel kitchen. She hurried away, annoyed with herself for being affected by someone in that way. She'd had a good shift so far, been feeling quite positive about being around people again, then an attractive couple had arrived and she'd turned into a self-conscious teenager. This was something, she realised, that could not be blamed on the grief.

–

Joe sipped his beer. He'd remembered Ffion as the woman from the beach and was finding it surprisingly difficult now to push thoughts of her from his mind. He made an effort to concentrate on what Demi was telling him about the large detached house she'd bought in Kent. She seemed different in some ways, had assumed a new air of sophistication in their time apart, but then he wondered if that was more to do with the travelling than with her rich husband with his land and money. When Demi had initially confessed to falling for someone else, Joe had thought it would be another Paralympian, a sporting hero that she'd met during training or competing, someone she'd shared long haul flights or hotel dinners with while they were away. Surprisingly, then, her husband was not someone she'd met in her sporting circles but at a social event. Hugo Cartwright came from land and money, had an old English name and an attitude, if the way he behaved on social media was anything to go by. Demi had always been so down to earth, so keen to promote sport to people of her own age and younger, had even talked about teaching in comprehensive schools too when she retired from professional sport. Then Hugo had come along and swept her off her feet and into his mansion. She had retired from competing now but she did guest spots as a sports commentator as well as running a fitness blog and working as a social influencer for several sporting brands.

As a romantic himself, Joe wondered if everyone wanted that feeling of falling in love truly, madly, deeply.

He'd been hurt by Demi's betrayal and yet he'd understood why she would be attracted by what Hugo could offer her. She had had a tough childhood; growing up on a council estate with her four siblings. Money had been tight. Her father had been on benefits and her mother had walked out on her husband and children when Demi was just six. It had left her with scars. Then she'd been left with her physical scar, the loss of her leg in a car accident when she was just fourteen. The driver had been drunk and crashed into a roundabout, rolling the car and leaving it unsalvageable. Demi had been rushed to hospital, her left leg so badly mangled that it couldn't be saved. But here she was, successful and well known after years of competing in sprints and long jump, flying the flag for women in sport. She was incredible and Joe was in awe of her, even after everything. Hugo had been able to offer Demi financial stability and a new life away from Swansea, while Joe lived on a teacher's salary and had no inclination to leave West Wales at all. So Joe did understand.

'Earth to Joe.' Demi waved a hand in front of his face. She hadn't yet told him why she was feeling low and as she'd chatted away, he hadn't wanted to bring it up and make her sad.

'Sorry?'

'You were gazing into the distance. Tough day?'

'Not really. I'm a bit tired and work has been busy but it's half-term next week so I'll have a chance to catch up with some things and hopefully some sleep too.'

'That dog keeping you busy?' Demi's upper lip wrinkled. That was her main flaw as far as Joe was concerned, far worse than the flirting. She didn't like dogs, never had done and it was something he couldn't comprehend.

'Odin's my best friend.' Joe shrugged, not caring what she thought about that.

'Odin?' She snorted. 'Where did that name come from?'

He felt sure he'd told her Odin's name before but perhaps she'd forgotten or had no interest in remembering.

'He's strong, brave and invincible.'

'Right, OK.' Demi was grinning. 'You still running with him?'

'Regularly. As well as walking him, playing Frisbee and snuggling on the sofa.'

'You snuggle him on the sofa?'

'Of course I do. That's what dogs are for.'

'So…' She licked her lips. 'There's no woman on the scene, then? I mean… if there was, you wouldn't be snuggling a flea-ridden dog, would you?'

'He doesn't have fleas…' Joe swallowed, reminding himself not to rise to this old argument. 'And in answer to your question; no, there's no woman on the scene.'

'I can't understand why you haven't been snapped up.'

What? Alarm bells started ringing in his head.

'Oh Joe, it's so good to see you again. I have missed you.'

Demi reached across the table and rested her hand on his, peering at him from beneath her long dark lashes. She was stunning, had grown into her beauty effortlessly as she progressed from skinny, sporty teen to strong, athletic woman, and yet as she gazed at Joe in what could be considered a suggestive way, he felt nothing. Except that perhaps Demi saw him like some kind of comfort blanket from her childhood that she wanted to cuddle up to when her insecurities were at their most restless then tuck away again in a box when she felt better.

He gently pulled his hand away, glad that there wasn't a flicker inside him – no yearning, no desire and no regret that she hadn't chosen him.

Demi had made her choice and that was fine with Joe because he knew now that he really had moved on.

'Joe… everything's just gone wrong since I left you.' Demi leant her elbows on the table and rested her chin on her hands and Joe sucked in a deep breath, wondering what on earth she was about to tell him.

–

Ffion took a deep breath, willed her blushes to stay away and headed for the corner table in the bar.

'Are you ready to order now?' she asked, holding up her iPad, something that had changed since she'd last worked there. In the past, she'd used a notepad but now it was all far more high-tech.

'Yes please,' the man named Joe nodded.

Ffion typed their orders into the iPad, checked that they didn't want more drinks then got them some cutlery. When she came back and set the table, Joe was peering at her.

'I think I've remembered where I know you from.' He seemed cautious, as if he did remember but didn't want to come across as pushy.

'You do?'

'The beach.'

Ffion snorted. 'The beach?'

'Yes. I was with my dog.'

Ffion felt her eyes widen and her shoulders stiffen. Then the blush flooded her cheeks again. *Of course, it was him!*

'It was you with that damned giant dog.'

The woman with Joe sniggered. '*Odin* been upsetting you, has he?'

Ffion met the woman's striking green eyes and realised what she'd said. *To a customer!* Perhaps she was a bit out of practice after all, because she knew the rules: you were never rude to a paying customer. Bad reviews spread like wildfire but good ones were harder to get and harder to share.

'Goodness, I'm sorry, I didn't mean to sound rude. For a moment there I remembered him knocking me over. He's so big and boisterous and… I'm sure he didn't mean any harm.'

'He didn't. He was playing and lost in the game. He's a big softy really. Honestly.' Joe's eyes were wide as if pleading with her and Ffion felt a spark of pity for him. Perhaps he was keen to impress his girlfriend, or perhaps she was his date, and he didn't want to look bad in front of her.

'It's fine.' She shook her head. 'There was no harm done. I was a bit winded but nothing more.'

'Good. That's good.' Joe was fidgeting with a beer mat, relief filling his eyes.

'Anyway, your food won't be long. Have a lovely evening.'

She picked up the menus and turned to go but something made her glance back at the table. Joe was still looking at her, his head tilted on one side, his expression curious. His companion was chatting away, but he looked sad, as if the topic of their conversation was worrying him.

Ffion bustled away to the kitchen, wanting to find her mam to let her know how she was getting on. Gwen had been worried about Ffion working so soon after returning to the cove but Ffion had been determined to show her that she would be fine. And she was. Absolutely fine. She'd even dealt with Joe, the man whose dog had knocked her flying, and only been a tiny bit rude. Plus, for the past three hours she'd been able to avoid thinking about how her heart ached or about what she was going to do with her life now. About how she slept alone these days and had no loving husband to warm her feet on or to cuddle her on the sofa as they watched TV.

The latter thoughts she batted away as she pushed the door to the kitchen open and entered the steamy air. Her life seemed to have come full circle and it was confusing; it left her feeling lost and wobbly, but it was also OK. She had put one foot in the right direction today and she was going to focus on that.

—

Joe had expected Demi to launch into a speech about why things in her life had gone wrong since she left him for Hugo, but she'd talked about a lot of other things instead, including her childhood and how challenging it had been. Her mind had seemed to jump from one topic to the next as if it couldn't settle. She'd been very busy over the years, rarely taking time out, and Joe worried that it had taken its toll on her.

Joe's heart went out to her as she spoke; she had been abandoned by her mum after all, and then lost a limb in the car accident, and both events had left their mark on her. She had touched briefly on her apparent marriage woes during the evening, but only briefly. She'd seemed a bit angry when she did speak about Hugo and had waved her hand dismissively a few times, then moved the conversation on.

Demi had achieved so much and was such a positive role model for young women. He had intended on asking if she'd be able to visit his school some time to speak about her career, or if she couldn't find the time to visit in person, then to speak to them via Zoom or one of the other video links available, but after listening to her he knew it wasn't the right time. He just hoped that talking to him this evening had helped in some way.

He finished his beer then got his wallet out. 'I'll go to the bar and pay, and then I'd better get going.'

'Sure.' Demi swayed in her seat and he felt a flicker of unease. She'd had a few glasses of wine, something he'd thought unusual as she rarely used to drink – her body was a temple and all that. But as he walked to the bar, he counted up the drinks they'd had in his head, and realised that she'd had two more than him and he'd been drinking low alcohol lager while she'd been drinking large glasses of red wine.

Drowning her sorrows, perhaps? Had he missed how upset she was about her past or her marriage problems? Concern seeped through him and he glanced back at the table, wondering if Demi was really holding it together.

He paid the bill then returned to their table.

'I need to pay my half. How much do I owe?' She opened her bag and started rooting around in it.

'It's fine, honestly. I'm pretty sure you paid the last time we went out.'

'Well OK, then, handsome. I'll pay next time.'

'Sure.' Her eyes were glassy and his concerns about her state grew. 'Uh… Are you all right?'

Her brows furrowed and she stood up, but as she did so, the strap of her handbag caught the glass on the table and sent it hurtling towards the tiled floor. It smashed instantly and Demi's eyes widened.

'Oops!'

She crouched down and reached for a piece but Joe jumped forwards. 'No! Leave it, Demi, you'll cut yourself.'

'It's fine, I've got it.' Ffion had appeared at their table with a dustpan and brush. 'Just step back, please.'

Joe led Demi away from the table and helped her into her coat, then hooked her bag over her arm. He reached for his own coat and put it on, trying not to look around him because the smash of the glass had drawn everyone's attention just like a dropped tray in the school canteen. At least no one was cheering, though.

'I need the loo,' Demi said, then she walked gingerly away, her bag sliding down her arm.

'We're very sorry.' Joe pulled out his wallet. 'How much for the glass?'

Ffion stood up, holding the dustpan. Her cheeks were flushed and a few stray hairs from her bun curled softly around her face. Something inside Joe fluttered. Her eyes were so brown, her hair so shiny, her skin so smooth. Standing in front of her, he was aware of how petite she was and how, if he stepped forwards and took her in his arms, the top of her head would fit right under his chin. His stomach flipped over and he took a deep breath. Whatever was he thinking?

'It's fine.' Ffion shook her head and her eyes slid away.

'Please. Let me give you something.'

'It's fine, don't worry. Happens all the time. As long as your girlfriend is OK?'

He opened his mouth to reply, felt the sudden need to tell her that Demi wasn't his girlfriend – because for some reason it seemed important she know that – but Ffion turned on her heel and marched away.

He feigned interest in the tablecloth, not wanting to stare at other diners while they ate and enjoyed their evenings and fighting the urge to scan the room for Ffion. When Demi returned, she patted his shoulder. 'We should go.'

'Come on, then.' He stood up and took her arm.

They went through the door and out into the night. The air was freezing after the warmth of the bar and Joe pulled his hat from his pocket and tugged it down over his ears, then buttoned his coat to his chin. He glanced at Demi and shook his head. Her coat was flapping open, her throat and chest exposed, and her teeth were already chattering. He reached for her coat and buttoned it carefully, trying to avoid accidentally touching her. 'Where's your hat, Demi?'

'I didn't bring one.'

'Why not?'

'I'm driving.'

He glanced over at the car park and saw her Mini Countryman.

'Oh no you're not.'

'I'll be fine.' She hiccupped.

'Really, Demi? You of all people should know better.'

'What's that supposed to mean?' She stepped back and glared at him.

'I'm sorry. I just… you know how life-changing drunk-driving can be.'

She paused for a moment, rubbed at her cheek. 'I do. God, I really do.'

'Shall I call you a taxi?'

Even as he said the words, he knew he couldn't do that. She was drunk and putting her in a taxi and sending her to… Where was she staying? With her dad or at a hotel? He hadn't thought to ask. But he couldn't take that risk in case something happened, like someone taking advantage of her when she was in this state. He'd have to take her home with him.

'A taxi?' Demi asked. 'Oh.' She wobbled in the breeze, her teeth chattering harder now. Joe removed his hat and put it on her head.

'You'll have to come home with me.'

'What about my car?'

'It'll be fine here and we can pick it up in the morning.'

'Good plan.' She laughed and took his arm. 'To your place it is, then.'

Joe cast one more glance at the hotel, wondering at the yearning he felt to head back inside and explain to Ffion that Demi didn't usually get drunk, and that he was very sorry that Odin had knocked her over at the beach. However, she would probably think he was mad and anyway, he had to get Demi home and put everything else from his mind.

Chapter Seven

Joe carried the tray of toast and coffee into his lounge and set it down in front of Demi. In her drunken state, she hadn't made it up the stairs and instead had passed out on his sofa after trying to kiss him and telling him she still loved him. Joe had been firm but kind as he gently removed her arms from around his neck before going to get a duvet, pillow and bucket. He'd set a glass of water on the coffee table and eased her onto her side in case she was sick in her sleep.

Then he'd sat there in the armchair in the dark, anxious about leaving her alone in case she was unwell. He couldn't help feeling responsible for her, even after all they'd been through. Something was wrong and Demi was struggling. She hadn't said that much about Hugo during the previous evening but he'd been able to see it in her eyes, to hear it in her laughter that seemed forced. Demi had always put a lot of pressure on herself to be the best at what she did and he knew that went back to her childhood. She was also able to appear confident and self-assured and he knew that not many people would be able to tell that she wasn't feeling good.

Didn't her husband care? Had he been able to read the signs? Couldn't he overcome any difficulties they were having and help Demi, ease her worries, support her and be there for her as Joe had tried to do in the past?

Sitting in the cool dark of the lounge, the ticking of the old clock on the mantelpiece and Demi's soft snoring the only sounds in the room, he'd felt the familiar sense of loneliness creeping in. Not having Odin there made it worse because the dog was such a comforting companion, keeping Joe firmly grounded in the present and focused on the moment. The sense of loneliness had always been there, ever since his mum had died when he was sixteen. She'd seemed invincible, even when she'd first been diagnosed with breast cancer and had vowed to fight it with everything she had. But in the end, it had beaten her. And that had left Joe with a deep fear, because if his mum could die then so could anyone. He'd thrown himself into school, sport and socialising as well as into his relationship with Demi, and he'd left himself little time to think. If he played his music loud, then the dark thoughts couldn't creep in. If he drank until he passed out, then he wouldn't sit up into the small hours wondering if there was anything after death. If he ran until his legs throbbed and his lungs burned, then nothing, not even his grief, could catch him. With time and with the love and support of his aunt Caryn and Demi, he'd been able to work though his pain and to come to terms with it, but that didn't mean that he never thought about his mum or that he didn't still feel afraid sometimes. That was just part of the human condition, surely? He simply had to remind himself to keep busy, keep going, be a good person, and to make the most of every day because nothing, not even tomorrow, was guaranteed.

And now, Demi was sitting on his sofa wearing a pair of his pyjamas, looking worse for wear.

'Drink some tea and try to eat something,' he said.

She grimaced. 'How much wine did I have last night?'

'A fair bit.'

'I am never doing that again.' She shook her head. 'Ouch. That hurts.'

'Paracetamol?'

'Please.'

Joe got her some from the bathroom then handed them to her with a glass of water. Once she'd taken them, sipped some tea and nibbled at her toast, she started to look a bit better.

'Do you want to talk about it?' Joe asked, cradling his own mug between his hands. 'I mean… you let a few things slip last night but you jumped around topics a fair bit.'

Demi raised her eyebrows. 'About what?'

He sighed inwardly. He was tired today and had lots to do and really didn't feel like having a long and difficult conversation but he also wanted to help Demi if he could.

'OK. OK. I know what you mean. Sorry, I'm just being an idiot.' She put her mug on the table then pressed her fingertips to the puffy skin beneath her eyes. 'I do need to talk but are you sure you want to listen?'

'I wouldn't ask if I wasn't.'

Demi wrapped the quilt around herself and nodded. 'So… things haven't been great recently.'

Joe sat back and let her talk, let his plans for the day drift away. Right now, being Demi's friend was what he needed to do.

—

Ffion got out of her dad's car and followed him and her mam up the driveway to Mari's house.

'It's a new estate, this,' their mam said as they looked around. 'Only two years old and the properties have already grown in value.'

'It's very nice.' Ffion admired the light brown bricks and the large white-framed bay windows either side of the white front door.

'One of the reasons Mari wanted to buy here was because of the sea views. As soon as she heard that they were building on the site of the former university campus, she knew she had to live here.' Her dad knocked on the door.

'A beautiful house and a sea view.' Ffion smiled. It looked like Mari had done well for herself.

The door opened and Bryn greeted them. As Ffion entered the hallway, she tried to hide her surprise. She hadn't seen Bryn in a while but he'd changed a lot. He was balding, with just a semi-circle of ginger hair running around the back of his head from one ear to the other, and he'd developed a paunch that his familiar shirt and jumper combo did nothing to hide. At just five foot six, he wasn't much taller than Ffion and she could look him straight in the eye.

'Ffion! Long time no see. How are you?' He kissed her on each cheek.

'Hi Bryn. I'm OK, thanks,' Ffion said. When people asked how she was these days, what else could she say? She was quite sure they didn't want her to launch into a monologue about missing her husband and being sad that her life hadn't worked out how she'd planned; how she should also have a husband, two children and a lovely home. Who wanted to listen to that?

Bryn gestured towards a doorway at the end of the hall. 'Mari's in the kitchen.'

'Great.' Ffion smiled briefly but her brother-in-law's attention had already moved on.

'How lovely,' Bryn said as Ffion's dad handed him the two bottles of wine they'd brought to go with Sunday lunch. 'These will go down well with the beef, Aled. Let's put them in the dining room.'

'Just popping to the loo,' her mam said, and Ffion suppressed a smile; her mam couldn't go anywhere without a trip to the toilet.

While Ffion's dad and Bryn went through a door to the right and her mam slipped through a door to the left, she went into the kitchen. The windows were clouded with steam and the room smelt delicious. Aromas of roast beef, potatoes and more met Ffion's nostrils and her stomach grumbled. It had been some time since she'd eaten a roast dinner and she found that she was actually looking forward to this one. Mari was an incredible cook, having spent a lot of time as a teenager in the kitchen of the hotel learning from the chefs.

Mari's back was to Ffion as she stirred something on the range cooker, while a small girl with dark hair sat at the kitchen table, head bent over a book, pencil in hand. It was the perfect cosy domestic scene and one she'd imagined for herself over the years.

'Hello, Mari.'

Her sister didn't move.

'Mari?'

The little girl looked up, her dark eyes appraising Ffion. 'She can't hear you. She's got her eyepods in.'

'Eyepods?' Ffion frowned.

'Yes, those things you put in your ears to listen to podcarts and music.'

'Podcarts?'

'Yes.'

The little girl nodded, her expression very serious and Ffion smiled. 'You must be Anwen.'

'I am.'

'Do you know who I am?'

'Ffion!' Mari had turned around now and removed her AirPods. 'Sorry, lovely, I didn't hear you come in. Since I had these for Christmas, I wear them all the time. There are so many podcasts to listen to.'

'Daddy says Mammy's quite ignorant now she's got podcart fever.' Anwen shook her head as if it was the worst crime in the world.

'Oh dear.' Ffion met Mari's eyes and they smirked at each other.

'Anwen, this is your aunty Ffion. You haven't seen her for a while in person but I have shown you photos, remember?'

'You were tiny little girls on the beach,' Anwen said solemnly, knitting her dark brows. 'And Aunty Ffion looked like me.'

'She did.' Mari looked affectionately at her daughter. 'Can you see it, Ffion?'

Ffion crossed the kitchen and gazed at the little girl. The pale skin, large dark eyes and brown hair with a straight fringe did look familiar. 'I can. You look a lot like me in the photos that Nanny and Grampy have.'

'They have loads of photos!' Anwen grinned, exposing a gap where her bottom front teeth were missing. Ffion smiled back, loving how singsong Anwen's accent was as much as at her comment.

'How's that homework coming along?' Mari asked as she peered at the workbook in front of Anwen.

'Nearly there!'

'Get it done then you can watch some TV after lunch.'

'OK, Mammy Bear.'

Ffion pressed a hand to her chest as she joined Mari at the cooker. 'That's so sweet.'

'I know. She started calling me that after we read a story about a bear family and it stuck. She usually does it when she's being cute or when she wants to wrap me around her little finger.'

'She's adorable and clearly very clever, too. Where's the baby?'

'Seren had a restless night so she's napping. I'll go and wake her up in a bit or she'll be grumpy at lunch.'

'Does that mean you had a restless night too?'

Mari grimaced. 'Can't you see the bags under my eyes? I'm sure I could pack potatoes in them.'

'Not really but you always were good with the concealer.'

Mari tapped Ffion's arm. 'Cheeky bugger.'

'Do you need a hand with anything?'

'You can mash the potatoes if you don't mind.'

'Of course not. Show me where everything is and I'll do that.'

While Ffion mashed, adding knobs of golden butter and ground black pepper to the potatoes, Mari finished off the gravy then set everything to keep warm. Their mother joined them in the kitchen.

'Bryn's showing your dad something in the garage, apparently.' Her mother rolled her eyes. 'New golf clubs, I think.'

Ffion looked at Mari but her sister avoided eye contact. 'Does he play a lot of golf?'

Mari shrugged. 'Not really. Just at weekends… when the weather's fine and sometimes during holidays.'

67

'Who's helping you with the children then, Mari?'

'I... I...' Mari covered her face with a tea towel and Ffion looked at her mother, who knitted her brows and shook her head sadly.

'Mammy, what's wrong?' Anwen had jumped down from the table.

Mari reached out and stroked her daughter's hair. 'I'm OK, bach. Just got something in my eye.'

'Anwen, come with Nanny and we'll go and wake Seren up, shall we?' Gwen took Anwen's hand and they left the kitchen.

'Mari?' Ffion placed her hands on Mari's shoulders and Mari lowered the tea towel. 'What's wrong?'

'Oh it's nothing. I'm just tired after last night. It's hard to keep everything ticking over sometimes, you know?'

Ffion nodded, but she didn't know. Not in the sense that Mari meant, although she could imagine how difficult it could be. Ffion's difficulties came from loneliness and not having the life she'd envisaged for herself, whereas Mari's came, it seemed, from working full-time, having two young children and a rather unhelpful and selfish husband. Mari was juggling a lot and Ffion was worried about her.

'Mari, I meant what I said the other day on our walk. I'm back now and I'll help you...'

Mari waved a hand and sniffed. 'I'm OK, honestly. But I am glad you're back because I've missed you so much. I'm sad about the reason why you're back, obviously, but we can see more of each other now and for me that is a massive bonus.'

Ffion hugged Mari tight, hoping that she could convey how much she loved her.

Ffion wasn't happy about why she was back either but now she was here, she would do what she could to help. It would take a lot of effort not to interfere if Bryn was being as lazy as it appeared, but perhaps Ffion could help to ease things for Mari by being around more. If Mari was struggling to let go of control around the house, as Ffion had previously suspected, then Ffion would try to help her with that too. She would also enjoy getting to know her nieces because that was something she'd missed out on over the years.

'Right, what else can I do to help with this dinner?' she asked, rolling up her shirt sleeves and looking around.

Mari pulled her back into a hug and Ffion knew that her sister really was happy to have her there.

—

'That was a delicious dinner.' Ffion sat back on her chair and patted her full belly. 'I haven't eaten that well in ages.'

Mari smiled. 'I'm glad you enjoyed it. You've got so skinny that I think you need a few more good meals inside you.'

'How do you stay so slim, Ffion?' Bryn asked.

Ffion swallowed, her dinner suddenly sitting heavy in her stomach. He wasn't being serious, was he?

'Bryn!' Mari tutted. 'You're such an idiot sometimes.'

'What did I say?' He asked cluelessly. 'I just thought you'd want to know her secret. You're always moaning about how you need to lose weight.'

Mari pressed her lips together then stood up and started clearing the table. Ffion stared at her brother-in-law for a moment, incredulity coursing through her. Could he really be that insensitive?

She glanced at her parents and they looked as uncomfortable as she felt but they stayed silent. Thankfully, Anwen and Seren seemed oblivious. Anwen was draining her drink and Seren was chasing a pea around the tray of her highchair with her thumb and forefinger.

'Daddy's an idiot.' Anwen giggled, breaking the awkward silence.

'Anwen!' Bryn stood up and shook his head. 'That's not appropriate.'

Anwen looked up at her daddy and her bottom lip wobbled. 'I only said what Mammy said.'

He sighed and marched away from the table and Ffion heard his heavy tread on the stairs then a door slamming above their heads.

They had opened the wine her dad had brought and enjoyed some with dinner but Ffion hadn't had more than a glass and she'd noticed that Mari had barely touched hers. Her parents had only had one glass each and yet they'd got through two bottles. Had Bryn consumed the rest?

'It's OK, Anwen.' Ffion got up and went to her niece. 'Shall we help Mammy with the dishes?'

Anwen grimaced. 'I don't like doing the dishes. I don't want to end up like Mammy doing all the yucky stuff. Daddy doesn't do dishes.'

'I'll do it, Ffion. You stay with the children.' Her dad got up and carried more plates to the kitchen.

'Do you have any books to show me?' Ffion asked Anwen. Mari had told her earlier that Anwen was always reading.

'Lots.' Anwen's face lit up. 'Do you want me to read to you?'

'I would love that.' Ffion smiled.

'I'll get my favourites.' Anwen got down from the table and ran from the dining room.

'Is it always like this?' Ffion asked her mam.

'Sometimes.' Gwen sighed. 'It's very difficult because your dad and I don't like to interfere. Of course I'd like to give Bryn a piece of my mind but it's not my place.'

'But Mari's running herself into the ground.' Ffion went around the table, tucking the chairs underneath.

'She is and I am worried about her. It's so difficult being a parent, though, Ffion. As I told you, we battled with our need to come and get you, knowing that you had a whole life in Scotland. We wanted to rescue you, but we weren't sure if it was the right thing to do. When your children are adults, you have to let go and let them live their own lives even if you want to wrap them up in cotton wool.'

She wrung her hands on the table in front of her and Ffion leaned across to give them a squeeze. 'I can understand that, and I know that if you'd said anything negative about Graeme to me then I'd have taken offence. Having said that, I do want to give Bryn a good talking to.' Ffion's jaw felt tight and she realised she'd started to grind her teeth.

'But is it your place to do that?' Her mam raised her eyebrows and Ffion saw the concern in her eyes.

'I guess not. However, I can be there for Mari more and try to help her.'

'Mari will be glad to have you around. In some ways, I'm grateful that I'm so busy with the hotel because if I wasn't then I'd be sitting at home stressing over you both. I want you and Mari to be happy and healthy and to have everything you want but I don't have the power to give that to you. All I can do is be there when you need me. Your poor dad has swallowed many a comment over the years when Bryn's been a knob and it's hard for him because he feels so protective of Mari too, but if he said anything, it could cause tension that would be difficult to overcome and that's not fair on anyone, especially the girls.'

'I get that...' Ffion sank onto a chair and folded her hands on the table. 'But—'

Something hit her in the side of the head.

She rubbed at her skin. 'What was that?' She turned in the direction the object had come from and saw little Seren grinning at her.

'Seren, was that you?'

'Knob!' Seren laughed.

'Oh god.' Gwen buried her face in her hands. 'I forgot that she keeps repeating things.'

'Bryn knob.' Seren smacked her hands against the tray of her highchair then picked up a pea and threw it at Ffion. It fell short and dropped to the carpet but Ffion gaped at her niece.

'Knob! Knob! Knob!' Seren chuckled.

'Don't say that word, Seren.' Gwen shook her head. 'It's naughty.'

'Notty knob.' Seren squealed with delight and Ffion turned to her mam and saw her lips twitching.

'Oh dear.' Gwen shrugged. 'Seems like that one's sticking around.'

Ffion started laughing. She was incredibly worried about Mari and would try to speak to her sister about things, but for now there were children to entertain and care for and, of course, she'd only just come back. She couldn't charge around like a bull in a china shop and start telling people how to behave when she didn't have the full picture. Her mam was right; if any of Ffion's family had started telling her how to live her life with Graeme, she'd have told them where to go. Such matters required sensitivity and tact.

'Aunty Ffion!' Anwen struggled into the room, her small arms wrapped around a pile of books.

Ffion went to help her. 'Gosh, what a lot of books!'

'They're my favourites.'

'Where shall we sit to read them?'

'In the lounge?' Anwen asked. 'We can snuggle on the sofa.'

'I like the sound of that.'

'Me!' Seren held up her podgy arms, so Gwen lifted her out of the high chair and she wriggled to be put down, then the four of them went through to the lounge.

Anwen put the books on the rug and sat on the sofa with Ffion. Seren stood gazing at them, one finger in her mouth, her mop of ginger curls shining like copper in the afternoon sunlight that poured through the window.

'Do you want to come and look at the books too?' Ffion asked the toddler.

Seren nodded then climbed up next to Ffion, placing a sticky hand on her arm. Ffion tried not to notice.

'I'll go and help Mari and your dad. You enjoy yourself.' Gwen left the room and for the first time, Ffion was alone with her nieces.

For the next hour, Anwen and Ffion took turns reading the books while Seren tapped at the pictures and occasionally said 'Knob!' Ffion was impressed with how well Anwen could read and with how patient she was with Seren. Whatever was going on with Mari and Bryn, they'd done a good job with their children.

When Seren rested her head against Ffion's arm and snuggled closer, Ffion had to swallow the lump that rose into her throat. Once upon a time she'd pictured a scene like this where she'd have children of her own cuddled up to her as they read stories, but Graeme would have been there too. She wished he could see her now; that he was sitting in the armchair opposite the sofa, smiling as Anwen used different voices for the characters – she'd clearly done this before and Ffion knew that Mari would have been reading to her since she was in the womb – while Seren sucked her thumb and dozed.

It was a wonderful way to spend a Sunday afternoon, and Ffion felt another small piece of her fractured self slot back into place.

Chapter Eight

After they got back to the cottage, Ffion was still so full that she felt the need to walk some of the dinner off, so she headed down to the beach. It was cold, but she was glad to be outdoors. She walked the length of the beach to the cliffs and then back again, breathing deeply and savouring the briny air and the soothing sound of the sea. The wet sand sucked at her wellies and the wind made her eyes sting but it was good to be near the water, to have some time to herself as twilight fell. Apart from a few dog walkers and two runners who appeared to be doing some sort of relay, Ffion had the beach to herself.

The day had been interesting. Seeing Mari in her home had brought some things to Ffion's attention and she couldn't shake off her concerns about her sister. She had two beautiful children and a lovely home, but Bryn was, as Seren had repeated many times, being a knob. Having been through a breakdown after losing Graeme, Ffion was wary about judging people and suspected that there must be more to it. She hoped there must be, because although she'd always been convinced that Mari could do better than Bryn, she also believed that people were entitled to choose for themselves and Mari had chosen him. There must be some redeeming things about Bryn for Mari to have fallen in love with him, married him and had two children with him. Perhaps they had temporarily lost their way and needed to find their direction again. Ffion hoped for her sister's sake that it would be possible for them to work things out.

She'd spent a lovely hour with her nieces reading Anwen's books, and her heart had squeezed when Seren had nodded off, her head of curls drooping until it rested in Ffion's lap. Ffion had felt like she should hold her breath, afraid to move and disturb the tiny girl, while Anwen had continued to read and to ask her questions about the story as if to check that she was paying attention. Anwen was very bright, her love of books delightful.

When Ffion's parents had said that they needed to get back to the hotel for the late afternoon shift, Ffion had almost cried with disappointment. While sitting in her sister's warm, cosy home, she could forget her own pain, the emptiness of her life. However, she'd known that Mari would still have a lot to do, and that time was precious, so she'd reluctantly slipped out from under Seren, promised Anwen that they would read more together soon, then donned her coat.

During the car journey back to the cottage, her parents had spoken more about Bryn and Mari, about how they were worried about what was happening there but didn't like to interfere, and it had strengthened Ffion's resolve to be there for Mari as much as she could.

Now, as Ffion made her way back to the cottage, she didn't think she'd want anything to eat for the rest of the day, but she definitely fancied a coffee. When she got to the front lawn of the hotel, she walked around the side and towards the car park. She heard voices approaching but didn't feel like speaking to anyone right then, so she ducked behind the large square bins, planning on waiting until whoever it was had gone before emerging and going to her parents' cottage.

'You sure you'll be all right now?' A man asked.

'Yes, I'll be fine. And thanks again.'

The voices sounded familiar so Ffion peeped around the bins. It was the customers she'd served the previous evening.

'You didn't have to come down here with me.'

'I was concerned about you.' He scuffed the toe of his boot against the gravel. 'Besides which, I needed some air and I have to go and get Odin. I didn't mean to leave him with my aunt all day.'

'Bloody flea-ridden dog.' The woman – was it Demi? – chuckled and Joe did too.

'Take care now, Demi.'

'You too.'

They stood there for a moment, gazing at each other, then Demi stepped forwards and embraced Joe before taking his face in her hands and moving in for a kiss.

Ffion pulled her head back behind the bins. She felt so awkward but couldn't go anywhere because if she moved, they'd know she'd been there, watching them. What would Graeme think of her? Hiding behind bins, spying on customers, giggling at a sweary toddler and fretting about her sister's marriage?

She snorted, nerves and embarrassment battling inside her, then slammed a hand over her mouth. She needed to be quiet but it was one of those times when she felt so anxious that she wanted to guffaw.

'What was that?' Demi said.

'No idea.'

'I thought I heard something.'

Ffion froze, trying to stay as still as she could.

'Just a cat or a rat, probably. Anyway, drive carefully and we'll speak soon.'

There was the sound of a car door closing, an engine starting, and a car drove over the gravel and left the car park. Ffion stayed where she was, holding her breath because even in the cold, the smell of the bins was revolting. When she finally felt it was safe to take a look, the car park was empty and the light was fading fast.

She moved out of her hiding place and hurried back to the cottage, hoping no one had been looking out of their hotel room window and spotted the crazy lady lying in wait behind the bins.

As she let herself into the cottage though, she couldn't help picturing Joe and Demi hugging and kissing and wondered how it would feel to experience that again. To have a man look at her with love in his eyes, strong arms to encircle her and a heart to beat in time with hers.

She'd had that once but right now she couldn't imagine ever having it again.

–

Joe had picked Odin up from his aunt's and they were both back at home. Joe was lounging on the sofa, the TV on with the sound down low, and Odin was lying in front of the log burner enjoying the warmth.

It had been an eventful twenty-four hours for sure. Demi was having a difficult time with her husband, Hugo Cartwright, as well as experiencing what Joe had heard described as burnout. Joe had met Hugo once at a charity fundraiser and thought him rather snooty. He was tall and thin and had icy blue eyes and white-blonde hair that always looked as though it needed a cut. When Demi had introduced them, Hugo had almost sneered at Joe, making him feel every bit the working-class man he was. And that was fine, because Joe wasn't pretentious at all, but he did feel it was a bit unnecessary for Hugo to look down on him in that way. Hugo might have been born with a silver spoon in his mouth but Joe had come from working people and he was proud of that. He did suspect though, that Hugo's sneering might have come from something else, a possible jealousy that Joe had once been involved with Demi.

Demi had told Joe that Hugo was being cold and distant at the moment and she was finding it difficult, especially as she needed her partner right now because she had hit a physical and emotional low. Joe felt sorry for her. They had known each other for such a long time and the last thing he wanted was for her to suffer in any way. This morning, she had poured out her fears and confusion and she had cried a lot, then her mobile had buzzed with a text from Hugo asking her to meet him to talk. Apparently, knowing that Demi had spent time with Joe had given Hugo a nudge in the right direction. Joe had advised her to ask Hugo to come to her rather than driving all the way back home to Kent with a hangover, and she had seemed to accept that it was a wise suggestion. Instead, she'd told Hugo she'd meet him the following day if he came to Wales, and Hugo had agreed.

Joe had taken her back to the hotel and seen her off then walked home to get his car to collect Odin. If he'd had work the next day, he might have left Odin with his aunt overnight – even though he'd have missed him – but as it was half-term, he wanted to have his canine companion home.

When he'd gone with Demi so she could collect her car, he'd had the strange feeling that someone was watching them in the car park. There had been movement behind the large bins and he was sure he'd seen someone. But then why would someone spy on them? Demi had kissed him briefly but it had been a kiss goodbye and there'd been nothing amorous in it at all.

He shook his head and stretched out on the sofa, turning up the volume on the TV. He had a whole week to catch up with marking, to work on the house and to spend walking and running with Odin, so he aimed to begin with a relaxing Sunday evening. In all honesty, after the emotional direction the previous evening had taken, it was exactly what he needed.

Chapter Nine

Ffion sat on her bed staring at the packet of pills in her hand. She'd had a restless night again, waking from dreams that made her heart ache. Graeme had been there and she'd held him close, breathed in his scent and asked him where he'd been. Such dreams were cruel because when she woke, the fact that she couldn't turn over in bed and hug him was agony. She wanted to feel his arms around her and to ask for reassurance that he'd never leave her, but she couldn't, and never would be able to again.

Being back in Cariad Cove had been a welcome distraction. She'd taken the two weeks since her arrival to settle in, spent some evenings working at the hotel and made the most of walks along the beach and the coastal path. But she needed a purpose. Not a permanent job – not yet, anyway, because she didn't feel ready for that – but she needed a challenge, something to get her out of bed in the mornings, something to push her to test her strength and determination.

But what?

She could swallow a pill and sleep all day. She'd been trying not to take them but she knew they were there, tucked at the bottom of her bag. The Zopiclone was a comfort blanket, although only a temporary comfort because when she woke from the sleep it induced, everything hit her all over again. At least when she slept without medication, even if she didn't sleep well every night, she was aware that she was dreaming. Some part of her subconscious knew that Graeme was gone and that he wouldn't be there when she woke and so she was protecting herself from the worst of her pain.

She stood up, walking over to the window. The waves crashed against the shore, sending spray up into the air, and she shivered. It would be freezing in the sea today. Perversely, she was overwhelmed with the urge to feel exactly how cold the water was.

To feel alive.

She dug around in a drawer until she found the black swimming costume she'd bought two years ago when she and Graeme had gone for a weekend at a spa resort. It had been a beautiful break, one of their last times together not overshadowed by his ailing health – a time of complete innocence, was how she thought of it now.

Stripping off her pyjamas, she pulled on the swimming costume then tugged a jumper and jogging bottoms over it. This might be utter madness but she didn't care. She needed to do something to shake off this torpor.

Downstairs, her parents were in the kitchen having breakfast, so she said good morning to them and told them she was off for a walk. They didn't need to know her plans; they might try to dissuade her and now she'd got the idea in her head, she couldn't not do it. She pulled on her coat and wellies then let herself out, shivering from nerves and the cold as she made her way down to the beach. It was deserted and she was glad because she didn't want anyone to witness her wild behaviour.

She walked along the sand for a bit then stopped. 'Graeme, what do you think?' His name felt unfamiliar on her lips; she said it out loud so infrequently these days, and yet her heart repeated it thousands of times every day.

The tide was in and it lapped at the toes of her wellies, tugging at her as if to encourage her.

'Do you think I should do it?' she asked, laughing and trembling. 'Would you do it too?'

His bright smile shone in her imagination, his loving gaze fixed on her face, and she knew that he would. They'd done it before, a long time ago, dared each other to go into the sea on a chilly December day. Keen to impress each other, they'd stripped down to their underwear and charged in holding hands, screaming as the cold hit their skin and with the sheer joy of being together, being alive.

'I'm doing this for you, *Graeme*!' This time she said his name louder, savouring its sound, its feel, his memory.

She kicked off the wellies, stepped out of the jogging bottoms and pulled the jumper over her head, setting them on the sand out of the reach of the tide. She was shaking violently now but she'd gone too far to stop.

'OK, my love. You owe me one…'

She took a deep breath, knowing that doing it gradually would only make it worse. It was imperative that she went into the water quickly and then got out. As quickly as possible.

'One. Two. *Three!*'

She ran into the shallows, squealing as the freezing water splashed her, bringing goosebumps to her skin and turning her nipples to tiny hard peaks. Her body told her to turn around and go and get warm again, but her heart and mind drove her on. She could do this!

When the water reached her waist, she sucked in a shaky breath and dived beneath the surface. Everything went quiet for a moment, then she heard the whoosh of the water past her ears. Opening her eyes, she saw fathomless blue-grey, dark swirling seaweed and the blurred rays of the morning sunlight that pierced the surface and faded before meeting the seabed. She held her breath, feeling her body acclimatising itself, wondering how long she could stay there, but something inside her gave and she pushed upwards and gasped, sucking in air.

Wading out of the sea, she squeezed water from her hair, then started to dress again. Her clothes clung to her wet skin and she was shuddering uncontrollably but felt like she'd been through some kind of cleansing ritual. The sea had wrapped itself around her and washed away the things she didn't need to cling to anymore. It had cleared her head, stung her eyes and her throat, left its salty kiss upon her lips. She was freezing, but experiencing a strong sense of renewal. If she focused on physical sensations there was less room to dwell on her grief, and she could allow her mind and heart some time out to heal.

She had set herself a challenge this morning that she had accepted and passed, she thought, with flying colours. That had to be a positive start to a brand-new day.

–

Joe had struggled to concentrate all day at work and it wasn't because it was the week after half-term and he had back-to-school blues. He'd gone for an early run with Odin along the beach, enjoying a good workout before breakfast. He'd run to the far side of the cove and back, throwing Odin's ball as they ran, laughing as the dog raced into the shallows to retrieve the ball then back out again, as excited as a puppy every single time.

On the way back, he'd seen a petite figure walking along the sand. She had stopped, undressed and then run into the water. Joe wasn't concerned because there were some crazy locals who liked to take a dip, even in the winter, but as he'd got closer, he'd become worried because the figure had been completely submerged by the waves. Just as he'd been about to investigate, the woman had emerged again and he'd paused, sure that it was Ffion from the hotel. Embarrassed at seeing her in a small black swimming costume, her pale wet skin gleaming, her hair slicked back and a smile on her face, he'd averted his eyes. She hadn't seen him – too caught up with her swim, it seemed – but the image of her emerging from the waves had played on repeat in his mind all day.

It had stirred him and intrigued him – he wanted to know how the water had been (freezing, he guessed), why she had done it (perhaps she did it every day), and a part of him wondered how it would be to hold her in his arms while her skin was wet and cold. If he kissed her, would he taste the salt on her lips?

The last thought was one he'd tried to shake away. After all, he didn't know Ffion well, had barely spoken to her and yet he kept seeing her. He wasn't going to deny that she was attractive, that there was a basic and primal urge within him that wanted to scoop her up and feel her slide her arms around his neck, but that was something he would push away. This wasn't a movie or a romance novel where heroes and heroines met and fell in love, where real life didn't get in the way with its codes of appropriate behaviour and the whole awkwardness of being human. After all, what would she think, this virtual stranger, if she knew for a moment what he was thinking right now? Her moment in the sea was private and she hadn't seemed aware of his presence; she had been taking a chilly swim for herself and only for herself. Just as he ran for himself, to stay fit and healthy, but also because of the freedom he felt when he ran and became one with movement, with the beating of his heart and his steady breaths, the regular rhythm of his trainers as they hit the ground and pushed him on.

Ffion was a stranger and would probably always be one. That was how life went. And yet, he knew now that she worked at the hotel, knew that she took early morning dips in the sea and knew that there was something in her gaze that suggested she was going through a difficult time. There was a chance that he would see her again, and have the opportunity to talk to her, as well as ask how she found the guts to dive into the icy depths of the sea.

There was always a chance…

—

'You did what?' Mari's eyes widened.

'I went for a dip in the sea this morning.'

'You're mad.'

'Perhaps.' Ffion smiled. Mari had asked if she wanted to meet that afternoon in Swansea for a coffee. Apparently, Bryn had offered to collect Anwen from school and Seren from the childminder. Ffion had been pleased that her sister was making some time for herself and had agreed.

'Ffion…' Mari licked her lips. 'I fibbed when I said Bryn offered to collect the children. I told him he had to because I had twilight training. I had such a bad night because Seren was up and down and then today was challenging in school. I felt like I needed a break so I rang him at work and said I'd forgotten about the training.'

Ffion reached across the table for her sister's hand. 'Everyone needs time out. And it seems like you're—' She bit her lip.

'Like what?' Mari's brows knitted together.

'Uhhh…' Ffion was conscious of what she'd spoken with her mam about and didn't want to express her opinion on Bryn to Mari and make things worse.

'Tell me.'

Around them the sounds of a busy cafe provided comfort. The clinking of cutlery, the grinding and frothing of the coffee machine, the low hum of the cake fridge and the murmur of conversations were soothing. Aromas of freshly ground coffee and grilled cheese, fresh bread and scones drifted through the air, and Ffion was lulled into a relaxed state by the wonderful familiarity of it all, by how life just kept on going even when her own world might have fallen apart. Sometimes she needed to be alone but at others being around people helped.

'Ffion!' Mari's voice was sharper this time and she pulled her hand back and ran it over her hair. 'Please finish what you were going to say.'

'Oh Mari, I'm sorry. I don't want to interfere and I certainly don't want to seem like I'm judging, but when we came over for lunch Bryn seemed a bit… Well… he left you to… to do everything. And then when he lost his temper, I thought he was out of order. I promised Mam I wouldn't say anything because I don't want you to hate me for commenting about your husband's behaviour…'

'Why would I hate you?' Mari rested her elbows on the table.

'Bryn's your husband. You chose to be with him and you love him and I'm just the sister who's been away for ages and… it's not my place to pass comment on your partner.'

'Bryn is being a dickhead.' Mari blinked rapidly. 'I know he is and I'm annoyed with him too. But I'm also scared… He seems so off with me lately and something's just not right. I don't know what or why or how we came to this point but I know we need to make some changes. I mean… I don't think he even finds me attractive any more.'

'What? How could he not?'

'Look at me, Ffion. I've several spare tyres and I'm so knackered all the time that I never want to… you know… have sex.'

Ffion sipped her coffee. 'Libido doesn't work on a command basis. You have two young children and a full-time job so of course you're bloody knackered. If he took a bit more responsibility for things and did his share, then maybe you wouldn't be so exhausted and would feel like having sex.'

'Maybe.'

'And it's not about him helping out more either, because caring for the children is just as much his respons-ibility as it is yours. He should do his bit.'

Mari finished her latte and put the tall glass on the table. 'I don't know how we're going to sort things out yet, but I do know that I want to do something for myself. I need to secure some "me time" so I can get my head around things. You heard what Bryn said about my weight and me moaning about it all the time.'

'Mari, you're not overweight.'

'I feel uncomfortable at the moment and it's knocking my confidence because even though I can't get my pre-baby body back, I can at least get a body I like. I have some gorgeous work clothes in the back of my wardrobe and I can't wear them because they don't fit. It's not about being skinny, it's about feeling like me.'

'I can understand that,' Ffion said. 'I don't feel like me either.'

'We're in a state, aren't we?' Mari sighed and rubbed at her eyes.

'You know... I was thinking that I want to do something for myself too. I need to challenge and motivate myself and I've been trying to think of a way to do that.'

They sat and gazed at each other for a moment, mulling things over.

'We are talking about exercise here, aren't we?' Mari asked. 'I don't want to jump out of a plane or bungee jump or learn to pole dance or anything like that.'

'I don't, either.' Ffion laughed.

'OK, then, how about joining the gym? We could go together, make a pact to go at least twice a week.'

Ffion pursed her lips. 'I'm not a fan of gyms. There are too many gorgeous people there who know what they're doing and it makes me self-conscious. Plus, it's not really a goal as such.'

'A goal? So you want something specific to aim for?'

'Yes.'

'I know... how about we take up running? We could aim to run 5k or something.'

'Running?' Ffion thought of the people she'd seen on the beach, of how focused they seemed, how they looked like they had a goal. 'That's a good idea. But will you be able to fit it in?'

'We could schedule it in. I really think I need this and you can help motivate me.'

'OK.' Ffion nodded. 'When shall we start?'

'Why don't we go shopping for some gear now? Then we can't back out. If we have the clothes, we have to do it.'

'Deal!'

They shook hands over the table, grinning at each other as if they were teenagers again who'd just agreed on a plan to pinch some cider from the fridge to take to a beach party.

Chapter Ten

'Are we really going to do this?' Mari asked as she stood in the lounge of their parents' cottage.

'We are,' Ffion said determinedly. 'I mean… we invested in the gear so we have to do it, don't we?'

Mari gave her a small smile but there was uncertainty in her eyes.

'This stuff wasn't cheap.' Ffion looked down at her black running tights and sweat-wicking fleece top that covered her sweat-wicking T-shirt and sports bra, then at the expensive trainers she'd bought when she'd gone shopping with Mari.

'It wasn't. Plus, I forced myself out of bed at five thirty a.m. on a Saturday morning to get over here, when I could have stayed in bed for at least ten more minutes before the girls started pestering me for breakfast.'

'They have you up that early?'

Mari blew out a breath. 'It's constant. I'm on call twenty-four hours a day.'

'That must be draining, Mari. I mean… I know that young children don't always sleep well but I had no idea that they'd wake you in the night *and* get you up so early.'

'Well, this morning Bryn will have to deal with it. If he can.' She tugged at the hem of her T-shirt. 'Oh god, what have I done? He doesn't know which cereal Anwen prefers and he might make the milk for Seren's porridge too hot and—'

'Hey, hey, slow down. Bryn's their dad and he must have picked some things up over the past six years. He'll manage.'

'I don't know if he will… and what if the girls need me? I feel so guilty because I miss them terribly through the week when I'm at work, and then some days I feel bad because I wish they'd just give me five minutes' peace so I could go to the toilet without someone asking if I'm having a stinky poo, or so that I could have a shower without being interrupted but… oh…' She sank onto the sofa, a dazed expression on her face. 'I'm a bad mother.'

Ffion sat next to her. 'You are a wonderful mother and you do so much for them but it shouldn't be a lone venture. Bryn married you and decided to have children with you and therefore it's also his responsibility to take care of them. You shouldn't have to do it all alone, you know?'

Mari blinked. 'I know that and the rational part of me tells me the same thing every day but then the doubts creep in. Bryn is just… he's not me and the girls are used to having me there. I'm their world.'

Ffion rubbed Mari's back in a circular motion as if trying to comfort a small child. Mari was clearly exhausted. Her need to stay in control was understandable because if she didn't stay on top of her life then who would? At the same, Ffion couldn't help but remember her sister when they were younger – she'd always had trouble delegating and wanted to do things in her own particular way. If she'd been ill after having Seren, then she'd probably have felt that she lost some of that control and might well have overcompensated afterwards.

'I'm worried because when I go home, I'm sure the sink will be full of dishes, the children might not even be dressed and they'll probably have ended up having biscuits for breakfast.'

'Would that really harm them for one day?'

'I guess not.'

'Dishes can be done later and children can be dressed later… or not. Who cares if they wear their pyjamas for a whole Saturday morning? Don't you remember you and me watching TV all Saturday morning because Mam and Dad were working? And we did all right, didn't we?'

'We turned out OK.'

'See… Anwen and Seren will be fine. And to be honest, Mari, Anwen is quite switched on for such a young girl. She'll whip Bryn into shape if he's slacking.'

Mari laughed. 'She probably will.'

'So… shall we get going?'

'OK.'

Ffion stood up then reached for Mari's hand and pulled her into a hug.

'Love you, sis.'

'Love you too.'

They headed outside and walked down to the beach. It was almost seven a.m. The horizon was gold, the water dark and calm as a pond and the sky above them painted with shades of butter, biscotti and cobalt dashes where the clouds had parted. It was breath-taking and it stopped Ffion in her tracks.

'What an amazing sunrise.'

'It's perfect.'

'No better time to start our new fitness routine.'

Mari yawned. 'Are we going to do this every Saturday?'

'We should aim to run every other day, really, Mari, if we're going to get fit. But... for starters, and because you're so busy, I think that if we can aim to run two or three times a week that will be a good start.'

'OK.'

'Let's do some stretching then get going, shall we?'

'Are you nervous?'

Ffion frowned. 'A little bit. Mainly because I haven't done any exercise apart from walking in years and I'm worried about how unfit I am.'

'Me too. I think I'm quite fit because I'm always on the go, running around after the children and at work I hardly ever sit down, but proper exercise where you get your heart rate up is different, isn't it?'

Ffion felt a flicker of doubt pierce her resolve and for a moment she thought about how nice it would be to head back to the cottage, make a pile of toast and a pot of tea and sit on the sofa with a good book. But then she realised she'd struggled to relax like that for ages, that a lazy Saturday morning was not the same without Graeme there to share it, and so if she did give up on running now, she'd regret it later. It would be like going back to square one, back to where she'd already been, and she definitely didn't want that.

'We need to do this.' She took Mari's arm and they padded down to the sand.

'Ready?'

'Have we warmed up enough?'

'I think so. I read that you should do a warm-up walk and some stretching and so we should be fine, right?'

'I guess so.'

'Ok then... off we go.'

They started to jog along the sand, the sea to their right, the dunes to their left, the hotel and cottage behind them. They went slowly at first, avoiding piles of seaweed and a beached jellyfish that looked like a large, translucent mushroom. Then they sped up a bit, flashing smug smiles at each other. This wasn't so bad, it was easier than Ffion had expected actually, it was…

What had happened to her breathing?

She sucked in air, trying to fill her lungs, but it was like she couldn't get enough. Next to her, Mari was panting and her face was turning red, and Ffion knew it had nothing to do with the sunrise.

She tried to slow down a bit but her legs felt heavy and solid and there was a terrible burning in her calves.

'This… hurts!' Mari gasped next to her.

'I know. How's… it… so hard?'

'Don't… know.'

But they kept going, reaching the halfway point along the beach and Ffion tried to distract herself by looking ahead at the dark arm of the cliffs where the land stretched out into the sea. She gazed at the water, thinking about how cold and refreshing it was, about how it felt as the sand sucked at her feet, pulled at her toes when she stood in the shallows and the tide played out its tug of war with anything it encountered.

'Can't… go… on.'

Mari stopped suddenly and Ffion staggered as she tried to stop her legs moving. They were like lead weights now, her toes were numb, and the rest of her was boiling.

Mari slumped to the sand and Ffion followed suit, her lungs raw.

'I hate it!' Mari cried. 'It's horrible.'

'I know!'

Ffion lay down and stretched her arms above her head. 'Everything in my body hurts and I feel sick. How can people do this?'

Mari flopped next to her and they lay there until their breathing had slowed, occasionally coughing and groaning.

'What are we going to do?' Mari asked, her voice filled with despair. 'I was so excited about trying to get fit, about doing something positive for myself and for my mental health. I've seen other women doing it and they make it look easy. Why isn't it easy, Ffion? Are we just rubbish?'

Ffion sat up and shook her head. 'We're not rubbish at all. That was just our first attempt. We absolutely can do this.' She forced determination into her tone even though her whole body was screaming in pain. 'If other people can do this then we can too. We're strong and resilient women, Mari. So come on, get up, and we'll walk this off then try again in a day or two.'

'OK.' The word wavered with doubt and Ffion felt terrible for her sister. She'd wanted to help Mari as well as herself but it had been a lot harder than she'd expected.

The sound of feet pounding the sand made Ffion turn and sigh. It was Joe and that huge dog of his, running towards them, making it look effortless. He slowed as he reached them and handed something to the dog.

'Good morning!' He stood before them, a dark shape with the rising sun behind him making him seem to glow around the edges. He was tall and broad, like some marauding Viking come from the sea to stake his claim. 'Are you ladies all right?'

He crouched down and the dog came and sat next to him. Now that it was closer, Ffion could see the yellow ball in its mouth.

'We're fine,' Ffion replied even though something in her lower left leg was growing tighter by the second.

'Have you been running?'

'We tried,' Mari said, her voice emerging as a whine. 'But we failed.'

'We didn't fail.' Ffion didn't want Joe thinking they'd failed at doing something he did with ease. For some reason she didn't want this man thinking she failed at anything.

'Do you run regularly?' he asked.

'This was our first time.' Mari just kept talking even though Ffion was now trying to send her a psychic message to shut up.

'First time, eh?' He nodded. 'Did you find it difficult?'

'No!' Ffion snapped and stood up, hands on hips, then yelped. 'Shit!'

'What's wrong?' He stood up and peered at her. 'Pulled a muscle?'

'I don't know. Oh my god that really hurts…' Her left calf was a ball of fire with hot needles stabbing at it repeatedly. The muscle felt so tight, she worried it might pop.

'It's probably cramp.' He reached for her hands. 'Come here, I can help.'

'I'm fine.' Ffion put her foot down then lifted it immediately. 'Ouch!'

He knelt down in front of her like some kind of medieval knight.

'Place your hands on my shoulders and I'll stretch your calf for you. Is it OK if I put my hands on your leg?'

Ffion glanced at Mari who was now wide-eyed and grinning.

'OK.' Ffion placed her hands on his shoulders and he took her leg in his large hands. He started to gently move her foot up and down then he ran his hands over her calf and soon, the pain eased. As the distraction of the burning ebbed away, Ffion became aware of how broad and muscular the shoulders beneath her hands were, of how the muscles moved as he manipulated her leg and foot, of how she could see the graduation of his short haircut and smell his spicy, woody cologne.

'How's that feeling?' he asked, looking up at her.

'Better.'

'Are you a sports therapist or something?' Mari asked him, dusting sand off her running tights.

'Kind of.' He smiled. 'I'm a PE teacher.'

'I'm a teacher too.' Mari's tone was warmer now, as if she found the presence of another professional reassuring. 'But I teach primary.'

'Tough job.'

'Sometimes, yes.'

Ffion turned her attention back to Joe, trying to ignore how close he was, how his hands felt on her leg, how handsome he was. Had she noticed that before?

She shook her head. This man had a girlfriend and Ffion was in no position to fall for someone. Ever. It was just the first time she'd had a man's hands on her since she'd lost Graeme and it was bound to be strange. Even with her sister right next to them and a large damp dog with a yellow ball in its mouth watching their every move.

'There. That should do it.' He released Ffion's leg and she put her foot on the sand and tested it.

'It's still a bit sore.'

'You had a nasty cramp. You should probably take it easy for a few days to rest it but keep massaging the area to keep the blood flowing into it.'

Mari sniggered. 'Sorry. Playground humour. I think I had too much oxygen when we were running and it's gone to my head.'

'You might not have had enough oxygen in your blood, actually,' Joe said, his tone serious. 'You should be careful when starting any exercise plan.'

'We'll be fine but thanks for your help and advice.' Ffion straightened her fleece and redid her ponytail.

'If you're serious about running you could try that Couch to 5k programme.' Joe looked at them both in turn. 'It's a great way to start running and helps you build up while providing motivation too.'

'I've heard of that.' Mari nudged Ffion with her elbow. 'A team of parents at the school do it and I think they have some sort of Facebook group.'

'Probably. It's very popular, as are the park runs.'

Ffion felt like a sulky teen and she wasn't sure why. This man had been nothing but kind. He'd eased her cramp with what she thought must be magic hands and was now sharing sensible information. Was it because the first time she'd seen him his dog had knocked her flying? Was it because he had an air about him that could be confidence or could be arrogance and she just didn't like arrogant men? Or was it something else entirely? She'd barely noticed a man since she'd fallen in love with Graeme and had certainly not noticed any since he'd passed away, but this man had landed on her radar and he was having a strange effect upon her. Yes, she could see that he was quite attractive – if you liked that sort of thing – and yes, he had a good job as a teacher, so must have some positive traits because everyone knew that teaching was a tough job. So why did she want to kick him in the shins, poke out her tongue and run away from him?

Did she resent him because she was *interested* in him?

'No!'

'Sorry?' He frowned at her.

She'd said it out loud.

'I… sorry… I thought you asked if we'd tried park run. We haven't, anyway.' She looked down and fiddled with the zip of her fleece, her cheeks burning.

'Well, have a think about Couch to 5k. It's worth a shot.'

Ffion looked up and found him smiling at her, his blue eyes bright as sapphires, his skin illuminated by the golden glow of the morning sky.

'We'll try that, won't we, Fi?' Mari asked. 'Thanks so much. I'm Mari, by the way.'

'Joe.'

'Hello, Joe. And this is my sister, Ffion.'

'We've met before.'

'You have?' Mari's eyebrows rose.

'At the… uh… hotel and… here.'

'You've met before?' Mari looked intrigued now and Ffion wanted to nudge her and tell her to calm down. Nothing interesting had happened.

'Odin knocked your poor sister over.' Joe shook his head. 'I was incredibly embarrassed.'

'Me too.' Ffion found a smile creeping to her lips now.

They stood there for a moment, all three of them smiling, then Joe said, 'Right, I'd better get going. I have a million jobs on my "to do" list for today. Anyway, rest that leg and check out one of the running apps. It will help you no end, I'm sure.'

'Will do.' Feeling awkward and lost for what else to say, Ffion gave him a thumbs-up.

'Bye, then.' He took the ball from Odin and threw it ahead. The dog bounded after it and Joe started to jog; soon they were almost at the hotel and Mari and Ffion were still watching them.

'Yum!' Mari rubbed her hands together. 'That is one gorgeous man.'

Ffion kicked at the sand, wincing as her sore muscle twinged.

'Oh come on, Fi. You can't deny that. I know you still have your Graeme goggles on but surely you can see that Joe's delicious? Much as I love Bryn, I can still appreciate a sexy man.'

'Don't objectify him.' Ffion folded her arms across her chest.

'I'm not! I meant that he seems gorgeous on the inside too. Not many men would stop to help a random sweaty woman and massage her leg to make it better.'

'I guess not.'

'He seems very nice. Yes, he's handsome but there's more to him than that. I got a good vibe from him.'

'He's all right, I guess.'

'You could do worse.'

'What?'

'Ffion, I know how much you loved Graeme. *Love* Graeme. But you're still so young. You're still grieving, I know, but you are entitled to move on, too.'

'Move on?' Ffion's chest tightened. 'Why would I even want to move on? I had… I had… I had a…' She hugged herself and stomped down to the water's edge.

Mari followed her and put an arm around her shoulders. 'I'm so sorry, Ffion. I didn't mean to be insensitive. I just worry about you and don't want to see you so sad.'

'I'm OK. I just find it so hard to think about moving on. I tell myself the same thing all the time, try to chivvy myself into accepting that my husband is gone and I should live my life. I know it's what Graeme would have said too. But it's not easy, you know. Kind of like running.' She flashed Mari a small smile, trying to lighten the mood. 'It hurts like hell and makes me feel sick but I know I need to do it.'

'Oh honey, sometimes life sucks.'

'I know it does. And I miss Graeme so much it hurts like someone stabbed me in the chest fifty times.'

'Just fifty?'

Ffion shrugged. 'Probably more.' Joe's face popped into Ffion's mind and with it, the memory of the woman at the hotel. 'Anyway,' she said quietly, 'I'm pretty sure Joe's with someone.'

'That's a shame.' Mari wrinkled her nose.

They stood there gazing at the horizon until the sky was fully light and the cold had started to seep in as the sweat dried on their skin, then they walked back to the cottage, hand in hand, just like they used to when they were children.

When they reached the cottage, Ffion dug the key out of the secret pocket in her running tights and unlocked the door.

'Let's get the kettle on and do some research about those running apps, shall we?' Mari asked. 'It's a good place to start.'

'And we have to start somewhere, right?' Ffion said, thinking not just about running but about rebuilding her life too.

Chapter Eleven

Another week had passed and Saturday had come around again. That was the thing with teaching, Joe was so busy and occupied through the week that before he knew it, the weekend was there and so it went on until the next holiday. Plus, as well as renovating the cottage room by room, he liked to spend time with his aunt and uncle, to get out for runs and to visit the Cariad Cove animal sanctuary, where he was going today.

The sanctuary was a ten-minute drive from the village, set on what used to be a working farm. It had been set up five years ago by Gwyneth Parry, a forty-something former estate agent from Carmarthen who had wanted out of the rat race and to settle in the countryside. She'd bought the farm in order to create a donkey sanctuary but had ended up rescuing a variety of other animals too. The sanctuary was run by volunteers and funded by Gwyneth herself and through the occasional fundraising event.

Joe had adopted Odin from there two years ago and since then he'd done what he could to help support the sanctuary. Odin had been rescued as a puppy with his litter mates from an abandoned warehouse in Neath. From the moment Joe had first visited the sanctuary and met him, he had fallen in love and known he had to adopt him.

Gwyneth had been down to earth and friendly, and, although tired – she worked long hours and put everything she had into animal welfare – she'd done the home check on Joe's rented house herself and been there to offer advice on raising little Odin.

Back then, Odin had been a ball of fluff with a big round tummy and Joe had felt sad at having to go to work and leave the puppy behind. He wouldn't have adopted a dog if he hadn't had support though and his aunt Caryn had been glad to have Odin during the day when Joe was at work. To ensure that Odin was properly socialised, Joe had taken him back to the sanctuary regularly so he could play and walk with some of the other dogs, and when he was there he helped out as much as he could. One of the advantages of not having any commitments was that he was free to come and go as he pleased. Demi had left him before he adopted Odin and before he bought his house, and he had kept as busy as possible since their split because it meant he had less time to think about what might have been. At times he felt relieved that he hadn't ended up staying with Demi, because if he was totally honest with himself, he could admit that they'd grown apart over the years and had ended up wanting different things. He also knew that it would take someone really special to secure a place in his heart and that they would have to love dogs as much as he did.

Joe pulled into the sanctuary car park and cut the engine. Odin was standing up in the boot of his Ford Kuga, ears pointing upwards, nose pressed against the window smearing the glass. He knew exactly where they were.

'Ready to see Gwyneth, boy?' Joe asked as he climbed out and went around to the boot. He opened it and Odin leapt out, tail wagging in wide arcs.

Joe zipped up his jacket and pulled on his hat. It was a bright and sunny March morning but the wind was brisk. He clipped Odin's lead to his harness then locked the car and they walked across the car park to the sanctuary entrance. He pressed the buzzer on the gate and gave his name, waiting as it swung open. Gwyneth was security conscious and took sensible precautions when it came to the safety of the animals in her care.

Once through, Joe checked the gate was locked behind him and they made their way around the farm building that was split into living quarters for Gwyneth and an office where she met visitors, interviewed volunteers and dealt with admin. The living quarters had a lounge, a large kitchen-diner with a seating area and a TV, as well as a conservatory leading to a small backyard. Three bedrooms and a bathroom were available for volunteers who stayed at the house if they were on nights or early shifts and Gwyneth had the main bedroom for herself. There were usually several dogs lodged at the house, including Gwyneth's large fawn one-eyed lurcher, Bobby, and her three-legged brindle boxer, Jethro. Both were rescue dogs that had come into Gwyneth's care and that she had been unable to part with – a hazard of the job, no doubt.

Joe knocked on the front door of the farmhouse and waited. It opened to reveal Gwyneth wearing dirty jeans, a baggy grey sweatshirt and wellies. The skin at the sides of her hazel eyes concertinaed as she smiled at Joe.

'Good morning, lovely one.'

'Hi Gwyneth.'

'What have I told you about not needing to knock? Come on through. I just made a pot of coffee.'

She led the way through to the large kitchen where Odin jumped straight onto a sofa in the corner and sat waiting, expectantly. As if summoned, Bobby and Jethro ran into the room and joined him, the three of them sniffing one another and wagging tails.

'There you are, boys. I told you Odin was coming.'

Gwyneth went to the counter and picked up a packet of venison dog treats then gave one to each of the dogs.

'Happy now, Odin?' Joe loved seeing how delighted Odin was to see his mates.

One at a time, the dogs jumped down and headed for the conservatory where the toys were stored.

'They're like children, aren't they?' Joe said, not for the first time. It was something he'd often laughed about with Gwyneth. Dogs could be just as happy to see one another as humans could and Odin adored playing with his friends.

'Always.' Gwyneth handed him a coffee.

'Oat milk, right?' He slid Gwyneth a teasing look. Every time Gwyneth made him a drink she told him it wasn't dairy milk. She was vegan and never ate any dairy products, but she drew the line at feeding the dogs in her care anything other than a natural raw meat diet. She'd told Joe that it wasn't easy serving up meat but dogs were supposed to eat it and therefore it would be cruel to deny them what their bodies needed. 'I really like it in my coffee.'

'Good.' Gwyneth carried her mug over to the sofa and sat down. Even though she was only in her mid-forties, her black wavy hair – that she usually pinned back – was streaked with grey, her skin weathered from time outdoors and her hands dry and chapped, but her warmth emanated from her like a sunbeam. She had the kindest heart of anyone Joe knew and would do anything for animals, even spend her last penny to help them.

Joe sat on the chair opposite the sofa and looked at the blank TV screen. It was covered with streaks of saliva from dogs running past shaking their heads and from the times when they went up to the screen to peer more closely at whatever animals were on there. Odin had a habit of sniffing the screen whenever Joe watched a nature documentary and David Attenborough's voice could rouse the dog from the deepest slumber.

'How was your week, Joe?' Gwyneth asked.

'Not bad. Busy, but I can't complain. What about here?'

'We had two new arrivals this week. A young female greyhound and a rabbit that didn't like being held, or rather squeezed, by its seven-year-old owner.'

'Oh dear.' Joe grimaced. 'Greyhound a failed racer?'

'She was. Only young and straight from the breeder. They didn't have room for her at the kennels in Ammanford, so I said I'd take her.'

There was a greyhound sanctuary in Ammanford but they were often running at full capacity and Gwyneth tried to help them out whenever they were struggling for space.

'Poor girl is terrified of men.'

Joe shook his head sadly. He didn't want to get into a rant but he knew full well how some breeders mistreated the greyhounds in their care and the bitches in particular often came away with phobias of men. It took time, patience and rehabilitation to help the dogs past their fears so they could be rehomed. Gwyneth had a specialist team who helped with this, and apart from two canine residents who'd been unable to go to homes because of long-term health issues, all dogs were rehomed when they were ready.

'She's in the right place, then.' Joe smiled. 'She'll soon come round and then it'll be from kennels to cuddles.'

'I hope so. I've been doing this for years but it still breaks my heart every time I see a frightened animal.' Gwyneth blew on her coffee then sipped it, cradling the mug between her hands. 'I'll never understand people.'

'Nor me.' Joe drank his coffee, listening out for Odin, guessing that the repeated squeaking was coming from one of the balls Odin liked to play with at the farmhouse. If he didn't have a basket full of toys and balls at home, Joe would wonder if Odin felt deprived of toys. However, it seemed that someone else's toys were always better.

'Where do you want me today?' he asked after he'd swilled out his mug and set it on the draining board.

'Exercising the dogs would be great, thanks. The list of who needs to go out is on the table. How long can you stay?'

'As long as you need me. I haven't got any other plans.' It wasn't strictly true because Joe had planned on painting his hallway this afternoon, but he also hated to leave the sanctuary when he could be useful. Gwyneth never took advantage but Joe did like to do what he could. 'I'll make a start, then.'

'Thanks. I've got a family coming from Cardiff today to meet Betsy.'

'Really? Lady Betsy has visitors? That's good news.'

'The best. They sounded lovely on the phone and have passed the home check. We matched them to Betsy and I'm crossing everything that they get on.'

'I'm sure they will. Betsy is beautiful.'

Betsy was a four-year-old black greyhound who'd raced briefly but had been injured on the track. She was sweet and funny. When she had arrived, a lot of her teeth had been rotten, and had had to be removed, which meant that her tongue tended to loll out of her mouth and she drooled a lot, but she loved to walk and play and have her belly rubbed.

'Before I head out,' Joe said, 'I've been thinking about what I could do to help raise funds this year.'

Gwyneth tilted her head and her eyes widened slightly. She was always trying to come up with new ways to raise money for the animals.

'How about if I do a sponsored run? I run anyway and I was thinking that I could do a run along the coastal path or something similar. I'd need to fit it in around everything else but if I get an online form organised soon, I can start getting sponsorship and hopefully raise a decent amount of money.'

'That sounds like a wonderful idea, Joe. I'd join you if my knees could take it.'

'I think you do enough.' He smiled at her. 'But I'm glad to help.'

He went through to the conservatory, laughing at Odin who was sitting on the window seat with a squeaky ball in his mouth. He looked at Joe as if to say, *What?*

'Come on, Odin. Time to hit the paddock.'

Odin dropped the ball and jumped down, then they made their way outside and across the yard to the converted stable that made up the kennels. A day of exercising dogs was a good way to spend his time and while he was doing it, he could have a think about his fundraiser and hopefully come up with some firm ideas.

Ffion pushed the trolley around the supermarket, gazing at the shelves of cans, packets and boxes. There was such a lot of choice and so much she hadn't tried.

She should have been starting Couch to 5k this morning with Mari, but her sister had phoned to say that Seren had been ill in the night and she didn't like to leave her. Ffion could understand that and hadn't suggested that Bryn pull his weight, as she could remember how she'd felt as a child when she was poorly, and it had usually been her mam she'd wanted. Instead, she'd decided to go to the large supermarket in Swansea and purchase some goodies for Seren and Anwen and something for Mari. Their parents were working today, as they usually did on Saturdays, and their mam had been particularly excited as they had a couple coming to discuss their wedding. It was booked at the hotel for the first Saturday of the Easter holidays so there was a lot to do over the coming weeks. The couple were both teachers who lived and worked in Swansea and who'd dreamt of having their wedding at the Cariad Cove Hotel for years. Ffion's parents wanted to ensure that everything was perfect for them.

Ffion had offered to work this evening at the restaurant but had the day free, so going to see Mari was a good way to fill her time. Plus, she had to admit, the thought of spending time with her beautiful nieces was pretty exciting and she hoped she'd get to read with them again.

She picked a few chocolate bars off the shelves and some bags of chocolate buttons then went to the next aisle and selected some bottles of fruit cordial. She wasn't sure what the girls liked so selected a variety of flavours, picking the low sugar alternatives wherever possible.

Growing up, her mam had been strict about sugary drinks, and so Ffion and Mari had only been allowed water or warm drinks through the week, and fizzy drinks and squash at weekends only. Ffion could appreciate that now because her teeth were in excellent condition and her dentist in Scotland had commented on this every time she'd had a check-up. It had become a joke between her and Graeme and he'd always asked to see her gold sticker when she returned from the dentist.

She gripped the handle of the trolley tight and closed her eyes. They'd had so much between them that she missed. The silly little 'in' jokes, the hugs and kisses, the ease with which they had existed together. How could all that be gone? She had lost so much. Graeme had lost his life.

'Excuse me. Are you OK?'

Ffion's eyes sprang open. An elderly woman had stopped next to her and was peering at her through round glasses.

'Sorry?' Ffion frowned.

'I asked if you're OK, sweetheart. You looked very sad and you've been crying…'

Ffion's raised a hand to touch her cheek and found that it was wet.

'Yes, thank you. I'm fine. I was just… remembering someone.'

The woman moved closer and spoke softly. 'I thought so. You had that look I've seen in my own reflection many a time since I lost my husband.'

Ffion swallowed hard. 'I'm so sorry for your loss. How long ago?'

'Three years but I miss him every day. He was my best friend.'

Ffion's heart clutched. 'My husband was, too.'

'I'm seventy-six now but I don't feel a day over twenty. Except for these bones of mine that creak and groan, especially on cold days.' She laughed. 'But yes, Alun was my world. I have children and grandchildren and they help with the pain but I'll never forget him.'

'Of course not.'

'But, my lovely… I try to take comfort in something that someone told me not long after he'd died.'

'What was that?' Ffion asked, desperate for a pearl of wisdom to help her to cope with her own loss.

'Grief is love's receipt. We can wave it in the air and know that we loved. It isn't the absence of love but the evidence that love is still there.' She laid a hand on Ffion's arm. 'You'll always love him but you're young and you'll love again.'

'Oh, I don't know about that.' Ffion smiled sadly.

'It's not moving on so much as accepting that it's OK to live, and loving people is part of that. Your husband wouldn't want you giving up, now, would he? I bet he'd tell you to honour your memory of him by living life to the full.'

Ffion scanned the woman's face, taking in her short white hair, round glasses and lavender blouse under a grey waterproof coat. She looked elderly, but in her eyes Ffion could see the young woman she once was, as well as the experience of a life lived well.

'Now take care of yourself, dearie, and perhaps I'll see you here again.' The woman patted Ffion's hand before wheeling her trolley away.

'Thank you,' Ffion called to the woman's back and smiled when she raised a hand.

She hoped the woman was right and wondered at how she'd bumped into her like that. Life worked in mysterious ways and sometimes, even though she wasn't religious, she had a feeling that Graeme was looking out for her.

And that thought sent her on with her day with a comforting lightness in her heart.

'Aunty Ffion?' Anwen tapped her arm.

'Yes, Anwen.'

'Why did you live in Scotland for so long?'

'I fell in love with a man from Scotland and moved there to be with him.'

They were sitting on the sofa in Mari's lounge and had just read four of Anwen's books. Mari was upstairs with Seren who was feeling very sorry for herself.

'But… didn't you miss your mammy and daddy?'

'I did. And I missed your mammy, you and Seren.'

Anwen frowned and poked her tongue through the gap in her teeth.

'When did you move there?'

'A long time ago. When I was twenty-one.'

'How old are you now?'

'Thirty-two.'

Anwen frowned. 'So you lived there for…' She held up her hands and counted on her fingers. 'A very, very long time.'

Ffion smiled. 'That's right.'

'But you lived there when I was born.'

'Yes.'

'So how could you miss me? You didn't meet me.'

'I did. I met you when I came back to visit your mammy and my parents.'

'And Seren?'

'I only met Seren once or twice.'

'Why's that?'

Ffion swallowed hard. She wanted to be honest with Anwen but all the questions were exhausting.

'Well, not long after Seren was born, Graeme became unwell.'

'Your husband?'

'That's right.'

'Did he die like the robin that we found in the garden?'

'He did.'

'I'm sorry.' Anwen closed the book on her lap and turned and wrapped her arms around Ffion. 'It must hurt.'

'It does.'

'I was sad about the little robin because it was so still and quiet. But I was sadder about losing my best friend because she moved away to America and... sometimes I cry about it. She left when I was five but I'm six now and we write emails and sometimes we speak on FaceTime but it's not the same as seeing her every day.'

'I guess it's not.'

'She has a big house and a dog and a swimming pool and she's happy so Mammy says I have to be happy for her.'

'It sounds like she has a good life out there.'

Anwen nodded. 'Mammy says that we have to be happy for other people even if we're sad for us. I'm sad that Ellen went but I'm happy for her. But your husband didn't move to America.'

'No.'

'He went over the rainbow bridge!' She threw her hands expansively in the air.

'The what?'

'It's what we do when we die. We go over the rainbow bridge and see everyone we love, so I'm sure your husband is with people he likes now and all the dogs and cats and rabbits and bearded dragons. He's probably got a swimming pool there too.'

'I hope so.' Ffion blinked back the tears that had sprung into her eyes. Anwen was a bright little girl and she clearly absorbed everything she was told. Ffion liked the thought that Graeme had walked over a rainbow bridge and was now swimming in a pool in the sunshine. It was better than the image she sometimes had of there being nothing after death. If only she could have some of Anwen's optimism and see the world through her innocent eyes.

'He is.' Anwen nodded emphatically then kissed Ffion's cheek. 'Don't be sad.'

'I'll try not to be.'

Mari appeared in the doorway. 'She finally dropped off, thank goodness.' She held up a baby monitor. 'I'll listen out for her on this.'

'Has her temperature gone down?'

'Calpol works like a charm. She'll probably be running around like nothing was wrong later on. That's the thing with little ones; they can seem so unwell one minute then be right back to normal the next. She had a restless night so part of it's probably tiredness.'

'You look like you could do with a nap yourself.'

Mari smiled. 'That would be nice but I have too much to do.'

'Like what?'

Mari shrugged. 'It doesn't matter.'

'Tell me.'

'She's worried about the bloody massive ironing pile mountain in the spare room,' Anwen said, shaking her head.

'Anwen, don't say bloody.' Mari rubbed at her cheeks.

'Sorry, Mammy Bear.'

Ffion looked from Anwen to Mari, trying to swallow a giggle at her niece's swearing. 'An ironing pile mountain, eh? Well, I'm an excellent ironer.'

Mari's eyes widened. 'Oh no. It wasn't a hint or anything. It's fine. I'll get to it.'

'I'd like to do it and while I do, Anwen can read to me.'

Anwen's face lit up. 'I will go and find my book about the rainbow bridge.'

'Brilliant.' Ffion clapped her hands. 'You do that. I want to know more about this rainbow bridge.'

Anwen left the room and Mari sank onto the other sofa as if standing required far too much effort.

'I'm really grateful, Ffion, but there's no need for you to do my housework.'

'I want to do it. I don't have any of my own to do and I find ironing quite relaxing. That's probably because I've never had to do much but even so… let me help you out.'

'Thank you.' Mari looked too exhausted to put up much resistance.

'You go up to bed and take the monitor and I'll keep an eye on Anwen.'

'Are you sure?' Mari was already back on her feet, the call of bed too great to fight.

'Absolutely.'

Mari gave her a quick hug then disappeared. It felt good to be able to help her sister and she'd do it as often as she could, but more than that, she loved being in Mari's home, spending time with her sister and the children.

Granted, Bryn was out again and she did feel a bit annoyed with him, but it also gave her the chance to spend time alone with Mari, Anwen and Seren.

'Found it!' Anwen ran into the room and grabbed Ffion's hand. 'Mammy does the ironing in the kitchen so if I bring this book, I can read it to you while you iron.'

'Excellent.'

Ffion allowed Anwen to lead her to the kitchen and show her where everything was stored, and she spent the rest of the afternoon listening to stories, answering Anwen's hundreds of questions and hoping that her sister was catching up on some much-needed sleep.

Chapter Twelve

The next morning, Mari arrived bright and early and they went down to the beach. Mari had downloaded an app to her smartphone and brought her AirPods, so she handed one to Ffion and opened the app on her phone.

'We can have one AirPod each and listen to the instructor as well as the music.'

'You had time to make a playlist?'

'After my wonderful nap yesterday, I felt so much better. I made a playlist in bed last night and filled it with motivational songs.'

'Like what?'

'We've got some Bonnie Tyler, Meatloaf, Kiss, Bon Jovi…' Mari scanned through her phone.

'Oh god!' Ffion smacked her forehead.

'What?' Mari looked up.

'I forgot you were a metal head.'

Mari laughed. 'Not really. Not any more, anyway. I listen to all sorts these days.'

'That playlist begs to differ.'

Mari shook her head. 'You didn't let me finish. I've also added Beyoncé, Ed Sheeran, Lady Gaga and more.'

'OK… that's a bit better.'

'We need to do some gentle stretching then the programme takes us into a warm-up walk before we start running.'

'Right.'

They spent five minutes stretching and then Mari started the app, before tucking her phone into a bum bag around her waist.

'Nice fanny pack.' Ffion giggled.

'What?'

'That's what Americans call it.'

'Fanny pack?'

'Yes.'

'Do not say that in front of Seren. I can just imagine her going to day care and telling everyone her mammy has a fanny bag. She'd probably forget the "pack" bit or change the word order and then it will be something like, "my mammy has a baggy fanny" and it will escalate and then all the children will go home saying the same thing and oh… I just can't deal with that. The looks I'll get when I do the school run will be dreadful.'

Ffion bent over and held her stomach as she guffawed at the scene Mari painted. 'That's so funny. Seren's just wicked, isn't she?'

'She's a mini terror in a lot of ways and yet she can also be an angel.'

Ffion wiped at her eyes. She'd laughed so hard her eyes had watered. It made a welcome change to wiping away tears.

'Oh no… it's starting!' Mari pointed at the bum bag.

'Come on, then.'

They began walking along the beach, a nice brisk warm-up walk, just like the instructor told them. Ffion made an effort to keep her chin up and shoulders back. It gave her the opportunity to appreciate the sunrise, the peach and gold that spread across the sky, a hazy lavender at the edges. The sea was calm, spread out like a khaki-hued silk throw. Something about the air was different today and Ffion wondered if it was because March had arrived, bringing with it the first hopeful signs of spring.

The warm-up walk came to an end and the female instructor told them to take it steady, aiming for a light jog for sixty seconds. She counted them down then off they went.

Ffion and Mari kept a steady pace, running in step, and Ffion focused on the feel of the sand beneath her trainers, taking slow deep breaths and keeping her shoulders relaxed. Before she knew it, the instructor told them to slow down and to walk again.

'That wasn't bad at all.' Mari smiled.

'I know. I don't feel bad.' Ffion looked down at herself as if to check. 'And we get ninety seconds to walk.'

'Yay!' Mari flashed her a grin.

They repeated the process seven times, running for sixty seconds then walking for ninety, and by the end of it, Ffion was tired but nicely warmed up.

Halfway through, they had turned to run back towards the hotel and now they reached the concrete ramp that ran from the sand to the hotel grounds. There was a small wall at the top so they perched on it and drank some water from the two small bottles that Mari had slotted into the special pockets on her bum bag.

'How do you feel?' Ffion asked.

'Good. I'm not sure I've got that runners' high I've read about but it was easier doing it that way than trying to run the whole length of the beach.'

'It's meant to build up slowly to running for thirty minutes at a time or the equivalent of five kilometres.'

'I can't imagine running for half an hour straight, though.' Mari bit her lip.

'Nor me but if we stick at it then hopefully we'll get there.'

'Hopefully.'

They tapped their water bottles together in a toast then drank.

'Hey, isn't that your friend?' Mari pointed at a figure running along the beach with a dog. There was someone running with him.

'You mean Joe? And by the way, he's not my friend.'

'Ooh, defensive much?'

'Mari, stop. You know I'm not interested in anyone.'

Mari nudged Ffion. 'I'm teasing you, sis.'

They both turned to watch Joe and his companion, and Ffion couldn't help admiring their long strides, the effortless way they moved together as if in tune.

'I could just watch him all day.' Mari giggled. 'But don't tell Bryn.'

'My lips are sealed.'

As Joe got closer, she saw him throw a ball for Odin and the dog bounded after it, retrieved it and took it back to Joe. When Joe looked up and spotted them, he waved. Ffion inhaled sharply. 'Oh god, he's coming over.'

'And who's he with?' Mari asked.

'No idea.' Ffion squinted at them, trying to work out if it was Demi or someone else.

She didn't have to wait long because soon Joe, Odin and the woman were standing in front of them.

'Good morning.' Joe said. 'Beautiful spring day, isn't it?'

Ffion and Mari stood up.

'It really is,' Mari agreed.

'Have you been running?' Joe asked, taking Odin's ball and throwing it away from them.

'We have,' Mari replied. 'We've started the Couch to 5k programme like you suggested.'

'Brilliant! Well done.' He tilted his head. 'How're you finding it?'

'Good.' Mari said and Ffion nodded in agreement.

'No more leg cramps?' he asked Ffion.

'Not today but we're only on week one, run one, so...' She shrugged, feeling his companion's eyes on her.

'This is Kim.' He gestured at his companion. 'Kim, this is Ffion and her sister, Mari.'

'Hello.' Ffion briefly made eye contact with the woman and tried not to bristle under her appraisal.

'Hi.' Kim raised her hand.

'Hi,' Mari said.

'Hadn't we better get going?' Kim nudged Joe. 'If we're going to have that breakfast you promised me.'

Joe's eyes lit up. 'I guess we should. But you can do the eggs. You're far better at them than me.'

'Your wish is my command.' Kim gave a small bow.

'Well, good luck with the running.' Joe flashed a smile at Ffion and Mari then whistled to Odin and the three of them set off towards the coastal path.

'Do you think that's his girlfriend?' Mari wrinkled her nose.

'I'm not sure but she seemed to be quite familiar with him.'

'Didn't you tell me that he was with someone?'

'I might have.' Ffion stared at her trainers, feigning indifference.

'Was that her?'

'No.'

'Oh dear.' Mari grimaced. 'Best stay away from him, then. Seems like he might be a player.'

Ffion shrugged. 'None of our business.'

'Very true if a bit disappointing, as he is rather dishy.' Mari sighed. 'However, speaking of breakfast…'

'I did promise you poached eggs, didn't I?'

'You did.'

'Come on then.'

They linked arms and made their way back to the cottage, and Mari chatted away about what she was going to buy to reward herself when she could run for ten minutes straight. Ffion's mind kept straying back to Kim who had been tall, skinny, blonde and gorgeous, if a bit cold – but then what did Ffion expect at sunrise on a beach? A warm hug and a hearty pat on the back? Kim didn't know her or apparently care to know her and why should Ffion care?

She didn't. Not really. She just felt a bit out of sorts because Joe had seemed like such a nice man and now it looked like he was involved with more than one woman. It wasn't Ffion's place to judge but it also made her feel a bit lost. While she had no intention of looking for love again, the thought that the first handsome man she'd noticed was a Lothario did not instil confidence in her to even consider trying to date anyone. She was far better off staying single, holding on to her memories of the love she and Graeme had shared and never, ever worrying about getting involved with anyone again.

–

Joe raised his fork to his mouth, savouring the runny egg on toast. Kim had made her delicious poached eggs while he'd prepared the rest of the full cooked breakfast. It was all quality produce from local farms and he could definitely taste the difference.

'You'll make someone a good husband.' Kim winked at him before stuffing a large mushroom into her mouth. When she'd swallowed it, she said, 'Because you cook a fabulous breakfast, of course.'

'Thanks. I'm glad you approve. My lasagne's not bad either.'

'Ooh, I'll have to try that too.'

Odin sat next to the table, a long string of drool hanging from his mouth as he gazed longingly at Joe's plate.

'I'll save you some eggy toast, Odin.'

'I will too, boy.' Kim stroked Odin's head. 'He's so lovely.'

After a long day at the sanctuary, Joe had got in his car to drive home when his mobile had started ringing. It had been Kim, asking him if he wanted to go out for a few drinks. Joe had been tired and in need of a shower, so he'd declined but he'd got the feeling that Kim was a bit low and instead, he'd invited her over for a few beers and a takeaway.

Kim was his head of department and they were good friends. She'd recently split from her girlfriend and Joe knew she was taking it hard. She'd been quiet in school and he'd found her crying in their small PE department staffroom a few times, so he'd told her she was welcome at his any time.

Kim cleared her plate then sat back and sipped her tea.

'Thanks for this, Joe.'

'For what?'

'For being such a good friend. I know I haven't been easy to work with lately and I'm sorry.'

'There's no need to apologise, Kim. I'm glad to help if I can. Everyone goes through a painful break-up at some point, unless they're incredibly lucky, and it helps to have friends around. I told you I'm here whenever you need a shoulder to cry on.'

'Cheers.' She inclined her head. 'It's tough, you know, because I was convinced that Robin was the one.'

Robin was a police officer who worked shifts so it had been difficult for Kim to see her as often as she would have liked. Joe had met Robin a few times and thought she seemed nice but when he'd seen her with Kim, he'd thought Kim seemed to be far keener than Robin was.

'You'll meet someone and when you do, you'll be glad that Robin didn't want to move in with you.'

Kim shrugged. 'I just thought it would be a way for us to see more of each other. It seemed like the next logical step but when she made all those excuses, I should have known. I guess that love blinds us to the truth we don't want to see.'

'It can do.'

'Anyway… who was that woman at the beach?'

Joe cleared his throat. What had Kim picked up on?

'The runner?'

'The newbie runner, yes.'

Joe cleared his throat. 'That's Ffion.'

'And?'

He frowned. 'And what?'

'You like her, don't you?'

He took a swig of tea to buy some time to think. 'She seems nice.'

'Don't give me that old chestnut.' Kim brandished her mug at him. 'You fancy her.'

'I wouldn't go that far.'

'And she fancies you too.'

Joe met Kim's teasing eyes. 'And how would you know that?'

'It was written all over her face.'

Joe thought back to seeing Ffion on the beach. She'd been glowing, yes, but he put that down to the fact that she'd enjoyed a run. She looked amazing in her running gear and he couldn't deny that he found her attractive, but he also wanted to be realistic about this. She always seemed quite reserved, as if she was holding herself stiff and protecting herself from something. It could be that she'd been hurt by someone or that she was just shy, but the look he'd caught in her eyes the few times they'd bumped into each other made him think there was more to it.

'I wouldn't know about that. I'm rubbish at picking up on signals. It would be nice to think that she found me attractive but I'm not going to hold my breath.'

'Accidentally bump into her a few more times then ask her out.'

Joe laughed. 'Advice from the woman who's had her heart broken?'

Kim winced. 'Ouch, Joe.'

'Sorry. I didn't mean that how it sounded.'

'It's fine. You're right. I'm not the best judge of character, am I?'

'Why don't we both agree to stay single for now and then we won't have to face the risk of heartbreak?'

Kim raised her mug. 'I'll drink to that but only until we both meet people we really like. I don't think we should give up just yet… Then we can drink to love and happy ever afters.'

'Deal.'

They clinked mugs and finished their tea but Joe was left wondering if there was anything at all between him and Ffion and if it would be worth pursuing. There was just something about her that made him feel drawn to her and unable to completely put her from his mind. Perhaps he would try to bump into her again just to test the theory.

Chapter Thirteen

'I can't believe I let you rope me into this.' Ffion applied some lip gloss then pressed her lips together before fluffing out her hair. 'I've never been one for big nights out.'

'I haven't been on a night out for yonks,' Mari said as she held Ffion's gaze in the mirror. 'But when one of the women in work invited me, I thought it would be fun, especially if you came, because we haven't had a night out together in as long as I can remember.'

'You're not wrong there.' Ffion straightened the collar of her black chiffon blouse and sighed. 'I also haven't dressed up in ages and it feels… strange.'

'You look gorgeous, Fi.'

'I feel a bit uncomfortable and these heels are already making my feet ache.'

She'd dug out the chiffon blouse and black vest top to go with her black skinny jeans and leather boots, not sure if she would be under-dressed or over-dressed. Mari had said her outfit was perfect and so she'd felt a bit better when they'd taken a taxi from Mari's into Swansea. The city was so different from when they were growing up. There were lots of new bars and clubs, restaurants and coffee shop chains that hadn't been there before. It looked good and Ffion was surprised that she was quite excited to be out. With Graeme's illness, followed by her loss of desire to do anything without him, Ffion really hadn't been on a night out in ages and something about actually making the effort and doing it made her feel a flicker of hope. Perhaps life did go on after all, and perhaps she could appreciate simple things like this – things that other people enjoyed – again.

'Right, let's go and get a drink.' Mari grabbed Ffion's hand and led her out of the ladies' and into the busy bar.

They made their way over to the group of women that they'd met up with – some of whom were Mari's colleagues – and took drinks orders then Ffion and Mari went to the bar. While they were waiting to be served, Ffion's eyes flickered over the people around her, from young women with poker-straight shiny hair and eyelashes so long they could have provided shelter for a small family, to men, most of them Ffion's age or younger, in tight shirts that showed off bulging muscles and jeans that looked like they'd been sprayed on. Everyone seemed to be having fun and she suddenly felt very out of place, as if she was alone in the middle of a crowd and would never fit in, like a penguin that suddenly found itself in the middle of a flamboyance of flamingos. She'd always felt that way to a certain extent, preferring cosy nights in to heavy nights out drinking and dancing, and Graeme had been the same. They were happy sitting at opposite ends of the sofa, their legs entwined, books resting on their laps and a nice bottle of wine open on the table with something delicious cooking in the oven.

She'd been so lucky to have that perfect companion-ship with Graeme and couldn't imagine ever finding it again. And wasn't that why some of these people were out? Looking for love, for someone to make them feel special, someone to take away the sense of loneliness that permeated every human being's heart, that made them seek comfort in others, in music, alcohol, dancing and noise? Noise could keep the emptiness and the isolation away, but it didn't last and what was left then? If you had love, Ffion thought, you had the best thing in the world to protect yourself. But now, with Graeme gone, Ffion was alone again and she didn't know how she'd keep the fear away.

'Ffion!'

She met Mari's concerned eyes.

'It's OK.'

'Sorry, Mari.' She shook her head.

Mari took her hand. 'I know this must be strange but I'm here, I love you and I've got you. You are not alone.'

Ffion nodded, a lump rising in her throat.

'I promise you that I'm always going to be here for you.'

'Thanks,' Ffion squeaked.

'So let's have a drink and a dance and enjoy this evening without worrying about what happened in the past or what might be. This night is for us and we are going to live in the bloody moment! Got it?'

'Got it.'

Ffion squeezed her sister's hand, deeply grateful that Mari understood and that she was there for her.

–

Joe sipped his pint and looked around at his colleagues. The music in the pub was so loud that the thump of the base was reverberating in his chest and he was already starting to feel a bit claustrophobic. He'd never been much of a clubber – hadn't been one at all, in fact, and at thirty-five he couldn't imagine that changing. He was of the mind that you either liked the club scene or you didn't. Joe would much prefer to go out for a meal with family and friends or to a quiet pub where they could hear one another talk. At the moment, he couldn't hear the conversation going on right next to him and so he'd given in and was sitting quietly, wondering how long politeness dictated he should stay.

Two of his colleagues, Sanjeev and Georgia, both history teachers, were getting married five weeks from tomorrow at the Cariad Cove Hotel. They were a lovely couple and had been together for eight years, having finally decided to tie the knot. Looking at Sanjeev and Georgia now, Joe felt a pang of something he couldn't quite define. He was happy for them; he had known them both for a long time, and wished them nothing but happiness. They'd been through some challenges as a couple, he knew, with Sanjeev's Indian family putting up some initial resistance to his relationship with Georgia, but once they'd got to know her, they'd come to care for her too. Besides, they'd been forced to accept that Sanjeev was thirty-six and Georgia thirty-seven, so they were old enough to know what they wanted, and old enough to make up their own minds about who they chose to marry.

Some of their male colleagues had tried to persuade Sanjeev to have a stag party or even a weekend away, but he had baulked at the idea. Instead, he'd suggested that they have a staff night out where he and Georgia could be together because he said he wasn't marrying her to get away from her at the first opportunity, and that he'd much prefer they celebrate their upcoming nuptials together.

'You ready to go to the bar?' Kim shouted across the table at Joe.

He checked his watch, surprised to see that it was ten fifteen already. Had they really been out for over two hours? Time had flown despite his yearning to go home.

'Yes, come on, Joe. Time for karaoke and a dance-off.' Kim grinned at him and he sighed. Her eyes were glassy and she was swaying slightly; she'd already had a few drinks and looked in the mood for a few more. He nodded, thinking he might just as well get on with it so at least he could be there to support Kim if she overdid it, or preferably, to encourage her to drink some water between cocktails because prevention was better than cure.

—

'Come on, it's time!' Mari grabbed Ffion's hand and pulled her to her feet.

'For what?'

'Karaoke!' Mari bounced on the spot as if someone had filled her shoes with springs. Ffion was a few drinks behind her sister but had watched with growing unease as Mari necked cocktail after cocktail. Then she'd silently reprimanded herself for being so uptight. Mari rarely went out and was clearly having a good time, and it would do her good to let her hair down.

But karaoke? She shuddered. Exhibitionism was not her thing at all.

As Mari dragged her down from the seating area and towards the small stage, the other women in their group cheered and clapped and Ffion grimaced. Perhaps she should have drunk a bit more to give herself some liquid courage. She grabbed her glass as she passed the table and flung the rest of the Cosmopolitan down her throat, hoping it would work quickly.

'What are we singing?' she asked Mari.

'"Jolene".'

'Really?'

Mari nodded. 'I need to get something out of my system.'

Ffion placed a hand on Mari's arm. 'What is it? You haven't seemed yourself at all this evening.' In reality, Mari had been OK until the alcohol had started to affect her and now she seemed a bit tense, as if she was forcing herself to have a good time.

Mari blinked, opened her mouth, closed it and shook her head. 'Not tonight, darling. Tonight… we have fun.'

'You can talk to me, you know.' As Ffion said the words a man stuffed a microphone in her hand and her last two words rang out through the club.

'Shhh, now. Let's have fun.'

Mari flashed a wild grin at her, then held up her own microphone and the music began. Ffion had been worried about everyone watching them but there were blindingly bright lights trained on the stage so she could only see the screen in front of her where the lyrics emerged.

Mari threw herself into the song, waving her arms about and belting the lyrics into the microphone. Ffion kept her voice quieter at first but soon the music wrapped itself around her and she sang louder. Whistles and cheers from the crowd made her smile and Mari winked at her. This was actually quite enjoyable. Ffion had never thought she had a good voice but it was surprising how a few drinks and some loud music could drown out that doubt. Or rather, drown her voice out.

When the song ended, she was disappointed, and turned to Mari to ask if she wanted to sing another, but her sister had tears running down her cheeks and Ffion was hit by a wave of dismay. What hadn't Mari told her?

She followed Mari from the stage and towards the toilets.

—

Joe was reeling. He'd been sitting in a booth with his colleagues, making excuses to avoid performing karaoke with Kim, when the first song of the evening had begun. He'd looked across at the stage to see Ffion and Mari standing there, microphones in hand, singing their hearts out. At first, Ffion had seemed a bit hesitant but she'd soon got into the spirit of things and then appeared to enjoy herself. Joe's eyes had been glued to her; in her chic black outfit with her long hair down, she was stunning. She had seemed to come alive with the music and it was like a weight had lifted from her shoulders; as if there was another person inside her who had been set free.

When the song had ended, he'd watched her turn to Mari, a big smile on her face which had quickly disappeared. From his seat, he hadn't been able to say for sure, but he suspected that Mari was crying.

Music could stir people's emotions and perhaps the song had special significance for Mari, he thought. When Ffion had rushed after her sister, he'd wanted to go and see what was wrong before realising how ridiculous that seemed. It might be the teacher in him, of course, because he was accustomed to acting in a pastoral role. He hated to see anyone distressed but wondered, what could he really do for Mari and Ffion right now? He was out with friends and if the shouts and laughter from the table opposite had been anything to go by, it seemed that Ffion and Mari were with their own crowd. No doubt their friends would help them out and all would be well again.

Kim was standing in front of the table now, her hands together as if in prayer, her lips pouting as she stared at him. He didn't want to get up on that stage but had a feeling that until he did, Kim wasn't going to give him any peace. Perhaps it would be better to get it over and done with so he could relax for the rest of the evening.

–

'Mari, what's wrong?' Ffion asked as they stood in front of the sinks. Mari was hunched over, sobbing hard.

'Stupid… I'm so stupid.'

'Why, Mari?' Ffion rubbed her back and gently brushed her hair away from her wet cheeks then handed her some toilet paper. 'You looked like you were having fun.'

Mari nodded. 'I… was… having a lot… of fun. Best night… in… ages.' She blew her nose then balled up the toilet paper in her hand.

'So what changed?'

'I can't handle drinking any more.' Mari dabbed at her eyes with the ball of dirty toilet paper so Ffion went into the stall and got some more, throwing the dirty piece in the bin.

'You've had two children and they're still young and, as you said, you haven't had a night out for ages. It's fine to get a bit emotional.'

'It's not that.' Mari turned and looked at her reflection. 'Oh dear.' She pointed at the mascara smudges around her eyes and the tear trails through her foundation and blusher. 'I look like a scary clown.' She snorted. 'A very scary clown.'

'You look like a woman with a lot on her mind. Whether you want to talk about it or not, I'm here.'

'Look at how things have turned around this evening. It started with me telling you it was OK to have fun and now you're looking after me.'

'That's what sisters and friends do, isn't it?'

Mari bobbed her head.

'So do you want to tell me what's wrong?'

Mari sighed. 'It's Bryn.'

'He's got the children tonight, hasn't he?'

'Yes. But… while I was getting ready, I heard his mobile buzz. He'd left it upstairs when he got changed after work. I saw part of a message on the screen.'

'OK.' Ffion tipped her head to one side, worried about where this was going.

'It said something about meeting up and… *she* knew she shouldn't be texting him at home… or words to that effect. I don't know exactly because I started having palpitations.'

'How do you know it was a she?'

'I don't. Not really. There was no name on it, just a number, and then I couldn't see the full message because it was just a preview.'

'It could be nothing at all, Mari.'

'I know. But… I also know that it could be something. Things have been different between us and Bryn spends a lot of time at work, golfing or going for a beer. We used to be so close and now… I just don't know any more.'

'This is Bryn we're talking about. I'm sure it's nothing.' Ffion hugged Mari, then stepped back and peered at her. 'Everything will be OK. Let's go and get another drink, shall we?'

'I'm sorry.' Mari's bottom lip wobbled. 'I… don't want to ruin tonight. I think that it all got a bit much with singing "Jolene" and the cocktails and being out and feeling old and…' She shook her head. 'Help me tidy my face up, would you?' She unhooked her handbag from around her body and handed it to Ffion.

Ffion got Mari's make-up out of the bag and set it on the sink unit then did what she could to repair the damage. She was quite sure that Bryn might be a lot of things but a cheat wasn't one of them. *Was it?* He could be an idiot, but surely he knew how lucky he was to have Mari and the children and he'd never do anything to jeopardise that?

Hopefully, she was right and everything would be OK.

–

Joe handed the microphone back to the compere then stepped down from the stage. He couldn't believe he'd just done that although his clammy palms were evidence of it. Three times! How Kim had persuaded him to sing more than one song, he wasn't sure, but once they'd got into the flow, he'd quite enjoyed himself. Kim had an amazing voice and knew all the dance moves to the hits she'd requested and Joe had laughed as she'd shimmied and twirled and kept singing through it all.

But now, thankfully, it was done and he could go and sit down.

As they walked back to their seats, he froze, because coming towards him was Ffion, her expression grave. He looked around, wondering if he should side-step her and hurry back to the table or if he should wave to get her attention. If he did try to duck away and she saw him, she'd think he was rude, but if he stopped, he'd have to speak to her and his mind had suddenly gone blank. Just as he ran out of time, she stopped at the bar and the moment was gone.

A hand on his back made him turn to find Kim grinning at him. 'Get back to the table immediately and accept your well-deserved praise.'

He swallowed his concerns and they headed back to their colleagues, then he took a bow as the teasing commenced.

–

Ffion and Mari carried their drinks over to the table along with a round of cocktails for their group. They sat down and one of Mari's colleagues asked if she was OK while some of the others looked on with concern. Mari mumbled something about not being used to drinking, loving Dolly Parton and getting over emotional at singing 'Jolene' with her sister. The colleague seemed to accept her excuse and soon, everyone had a fresh drink, a new couple took to the stage and the club filled with music again.

Ffion sipped her drink and looked around them. The bar was busy now. It had three floors: the ground one was a cocktail bar that served light snacks, the middle one was the karaoke section and the top one was a dance floor. She hadn't danced in ages and wondered if they should try to get up there before the evening ended. It might do Mari good to have a dance around.

Her eyes landed on a table across the room and she smiled. The men and women sitting there looked so happy and relaxed, as if the evening out was exactly what they wanted it to be. Were they work colleagues, friends or both? Were they family, or out for a couples' evening?

Then she saw him.

Joe…

He was nodding intently as a man spoke to him. He looked happy, as if he was having a good time and something bloomed in her chest. It was good to see him, like spying an old friend across the club. He was such a handsome man, tall, fair and athletic. Her encounters with him had shown him to be friendly and caring. And yet, she'd seen him with two women in recent weeks, so was he as genuine as he seemed?

She started as he looked up and met her gaze.

Her heart fluttered and her stomach clenched.

Then he waved at her before mouthing something that looked like, *I'm coming over.*

Chapter Fourteen

Joe couldn't help himself; he had to go and speak to Ffion. Seeing her at the club, watching her sing and sway to the music, being in the same place at the same time all made him feel like this was meant to be. Not in a soppy, romantic kind of way but because he was a pragmatist with good manners; locking eyes with her like that and not going to say hello would be rude. At least, that's what he told himself as he got up and strode over to her.

Up close, she seemed even more beautiful. Her shiny hair fell to her shoulders in soft waves. Her eyes were such a dark brown they seemed black in the dim lighting and she looked so petite in her black outfit that he felt certain he could have swept her up in his arms and carried her round all night without tiring.

'Hi.' He smiled at her, feeling a blush rising in his cheeks. 'It's warm in here, isn't it?'

She nodded. 'Lots of bodies.'

'Not really my scene, to be honest, but I'm here with some friends.' He gestured behind him. 'Two of them are getting married so they're having a joint hen and stag do.'

'Nice.' She glanced behind him. 'I'm here with Mari and some of her colleagues.'

'Is Mari all right? I saw you doing karaoke and then you both rushed off.'

'She's OK.' Ffion pressed her lips together as if letting him know that was all she'd say on the matter.

'Alcohol and music.' He shook his head.

'What?' A small line appeared between her brows.

'They can make the strongest of us emotional at times.'

'That's true.' She sighed and seemed to relax a bit.

'Can I get you something to drink?'

Just then, a group of women accosted them, surrounding them like a cackle of hyenas and making as much noise as one too, Joe thought.

'Come on, Ffion. Time to boogie-woogie.'

'Oh…' Ffion looked around as if torn between accepting a drink from Joe and hitting the dance floor. 'Uh… I did want to have a dance before the night is over.'

'Come on!' It was Mari. She took Ffion's hand. 'Hey, Joe.' Her smile was brief and her eyes were puffy. 'Let's go and dance it all away, shall we?'

Ffion looked back at Joe. 'I'll uh… see you around.'

'Actually…' Joe glanced at his friends again. 'I think we're heading up there too. So I might see you on the dance floor. But I have to warn you… I have moves like John Travolta in *Saturday Night Fever*.'

Ffion smiled. 'I'll look forward to seeing that.'

Mari led her away and Joe stood there with a stomach full of butterflies, wondering how on earth he was going to pull off said dance moves. He was about as good a dancer as an elephant on ice. Still, if he could amuse Ffion while he tried, that wouldn't be a bad thing.

–

Ffion stood at the edge of the dance floor with her latest cocktail in hand. It was strong and she was feeling relaxed.

In front of her, Mari and her colleagues were letting loose, swaying, waving their arms and strutting around. Some of them were very good dancers, or perhaps it was the cocktails making her see things differently. It had been quite an eventful night and she'd be glad to get back to Mari's to go to bed, but she was having a nice time, even if her ears were ringing from the loud music and her feet were throbbing from standing in heels.

'What're you having?'

She turned to find Joe peering over her shoulder. He was so tall that she had to crane her neck to look up at him, even in heels. He was also incredibly handsome, far more attractive than she'd realised. Or was the alcohol making him look even better too?

'A Screaming Orgasm.'

His eyes widened then landed on her glass.

'Ah… right.'

'It's good. Want to try?'

Mischief filled his gaze. 'I'd love to share your screaming orgasm but it looks like you need another.'

She looked at her glass and frowned. It was empty already.

'Do you want another one of… those?' he asked. 'I need to go to the bar anyway as it's my round.'

Ffion was about to decline but then thought it wouldn't do any harm.

'Go on then.' He took her empty glass and headed for the bar.

Ffion watched her sister. Mari was twirling around now, her eyes closed, her hips gyrating. She looked so much like she had at sixteen, although her hair was shorter and she was softer, curvier. Ffion loved her so much and had missed her more than she'd cared to admit. How could eleven years have passed with them barely seeing each other?

She knew how. Time flew. They'd both been busy with their lives. Perhaps on some level they'd known that they'd always be there for each other and that their relationship would be a safe haven for them whenever they needed it. Whatever the truth, Ffion was happy to be here with Mari, to watch her enjoying herself and to recapture, if just for an evening, the sense of who they'd been before life had changed them both.

Joe soon returned with a tray of drinks that he deposited on a nearby table – receiving a round of applause from his friends – then he came back to her side.

'I hope you enjoy this screaming orgasm, Ffion.' He grinned. Alcohol had softened his edges and his smile was slightly lopsided, his eyes glassy.

'Thank you. I'm sure I will.' She sipped it through the paper straw. 'It's good.'

Joe rubbed his forehead. 'I'm sorry. I feel so cheesy grinning about saucy cocktail names. It's almost indecent. In my job, I spend a lot of time with teenagers so I'm used to their humour.' He shrugged. 'Still, that's no excuse.'

'It's fine. It's funny.'

'Really?'

'Really.'

They sipped their drinks and watched the dancing. Ffion was conscious of Joe at her side, of his body heat and his scent – citrussy with an undercurrent of something else that she couldn't pinpoint – and of how every so often his arm brushed against hers as he moved to allow someone to pass.

'Would you like to dance now?' he asked, showing her that his glass was empty.

She swallowed. It had been so long since she'd danced, so long since she'd let go in that way and it scared her. When her grief had consumed her, she'd struggled to push it down, to stopper it in some way because she'd felt that if she didn't, it would burst from her in a torrent that would only cease when she was completely drained. Dancing was such a physical act that she feared it might trigger her, bringing everything to the surface again and she'd never regain control. Though she'd never been keen on clubs, she'd often danced around the kitchen with Graeme as they cooked dinner; laughing, hugging, kissing and drinking good wine. They'd shared such happy times and remembering them hurt like someone had dragged a rake across her chest then pressed it hard against her throat.

She blinked rapidly. Undecided. Then her hand was encompassed in another, fingers laced through hers. Joe was watching her intently.

'Are you all right?' he whispered.

Resolve filled her. The pain was there, regardless, so she would dance, feel the music and let go. If she lost herself again, so be it. When you'd lost everything and been to the edge, what else was there to fear?

'Let's dance.'

She pulled him towards the dance floor then released his hand. Simple Minds' 'Don't You Forget About Me' came on and she started to rock her hips, smiling as Mari joined her, arm around her shoulders. They twirled each other round, singing loudly, their voices swallowed up by the club ceiling, feeling their younger selves reclaiming their bodies.

Joe was nearby, doing an awkward shuffle, his moves surprisingly nothing like John Travolta in *Saturday Night Fever* at all. But still, he was trying. It seemed that he wasn't quite the athlete on the dance floor. He was as human as the rest of them, apparently a nice guy, cute and a bit of a geek.

Mari danced up to him and boogied around him, holding his hand to duck under his arm, twirling around and around. Joe laughed, throwing his head back, wobbling as he tried to keep Mari upright.

Then the music changed… 'Take My Breath Away', by Berlin. Ffion slowed her movements, wondering whether to leave the dance floor. Mari had suddenly disappeared and now Joe was right in front of her, eyes locked on hers, his chest rising and falling quickly as if he was out of breath.

He held out a hand to Ffion.

She stared at it.

He stepped closer.

And she was in his embrace.

It happened so quickly that she couldn't recall how, but his arms were encircling her waist and hers found their way around his neck. It was like their bodies had reacted before their minds could stop them. Ffion knew that this wasn't right but she couldn't think why. It was good to be held, to feel strong arms around her, another heart beating close to hers, to be held after so long…

'Hello, you two!' The breath was hot and smelt of beer.

Ffion pushed at Joe and stepped backwards, unsure why Kim was standing next to them, grinning. Through the haze of alcohol, she tried to remember. Was Kim his girlfriend? Or was Demi? If Kim was, then was she mad? Had she seen Ffion fall into Joe's arms?

'I'm sorry.' Ffion shook her head. 'I didn't mean to…'

Ffion glanced at Joe, wondered why he looked confused, why he wasn't apologising profusely to Kim for dancing like that with another woman. This was all too much. Far more than Ffion could deal with. She turned and staggered away, her head pounding with every step. She located Mari, told her she needed to go, then grabbed their coats and bags and dragged her sister to the ground floor and out into the night.

Mari didn't put up a fight; she was clearly drunk and exhausted, and Ffion was grateful because she didn't want to explain. All she knew was that she needed to get away from there, to be alone, somewhere quiet.

Guilt consumed her on the taxi ride home. What had she been thinking? She hadn't been thinking, had surrendered herself to the moment. Not only had she slow-danced with someone else's partner, she'd made a fool of herself, had let Graeme and all they'd been to each other slide to the back of her mind. For the sake of a dance, for the sake of being held, and feeling – if just for a moment – alive again.

She bit down on her lip, tasting metal, lip gloss and Amaretto. All she wanted to do was lie in bed and close her eyes, block out the world and forget, but she had a feeling that a restless night lay ahead and that forgetting would not come as easily as she would like.

Whatever would Graeme think if he could see her now?

Chapter Fifteen

Joe woke the next day wondering if the council was digging up the road outside because the pounding in his head was so bad. He winced at the morning brightness, at the fact that the room was warm and stuffy and at the disgusting taste in his mouth.

He lay there for a moment trying to work out where he was, then realised that he was in his aunt Caryn's spare bedroom. Joe had often slept there when he'd been growing up. Caryn had kept the décor neutral, the walls white and the furniture grey and always had fresh bedding ready. She'd told him it was his whenever he wanted it and he took advantage of this from time to time – if he had a late parents' evening or school event like the annual leavers' prom or the celebration of achievement. Sometimes he stayed there if he went out in Swansea with his colleagues (which was not very often) and sometimes he stayed for occasions like Christmas and birthdays. It was comforting to have a place to retreat to when he needed to be with family and he felt very lucky to have his aunt and uncle. And, of course, the best thing about it was that Odin loved being there too.

He pushed up onto his elbows and looked around. Where was the dog?

The sudden movement made the room lurch so he lay back down and pressed his hands to his eyes. Why did he feel so rough?

Cocktails… Ugh.

Never again!

There was a scratching at the door then it swung open and Odin plodded in. He approached the bed and sniffed at Joe's ear before giving it a good lick, making Joe wince.

'Stop it. That tickles.' Joe laughed then stopped because it made everything hurt.

Odin sniffed him again then jumped up onto the bed and curled up at the bottom. It meant that Joe's legs were trapped because Odin was so big but he didn't mind. He didn't feel like moving much anyway.

He snoozed on and off for a bit but he was thirsty and his headache wasn't going away. He didn't like taking tablets but with a headache this bad, he knew that if he didn't take something, it would linger all day.

Getting up slowly, he looked down at himself. Thankfully, he was wearing his boxers but he had no recollection of coming back the previous night, of undressing or getting into bed. What a terrible state for a grown man to be in. It wasn't like he was in his early twenties any more, was it?

He stood up and located his clothes, pulling on his T-shirt and jeans. Odin flopped over on the duvet, taking up more bed. 'You make yourself comfortable, Odin. I'm going to find some paracetamol.'

In the bathroom, he swilled his face with cold water, swallowed two of the painkillers he found in the bathroom cabinet then used the toilet before heading back to the bedroom. Odin was snoring now so he left him to it and padded down the stairs.

In the kitchen, his aunt was at the table, her iPad in front of her as usual.

'Ahhh… Good morning, nephew.'

'Morning.' He smiled sheepishly.

'How's your head?'

'I just took some tablets.'

'Bad, eh?'

'Yeah.'

'Seemed like you'd had a good night when you got back though.'

'Sorry… Did I wake you?'

'It's fine.' She waved a hand.

He lowered himself into a chair. 'I think I had a good time.'

'Coffee?'

'Please.' He sighed. 'I know there were beers. I know there were cocktails… and I know there was dancing.'

'Oh no…' She grimaced. 'You didn't show them the old two-step, did you?'

'I think I did.'

She giggled. 'Drinking with your colleagues is never a good idea.'

'It was all in aid of a good cause… a kind of send-off for the bride and groom.'

'I'm sure they had fun.' She set a mug of coffee in front of him. 'I know what'll help.'

'What?' He peered at her.

'A breakfast wrap.'

'That would be amazing.'

'Coming right up!'

She got to work and Joe sat as still as possible, sipping his coffee and waiting for the paracetamol to kick in. He'd shower after breakfast and hopefully feel better. It was true though, that hangovers got worse as you got older, he thought. In his twenties, he'd have gone out and drunk what he had last night and barely felt it the next day, probably even have gone for a run. Now, the thought of running when he felt like this made his stomach churn. It would not be a good idea until he'd got several pints of water into him and a good breakfast to soak up some of the booze and raise his blood sugar.

Caryn set a plate on the table and his mouth watered. She'd made him two of her special breakfast wraps consisting of an omelette with fried bacon, mushrooms and tomatoes all topped with grated mature cheddar. When the omelette was ready, she'd divided it between the soft white wraps. It was filling and delicious and never failed to set Joe up for the day.

He took a bite and chewed.

'Aunty Caryn, you are the best.'

She sat opposite him. 'Yeah, I know.'

'Thank you so much.'

'Not a problem. I like taking care of you and let's be honest, someone has to.'

When he'd polished off the wraps, he had another coffee. The sun was warming the kitchen and he felt sleepy again now that his stomach was more settled.

'So did you have a good time?'

He nodded. 'We went to that new bar where they've got three floors and... ah... I did karaoke.'

'You?' Her eyebrows rose.

'Unfortunately. Then we went up to the next floor where there was dancing.'

'You were so funny when you got back. Darryl was laughing at you because you couldn't get your key in the lock so he had to let you in. Then you were staggering around the hallway so he helped you upstairs and into the bathroom. I made you some toast to try to get you to eat something but you stripped off your clothes and fell into bed as soon as you got upstairs.'

Joe felt his cheeks glow. 'I'm sorry. That's not something you want to see.'

She shrugged. 'I've seen it all before, Joe, but don't worry, the room was dark and you kept your underwear on.'

'Thank goodness.'

'Odin watched you for a bit then came downstairs and asked to go out before bed. He went straight back up to you though, clearly wanting to keep an eye on you.'

'He wasn't there when I woke up.'

'I let him out this morning so he could use the garden and have his breakfast.' She raised her eyebrows. 'Did you dance with any nice young ladies?'

'Ha! No.' Joe shook his head and sipped his coffee but it went down the wrong way and he coughed.

'You OK?'

'Fine.' He'd just remembered dancing with Ffion. Holding her in his arms and feeling the soft brush of her body against his, the vanilla and jasmine scent of her perfume, sweet, sexy and moreish.

'What's wrong? You've gone bright red.'

'Things are coming back.'

'Oh no! Hangover anxiety is horrid. I'll make more coffee and you can tell me what you're remembering.'

Caryn got up and went to the kettle and Joe gazed into his empty mug. He'd repay his aunt for being so kind to him today, he always did. He'd take her and Darryl out for a nice meal, or buy them some flowers and chocolates.

They always told him not to and that he should save his money, but Joe believed that kindness should be repaid.

He let his mind wander back to last night. Feeling Ffion respond to his touch. Realising, in spite of the alcohol flowing through his veins, that he really liked her.

And then… she had pulled away as if something had burnt her. Had stared at him like he had two heads. Had stormed off without another word.

But why?

Kim had joined them, looking like Joker from *Batman*, someone else's lipstick smeared around her mouth, over her cheeks and neck. She'd met a woman she liked and they'd gone up to the dance floor, ending up outside together under the pretext of getting some fresh air. Kim had come to tell him, full of the joy of having a good snog, and the spell that had enveloped him and Ffion had been broken.

Was it Kim's return? Was it something Joe had done? He wished he had her number so he could find out. And yet… thinking of what he'd seen in her eyes made him wonder if it was worth pursuing. He liked her − more than liked her − but she didn't seem to feel the same. She had seemed angry, irritated, scared even, and had left him there without a backwards glance.

Perhaps he should let it go and forget her. After all, what did he know about her? She could have baggage from her past, could be afraid of falling in love, could be any one of a number of things that his tired and hungover brain couldn't face mulling over right now.

Ffion had chosen to leave and Joe had no right at all to do anything other than accept that she wasn't interested in him.

That was how these things went sometimes. He just wished she hadn't felt so good in his arms, as though she belonged right there with him.

Chapter Sixteen

Four weeks had passed since Ffion had gone out in Swansea with Mari and her colleagues. They'd continued running, working their way through the Couch to 5k programme, although during the week Mari ran closer to home while Ffion ran on the beach. She timed her weekday runs during school hours, not wanting to admit that it was to avoid bumping into Joe, and when Mari joined her at weekends, they ran different routes around Cariad Cove. She hadn't told Mari why she'd wanted to leave the club or why she'd been upset, as on the night, Mari had seemed oblivious. They'd both been quite tipsy, Mari more so than Ffion, and when they'd got back to Mari's home, Ffion had poured a large glass of water and gone straight to bed. The next day, she'd been up at dawn, unable to sleep in the strange bed, her burgeoning hangover making her restless.

Bryn had gone to the closest McDonald's and they'd eaten in Mari's dining room, the children delighted to have fast food for breakfast. Ffion had felt a bit better after she'd had food so she'd taken the children to the park with Mari and made the most of the fresh air and the morning sunshine on her face.

She'd stayed all day with them, reluctantly leaving after dinner because she'd told her parents she'd work in the bar that night. The following morning, she'd recovered enough to run with Mari, and although it had been a tough run, with Friday's excesses making their mark on her, she'd done it and felt proud afterwards as Mari high-fived her.

Ffion was finding it easier being back in Cariad Cove than she had expected. Staying with her parents was comfortable. They worked long hours and so she had time to herself, but they were close by when she wanted company. She had her suspicions that they were leaving her alone when they thought she needed space, conscious that she would need time to think and breathe, but they also reminded her every day that they were there if she needed them. In addition, it had been nice to catch up with the hotel staff. There was a real sense of the staff being a team and Ffion liked the regular rhythm of the days at the hotel, helping out in the restaurant and the bar and enjoying the distraction of being busy.

And then there was the beautiful Welsh cove itself. Being able to get out and walk or run, to sit on the sand and gaze at the water that changed colour as the weather improved was deeply comforting. Whenever she spent time on the beach, she felt aware of how she was just a tiny part of the world, insignificant in many ways, and yet her story was significant – to her, to Graeme and to those who loved them. What had happened was devastating, but she had loved and been loved, and she would never regret that. Never forget that.

Of course, staying with her parents was not a long-term solution and she'd have to think about where to go from here. Would she look for work with a local council, search for a property in Cariad Cove, in Swansea or elsewhere along the Gower Peninsula? Before she'd come home – she found that she was thinking of it as *home* again – she'd felt overwhelmed by everything and unable to think beyond the minute, hour or day. But now, something was rising inside her that whispered that she would be able to face life again and surprisingly, it wasn't terrifying. It was scary, yes, but the future no longer looked like such a large black hole. Now it was grey, somewhat hazy, but it was there, and she thought sometimes that she could see glimmers of light, fragments of hope. Things that had resembled enormous obstacles that she would never be able to break through now looked more like opportunities if she faced them the right way. As her body gained strength, her mind did too and she understood the things she'd been reading for years about how body and mind worked in tandem; that if one was weak then the other could be too, but if both were strong and in tune, then the world would open up. She wasn't quite there yet but she had hope that she was on her way.

And as March burgeoned into April, spring arrived in the Gower Peninsula, bringing beauty and renewal. She walked the coastal path, a place where nature ruled supreme and where she felt a deep sense of belonging. Her eyes were drawn to the spring flowers that bloomed on the clifftops, resilient and beautiful, from the bright yellow coconut-scented gorse to the pink sea thrift and wild thyme, all signs that winter had gone and nature was regenerating.

Ffion was starting to feel like she was renewing too. This struck her as strange at times because she was back in the place where she'd begun, and it could have been seen as going backwards, but for Ffion it was having a restorative effect. With her new exercise regime, she felt fitter, fresher and healthier. Running gave her a sense of purpose, something to look forward to, a goal to reach. She was only on week five of nine, but already her body was changing, adapting, and she liked how she felt after a run, how her appetite for food had improved so that she even felt hungry when she woke in the mornings. To some, this might be more of an irritation but for Ffion, who had stopped caring about food, unable to taste anything other than her pain, regaining her enjoyment of sustenance was a gift she would never take for granted.

And now she was getting ready to run, had checked what lay ahead for her today, and felt a jolt of anticipation then a flutter of nerves as she'd seen that today's run involved eight minutes of running, five minutes of walking then another eight-minute run. It would be challenging, would take effort and perseverance, but Ffion was determined to do it and to celebrate the sense of achievement she knew she'd feel at the end.

Today though, rather than run along the beach, she thought she'd try the coastal path. It was a sunny morning and she'd get to enjoy the views of the sea and the craggy coastline, to fill her lungs with clean air and to feel her heart pounding for a reason that did not involve grief.

–

Ffion walked for five minutes to warm up. She'd recently bought her own bum bag and she put her phone inside it along with a small water bottle. She'd also treated herself to AirPods and she connected them to her phone then set off.

She warmed up quickly in the beautiful spring sunshine and shrugged out of her fleece top, tying it around her waist. Birds sang in the trees, a gentle breeze blew in from the sea, and the scents of the fertile earth, of flora and fauna reached her as she passed through the shaded areas of the path. Patches of bluebells caught her attention, their violet-blue flowers contrasting with the greenery surrounding them. She knew that if she crouched next to them she would be able to smell their sweetness, to touch the velvet soft petals and to remember walks with Graeme in woods where bluebells bloomed and where they had pledged their love. She smiled at the memory, as sweet as the flowers themselves, then walked on.

The warm-up was coming to an end and it would soon be time to run. *For eight minutes!* Could she do it? Would she make it?

The voice in her AirPods told her it was time to get ready. It counted her down just as she reached the start of the coastal path. She took a deep breath and set off. The sun was almost at its highest point in the sky and it glinted on the water, giving the sea a glassy appearance. She kept her eyes ahead, aware that if she didn't have her music on, she'd be able to hear the sounds of the water lapping at the cliffs below, the suck and squelch as the waves pulled at the rocks and churned the sandy seabed.

The first two minutes were hard; her calves felt heavy and burned, her lungs pulled in air desperately and her heart pounded, but she knew this would pass. It was a feeling of awkwardness, of sluggishness as her body moved from one state to another.

Her feet soon found their rhythm and she followed the gentle peaks and troughs of the path, keeping a steady pace to avoid overdoing it and watching for any stray rocks or obstacles that might lie in her way. As the endorphins kicked in, a sense of euphoria flooded through her and goosebumps rose on her skin. *This was it!* This was why she would keep running. This sense of freedom felt unbelievably good.

She reached a steep dip in the path and slowed slightly to negotiate the change then jogged up to the top, emerging into an open space where there was a picnic area. She was admiring the view from the picnic spot, when suddenly something shot towards her and she staggered forwards, arms flailing as she tried to find her balance.

It came again, a flash of white and a screeching that made her hair stand on end. The cry had been so loud that she'd heard it despite her AirPods and she wondered if she'd been catapulted into a horror movie. She raised her arms to protect her head, wondering what had attacked her, when it came again. And again. She sped up, keen to escape, and only turned back when she felt she'd put a safe distance between her and her attacker.

The voice in her ear told her that the first run was done and she sighed, relieved that she'd made the eight minutes but sad that it had been interrupted. Gazing back at the picnic spot, she saw a large seagull circle the area then land on the bench, emperor of all it surveyed.

Ffion started to laugh. The bird had seemed enormous as it swooped at her, but it was just a seagull. Of course, growing up on the coast, she knew the stories about how greedy the birds could be and how they'd steal food from your hand if you weren't alert, but she'd never been attacked by one before. And she wasn't carrying any food. So that one must have a nest nearby with eggs or chicks in it.

The smile fell from her lips. She was supposed to run back that way.

How on earth would she get home?

Ffion paced back and forth, trying to keep her muscles warm while she worked out how to return along the path without angering the seagull. She could run really quickly and hope it didn't manage to get her, or she could crawl commando-style past the bench and hope it didn't spot her, but the idea of tripping and lying prone and vulnerable or being pecked as she crawled was incredibly unappealing.

The bird was perched on the bench now, fat and proud, clearly revelling in being in charge of its territory. But people used this path all the time for walks, runs and more. A grumpy seagull shouldn't be able to keep the spot to itself. It could even drive someone over the cliff and that would be dreadful.

The five-minute walking time seemed to be ticking away a lot faster than usual and it felt like a doomsday timer. She needed to make a decision. Following the coastal path all the way was not an option, not today anyway, so she'd have to return the way she came. There was nothing else for it. She took a deep breath, preparing to run as fast as she could past the bird, hoping that by the time it got airborne, she'd be long gone.

Just as she was about to set off, she heard footsteps, the regular pounding beats of a runner. She held her breath. Should she alert the runner in some way, warn them about the aggressive bird, try to make a break for freedom while the bird was distracted with them?

The figure came over the brow of the small rise in the path, strong legs carrying him easily along, eyes hidden by dark glasses, but she could tell as soon as she saw him.

It was Joe.

Joe had taken advantage of the Thursday finish for Easter by heading out Friday morning for a run. It would be a great way to start the holidays and it was a perfect day to run the coastal path.

He had his AirPods in and music blasting; the air was cooling his warm skin and he felt strong and alive, looking forward to the spring break. Then something passed his head and screeched so loudly he could hear it over his music. It swooped again and again but he kept running, arms raised above his head protectively, eyes scanning the scene for the culprit responsible for each attack.

In front of him, he saw a figure waving at him to hurry up, so he increased his speed and soon escaped the wrath of what he now realised was an irate seagull. He pulled out his AirPods and removed his glasses, panting from exertion, bending over his knees to catch his breath.

'Was that a seagull?' He looked up and met familiar brown eyes in a pale face, straightened up slowly and rested his hands on his hips.

'Ffion.'

'Hi Joe.'

'Did it get you, too?'

She grimaced. 'Frightened me half to death.'

'Me too.'

'Bloody thing.'

Her lips twitched and a snort burst from her. Joe started to laugh too.

'I was having such a good run.' She pouted.

'Are you still doing Couch to 5k?'

'And loving it.'

He hadn't seen her since the night out in Swansea but now he let his eyes roam over her face. Her hair was pulled back into a ponytail with a headband keeping it from her face and she looked well, better than before. Even her eyes seemed different, as if some of the anguish he'd previously seen in them had dispersed.

'You look really good,' he said before he could stop himself. 'What I meant was… that the… uh… the running's agreeing with you.'

She held his gaze then replied softly, 'Thank you. It's helping a lot.'

He played her words over in his head. *Helping…* with what?

There could be all sorts of reasons why running was helping her but he wished he knew exactly what she meant.

'I need to get back.' She tipped her head in the direction of the picnic area. 'But I'm not sure I want to face being attacked again.' She looked around them. 'Where's your dog? He'd deal with the bird, surely?'

'He's with my aunt today. She's taking him into a care home as part of an outreach programme where they take dogs to meet the elderly residents. It has lots of benefits for the people involved and Odin enjoys having a fuss made of him.'

'Like therapy dogs?'

'Yes. Odin has ulterior motives though… as well as the attention he gets, he loves all the biscuits they sneak him.'

'That's funny.'

'He's a good dog. In spite of what you might think after he knocked you over – which I am still mortified about – he's a gentle giant and he loves just about everyone he meets.'

'I know that he didn't mean to knock me over. It was partly my fault anyway for not being with it. So… we still have the problem of the harpy of the picnic spot.'

'We do.' He looked across the grass at the gull. How could he get them both safely past it? He couldn't exactly carry on with his run and leave Ffion to try to pass the bird herself. It would be awful of him to leave her to be attacked, plus he'd have to deal with it on his way back anyway, so it made more sense to team up now.

'What was that?' Ffion cocked her head. 'It sounds like voices.'

Joe peered past her to the path and sure enough, he could hear people.

A man appeared then, wearing walking trousers, a fleece and a baseball cap, with a rucksack on his back and walking sticks in his hands. Behind him came more people dressed the same.

Joe looked at Ffion.

'Ramblers!' they said at the same time.

'I reckon we should make a break for freedom while they troop past the bird,' he said.

'Good plan.'

He reached for her hand and she froze, eyes darting down to where they were joined.

'Ready?' he asked.

'Ready!'

They walked quickly, breaking into a run as the ramblers passed the bench. The screeching began. Hands still linked, they soon made it to the rise in the path then raced down the other side. When they reached the flat again, they stopped, laughing hard and gasping for air.

'Oh my goodness!' Ffion was holding her stomach. 'Did you see that one woman waving her stick around like a sword?'

Joe grinned. 'And the short man hiding behind the tall woman.'

'We shouldn't laugh, really.' Ffion's expression changed and the smile fell from her lips. 'Someone could be injured.'

Quashing his disappointment that the mood had changed, Joe reassured her. 'I'm sure they'll be fine. Safety in numbers and all that.'

Then they started to laugh again, both slumped onto the grass, giggling until they were spent.

—

Ffion gazed out at the water. They'd shuffled forwards so they were sitting near the cliff edge. At this point of the path, the drop wasn't that high and they could have jumped down to the water easily. Endless turquoise spread out before them and the sun warmed their skin. She was conscious of Joe, of the freckles on his strong forearms and the scent of his skin, salty with sweat but also with a pleasant citrus note that she suspected came from his shower gel and something else, like coconut sunscreen.

Laughing about the ramblers had felt naughty because they hadn't warned them about the seagull, but then there had been eight of them armed with sticks so she suspected they'd been OK. She and Joe though, in running gear and nothing else, had only their arms to fight off the seagull and she hadn't fancied their chances. She'd have to speak to her dad when she got home about who to call about the bird. Surely it wasn't safe for it to nest there, so it might need to be moved before it or any chicks it might have got hurt or before it seriously hurt someone. After all, one of its victims might run in the wrong direction and fall off the edge of the cliff.

'Ffion?' Joe was gazing at her; she could see him from the corner of her eye.

'Yes?'

'You know… the last time we met?'

Her stomach dipped.

'Did I do something to offend you?'

She turned and looked into his blue eyes, and her heart stuttered. He didn't look like a cheat, didn't seem like a flirt or a player or any of those things. Yet she had seen him with two women. There could be even more women in his life. Perhaps it was the fact that he seemed so nice and genuine that made him more powerful in his deception. So why was her heart screaming at her brain to listen to him and accept what he had to say?

'I don't know, Joe, did you?'

He grimaced. 'What? Not the old *if you don't know what you've done then I'm not going to tell you…*'

She cocked an eyebrow and sniffed. 'Excuse me? That's hardly the case here, is it? I think you do know what you tried to do. What you've done.'

His brow furrowed and he stared out at the sea then rubbed his hands over his head.

'I'm really trying to think but I have no idea.'

'OK, I'll make it easier for you. But first, you should know that I'm not angry at you or irritated or anything. In fact, I don't feel anything towards you… at all.'

His face fell and she regretted her words instantly. There was no need to be so harsh.

'OK.' He seemed to fold in on himself and she had to fight the urge to put a hand on his arm.

'Joe… I know that you're seeing two other women. That's two, *at least*, to my knowledge anyway.'

He spluttered, 'What?'

She shook her head. So he was going to feign innocence?

'Demi? Kim?'

He sniggered and she bridled with indignation. 'Don't laugh. It's not funny at all. Those poor women are being conned by you.'

'I'm laughing because it's ridiculous. Demi is a friend. She was my girlfriend but that was over a long time ago. So no, I'm not seeing her. And as for Kim…' He held up a hand and pointed at his fingers one by one. 'She's a colleague, a good friend, and she's gay.'

Ffion opened her mouth to retort then realised that there was nothing to say to that. If he was telling the truth, which he might well be, then she was very much in the wrong.

She turned away from him to look at the water again.

'But… what about Demi? I saw you embracing in the hotel car park.' Her cheeks flooded with heat as she realised she'd just admitted to spying.

'Did you? When?' He frowned.

'Oh… a while ago.'

'You must mean when we went to get her car. I didn't see you there.'

'No… uh… I looked out the window and saw you.' *Now who was lying?*

'Well, that was just because Demi was upset. She's having… a difficult time… and needed to reach out to someone. Demi is married.'

166

'She's married?'

'She is.'

'And Kim's gay?'

'She is, and when you saw her at the club she was grinning like that because she'd just snogged another woman. A woman she's been on dates with since then.'

'Oh.' Ffion stretched her legs out in front of her and placed her hands on her knees. 'It seems I owe you an apology.'

'You don't need to apologise. You haven't done anything wrong.'

She met his eyes again and almost gasped at how beautiful they were. Their blue was so intense they seemed to hold the sky within them.

'I judged you because I thought I knew something… but I was mistaken.'

'It really doesn't matter. I am sad that you've thought that for the past few weeks though. We could have been having some fun.'

'Sorry?'

'Well… I… uh… I like you, Ffion. I don't know much about you but I'd like to know more. You're very pretty, we can laugh together – as our seagull encounter has just shown – and I think we could be friends… possibly more, if you like me too. But,' he held up his hands, 'I completely understand if you're not interested in me in that way.'

Ffion chewed on her lip, her whole body tense as a coiled spring.

'Joe… there are things you don't know about me. My life is complicated. I'm not a normal thirty-two-year-old woman.'

'What's normal?' he asked. 'Don't we all come with baggage?'

'Mine is heavy.'

'Look… I don't want to put any pressure on you. How about if we agree to be friends? I can see that you're enjoying running and I'd like to help you with that. After all, I'm a PE teacher and an experienced runner.'

Ffion took a long deep breath. He was offering her friendship. What could possibly be wrong with that?

'I'd like that.' She smiled and held out her hand. 'Hello Joe, nice to meet you.'

'Likewise.' He smiled back. 'Now… shall we finish our runs?'

'I'll need to warm up again.'

'Of course you will. So let's walk back down to the beach then we can run along the sand.'

Then they walked back to Cariad Cove, Ffion and her new friend, Joe.

Chapter Seventeen

Over the next week, Ffion kept running. She ran with Mari and she ran with Joe and Odin. It was the Easter holidays so Mari and Joe had some flexibility in their days. Ffion chatted to Joe as they ran — or rather, he chatted and she grunted, because while he made it look effortless, she had to focus on breathing. When they slowed for the walks in between the running, they shared details about their lives, like music and movies they enjoyed, favourite food and drink and where they'd gone to school and university. It was nice to get to know him in this way; gently. She felt like Ffion, the person, rather than Ffion, the widow, when she was with him. Joe seemed happy to get to know her and there was no pressure on either of them. She was really starting to like him.

Joe was enthusiastic about his dog, his aunt and uncle, his job, and volunteering at the local animal sanctuary. She liked listening to his stories about pupils from the Swansea school where he worked and they often made her laugh. Teenagers could come out with some funny things and Joe had a way of telling the stories that made them funnier. Some of Ffion's favourite stories were about the excuses pupils gave to avoid doing PE, like the boy who claimed he'd cut off his little toe with the garden strimmer. He'd removed his shoe to show Joe a bandage with a considerable amount of red on it. Joe had been shocked and rushed the boy to the school first aider who had removed the bandage to find that the 'blood' was cherry juice and the toe was perfectly intact. There was also a girl who came to school with a broken arm in a cast. The cast fell off as she was walking through the gym and it turned out to be made of papier-mâché. Then there were the answers that pupils wrote to exam questions, some of them ones that colleagues had shared with him. In Science, when asked: 'Explain what hard water is', one pupil answered: 'Ice'. Another question asked: 'Describe what happens to a boy during puberty'. The answer given was: 'He says goodbye to childhood and enters adultery'.

Mari had commented on how upbeat Ffion seemed when they met for a run one day and Ffion had felt her lips twitching. When Mari pushed her to talk, she'd explained that she had also been running with Joe. Mari had waggled her eyebrows and beamed, but Ffion had explained that she was just friends with Joe and that he was helping her to keep up the running on the days when she wasn't with Mari.

Mari was also looking better and told Ffion that running was helping her deal with juggling everything because she felt more energetic and was sleeping better – even on those nights when Seren woke, as she was able to drop back off quicker. Bryn was still being pretty much the same, and Mari said she had almost confronted him several times about the message on his phone, but she'd chickened out. She was also so busy with work and the children that she often didn't have time to think about it until she was in the shower or the bath, and then she'd try to put it from her mind and think about the children and running instead. Things had a way of working out, she'd said, and — hopefully — all would be well. Ffion worried that Mari was burying her head in the sand but didn't want to push her sister to find out what was going on with Bryn because it had to be Mari's decision to ask.

On the Thursday of the first week of the holidays, Ffion and Joe met for their run as usual. As they were doing the warm-up walk, she glanced over at him and something inside her flipped. She pressed a hand to her stomach, surprised at her physical reaction to his presence.

'You OK?' he asked.

'Yes. Bit of a stitch,' she fibbed.

'Do you want to stop?'

'No. I'll be fine in a moment.'

'It could be wind.' He smiled roguishly.

'No… not at all.' She laughed; his frankness was refreshing. He'd said to her before that he thought people were silly to be so sensitive about things like bodily functions. Being a teacher, he was accustomed to hearing pupils fart, especially in lessons after lunch, and although some pupils did it deliberately to amuse their classmates, some simply couldn't help it.

'Everyone farts, Ffion. If you have wind, let it out. I promise I don't mind. We're on the beach, remember, and it will blow away.'

She shook her head. 'It's not wind!'

'You sure?' He stopped walking so she stopped too, then he stepped closer to her. 'Perhaps I should tickle you a bit just to check.'

He held up his hands and wiggled his fingers.

'No. Definitely not.'

'But if I tickle you then the wind will probably be expelled as you lose control and you can run unhindered.

I'd hate to think of you struggling to hold in a fart as you run.'

She stepped back. 'No. Do… not… tickle me.'

He wiggled his fingers again and she looked around but there was nowhere to hide so she started to run. He soon overtook her and blocked her path, waving his hands in front of her and she giggled. He reached out slowly and gently encircled her waist with his hands, his eyes wide, a grin on his face.

'It's not wind, I promise.' She was tense, ready to duck out of his hold if necessary.

'Just testing.'

He removed his hands but he held her gaze. She found herself wanting him to step closer again, to place his strong hands on her and tickle her until she was helpless. It had been such a long time since she'd been tickled to the floor, such a long time since she'd wanted to be tickled in that way. Something about Joe made her want his touch, want to be near him, want to trust him. His eyes were so kind; he made her laugh; he made her feel safe. She hadn't felt safe in years and she had missed the security that came from knowing that another human being had her back. Yes, she had her parents and her sister and knew that they were there for her, but being in a relationship was different; it was more intimate, more intense, a deeper connection on levels that only being in love with someone could bring.

Joe raised his hand and gently brushed her cheek, then tucked a few strands of hair behind her ear. Ffion's knees almost buckled.

'No more threats of tickling, I promise,' he said softly. 'Shall we finish our walk?'

Ffion inclined her head, afraid to try to speak in case her voice betrayed her. She was shocked to feel this way, and angry with herself because it felt like such a betrayal of Graeme that a part of her wanted this, wanted Joe, wanted to fall for this man and surrender to the moment.

Instead, she took a deep breath and they set off, the breeze warm and fresh, the sand firm crunchy grains beneath their soles.

'Joe?'

'Yes?'

'Are you sure you don't mind coaching me like this? I mean... you can run for miles so don't you find the stopping and starting of Couch to 5K frustrating?'

'Not at all. It's kind of like a warm-up for me and any exercise is beneficial.'

She nodded, feeling a bit disappointed but not sure why. What had she wanted him to say? That he loved spending time with her? That being with her was better than runners' high?

'Besides which, I really like your company. I've enjoyed our chats and seeing you getting a lot out of running and I want to see you complete the programme. In fact, I've been thinking about it all quite a lot recently and I have some ideas I'd like to discuss with you.'

'I'm listening.'

'I was thinking that it would be nice if we could meet for coffee, possibly brunch to chat about them.'

'Oh.' The voice in Ffion's ear said that it was time to run. She was only wearing one AirPod so she could hear Joe. 'Time to run,' she said, so they upped their pace.

'No pressure though, Ffion. I just... thought it would be nice to have a bit more time to speak. When we're running... it's difficult to talk much.'

'You mean… I get… out… of breath.'

'Well, sometimes. And you need to focus on breathing anyway.'

'You can… talk… though.'

'You're doing really well, Ffion. What I meant was that we talk when we're walking but when we're running, it's mainly me talking and… I'd like to hear more about you.'

'OK.' She inhaled deeply, exhaled slowly. 'Let's do it.'

'Brilliant. How does Monday sound?'

'Great.'

Ffion's calves were getting heavy. She tried to focus on the air caressing her skin, the birds flying overhead, the tide as it went out leaving a bed of wet gleaming sand, the rocks ahead that looked such a long way away.

'You all right?' Joe asked.

'Struggling a bit. It's the ten minutes.'

'You're nearly there. Just keep going. Slow down a bit though, as you're racing at the moment. You only need to jog, you know.'

Ffion slowed her pace, not having realised she'd increased her speed. It must've been the talk about meeting up with Joe outside of their running. Granted, she hadn't been running with him that long but it was a safe way to be with him. With her running tights and top, trainers and headband, she felt almost like she was wearing armour or a uniform. She was Ffion the runner, the woman who wanted to get fit and strong, who was pushing her body to be its best.

If she met Joe outside of that, who would she be?

Who was she now?

She'd avoided speaking to Joe about Graeme. He hadn't asked about relationships and she hadn't offered any information. She wasn't about to pour her heart out to Joe anyway, because as nice as he was, she didn't know him that well and speaking to him about Graeme would feel a bit like betraying her husband. Also, though she hated to admit it as it made her feel guilty, she didn't want Joe to see her as the grieving widow, someone to pity and tiptoe around. She'd had that from people since Graeme had been diagnosed, had felt isolated by his illness and by losing him. Ffion often thought she had lost herself through the process of losing the man she loved.

As Graeme's health had waned, he'd no longer been the man she'd fallen for. Though she'd held him and kissed him and cared for him with everything she had, she'd been unable to stop him slipping away and the guilt at not being able to save him had been overwhelming. The illness had eaten away at who he was; it had made him forgetful, caused him to lose the very essence of his being and it had broken her heart. Her parents, her friends, even her in-laws – dealing with their own pain – had looked at her differently, afraid that she might crack and fall apart completely. She had been treated with kindness and compassion but not as Ffion, as the woman she was – the person with qualifications, a career and a need to feel whole again.

Joe, however, knew none of this and he treated her the way she craved; he regarded her without the shadow of her loss. If she told him the truth, then surely he would change towards her and she would lose this.

She didn't want to lose what they had.

And yet she knew that she couldn't keep her past from him if they were going to move on with their friendship. This had been a temporary escape from the pain and reality, a much-needed respite, and, as with the running, it had helped her. She would have to tell Joe the truth and see how he took it. He was a sensible man and she was asking for nothing from him, so there was nothing for him to fear.

'You've done it!' Joe slowed down to a walk and Ffion followed suit.

'What? Already?' Goosebumps rose on her arms.

'Ten minutes. Well done, Ffion.'

He held up a hand and she high-fived it.

'I did it! I really did it!'

'Ten minutes is amazing. You're amazing. Just look at what you've achieved in mere weeks.'

'Thank you so much.'

She pulled out her water bottle and took a drink, gazing at the sea and blinking hard. *Ten minutes!* She had achieved something that weeks ago she'd never have believed possible.

As she turned back to him, a tear leaked from the side of her eye and trickled down her cheek. She brushed it away, embarrassed at her emotional state.

'I don't know why I'm getting emotional.'

'It's OK to feel that way. Running is like a magic key. It can unlock things inside you that might have been stored there for a while. You might be letting go of something that's been troubling you or something that's been buried deep. Or...' he shrugged, 'you might just be proud of yourself for achieving such a fantastic goal. Not many people can get to ten minutes. It takes tenacity and determination.'

She sniffed and wiped away a few more tears. 'Thank you. We'd better get on with the walk as there's another ten-minute run coming up.'

He squeezed her shoulder. 'You can do this, Ffion. I believe in you.'

She swallowed hard.
Joe said he believed in her.
She believed that he did.
And it felt so good.

Chapter Eighteen

Joe and Ffion had messaged over the weekend about where they could meet for coffee, then coffee had become lunch or even afternoon tea if they could find somewhere they fancied going. Ffion had run with Mari but not told her sister she was meeting Joe outside of running. She wasn't sure exactly why, but part of her worried that Mari might read more into it and that in turn would make Ffion feel guilty or embarrassed and she'd end up cancelling. She told her parents she was going for a drive and to do some shopping and they'd seemed relieved that she was doing something. It was strange at thirty-two to feel the need to explain where she was going to her parents, but living under their roof again meant that she felt she owed them that courtesy. Just leaving without a word would have felt wrong and she knew they were worried; she could see in their eyes that concern was, for them, an ever-present passenger. They wanted to know that Ffion was OK and she wanted to give them that relief.

She'd browsed the internet to see what new places to eat had sprung up in her time away from Wales and there was plenty of choice. In the end, she settled on a country house thirty minutes' drive inland from Cariad Cove. It had excellent ratings, offered a delicious-looking afternoon tea, and was set within beautiful grounds, so she thought it would be private enough for them to be able to speak without (hopefully) being spotted by anyone they knew.

Before she left the cottage, she put on a long-sleeved black midi dress with a daisy print and brown knee-length boots. She washed and blow-dried her hair and even put on a slick of lip gloss. It was pleasant to make an effort, because aside from the night out with Mari's colleagues, she lived in her hotel uniform of black trousers or skirt and white blouse, her jeans or her running gear. But she was doing it for herself, she decided, not for Joe.

The drive was soothing as she passed many familiar landmarks and new ones that hadn't been there before. When she reached the country house, she drove along the gravel driveway feeling like she was entering the set of a Regency movie. She parked and got out, admiring the house's red brick façade with white sash windows and a grand entrance. Signs directed her to walk around the house to the tea rooms, so she did, taking in the scents of honeysuckle and early roses that climbed a trellis at the side of the house. The path consisted of pale shingle that crunched underfoot and the grass off to her right was bright green and evenly mown. Birds sang in the established trees of the gardens and it was mild enough for Ffion to remove her coat, which she tucked over her arm.

When she reached the entrance to the tea rooms, she took a deep breath before going inside. All she had to remember was that this wasn't a date; it wasn't even close. This was meeting a friend for tea and cake, to discuss running and some idea he had, and hopefully to hear some more funny stories about the school he worked at. This was nothing to worry about, not a high-pressured situation and she would be just fine. After all, she wasn't planning on telling Joe all about her past and so there was nothing to worry about.

'Relax…' she whispered to herself. 'You've got this.'

Inside the tea rooms, she blinked as her eyes adjusted after the brightness outside. Aromas of cake and coffee made her mouth water. The low hum of conversation and the clinking of cutlery, as well as classical music that was being piped into the room from hidden speakers, created a pleasant ambience in the room.

'Good afternoon.' A tall man with a shiny bald head smiled at her. He was wearing a white shirt, black bow tie and black trousers, with shoes almost as shiny as his head.

'Afternoon.'

'Do you have a reservation?'

'Yes. Under Campbell.' She winced as she said the name. When they'd married she'd wanted to take Graeme's name, liking the idea of having the same surname as him, and had loved seeing it on her bank cards, post and email address. Taking Campbell made her feel like she was becoming part of his family, adopting his Scottish heritage, and that she'd belong there. Graeme hadn't minded either way, told her to keep her own surname if she preferred, but for her it had been symbolic and so she'd become Ffion Campbell. She hadn't said the name for some time and it felt strange on her lips, almost as if she were impersonating someone, possibly the woman she used to be.

He checked the iPad he was carrying. 'Right this way, madam.'

She followed him through the tea rooms, avoiding eye contact with people sitting at tables, not wanting to make anyone uncomfortable as they stuffed a sandwich into their mouth or licked cream or icing sugar from their lips.

Joe was already settled at a round corner table near a large window that overlooked a pool and fountain. He looked very handsome in dark chinos and a pale blue shirt open at the collar. It set off the blue of his eyes and made them seem to sparkle. Her belly did a loop-the-loop, making her think of first date nerves.

Joe stood up and pulled out a chair. 'Hello, Ffion.'

'Hi Joe.' She was about to hang her coat over the chair when the waiter held out a hand.

'Shall I take that for you?'

'Uh… thanks.' She handed it over then sat down as Joe tucked her chair in and took the chair opposite her.

'You look lovely.'

'Thank you.'

'I don't think I've seen you in a dress before.'

'I tend to live in jeans or my running gear these days. They didn't really seem appropriate for a place like this so I made an effort.' They looked around, absorbing the details from the floral wallpaper to the wall plaster motifs of rosettes and friezes in yellow, orange and green. 'It's lovely here.'

'I'm ashamed to admit that I've never been here before, seeing as how I've lived so close to it all these years, but it is very nice and the food looks wonderful,' Joe said.

'It was a good choice, then.'

'Definitely, although,' a small frown appeared on his brow, 'I do hope I won't embarrass us by using the wrong fork or glass.'

Ffion giggled. 'I'm sure you won't. Anyway, afternoon tea consists mainly of cakes and finger sandwiches so you shouldn't need to worry about cutlery.'

He wiped a hand over his forehead dramatically. 'Thank goodness for that. You can take the boy out of

Swansea, but you can't take Swansea out of the boy.' He winked to show he was teasing.

'Shall we take a look at the menu and order, then we can relax a bit?' she asked.

'I can't wait. I skipped lunch for this.'

Ffion picked up a flowery menu and resisted the urge to fan herself with it. The tearoom was warm but not unpleasantly so, yet she was feeling a trifle flustered. Her stomach was tight and her heart was racing, which was silly as she hadn't come to tea with the queen. This was her friend, Joe, and there was no pressure. It wasn't like he was going to take her hand and kiss it or something, was it? Like they were going to hurry out into the maze and get deliberately lost just so he could push her against the hedge and kiss her like they were starring in some raunchy Regency TV series.

Nothing like that was going to happen, so she needed to relax, eat cake, drink tea and put all such worries from her mind. What she couldn't quite convince herself of, though, was that the thoughts were unwelcome, because the idea of kissing Joe was growing in its appeal.

—

'This cake is incredible.' Joe held up the cherry Bakewell slice and gazed at it before taking another bite.

'I know.' Ffion covered her mouth with her hand, clearly not wanting to spit cake crumbs all over the table. 'I'm going to have to come here again. Mari would love this place.'

They'd ordered a full afternoon tea and it had come on a tall cake stand along with a floral china teapot and proper cups on delicate saucers. Joe felt clumsy as he held the cup between his thumb and forefinger, afraid that if he gripped too hard he would crush it, but the food was delicious and he tucked in with gusto.

He noticed that Ffion took her time, selecting carefully then eating slowly. She sipped her Earl Grey between bites, and he wondered if she was conscious of calories or just a slow eater. He knew that he sometimes wolfed his meals down in the same way he had done since he was a child. He'd always been so eager to get back outside to play, to watch TV or to return to his computer games that meals had been something he raced through as quickly as possible. He enjoyed food but didn't see the point in taking his time over it. Today though, he made an effort not to grab at the finger sandwiches and small cakes and swallow them whole, to leave one of each for Ffion to try, and not to appear greedy or hasty. The bonus of taking his time was that he got the chance to look at her pretty face with its symmetrical features, her small straight nose and her thick dark lashes. The more he saw her, the more he found himself wanting to see her, and yet he knew that she only wanted friendship from him. It was disappointing but he respected her honesty and he realised now that he would prefer to be her friend than not see her at all.

When they had ordered another pot of tea, Joe sat back and folded his hands over his stomach. He wasn't stuffed but he was comfortably full.

'That was delicious. I think I'll come here again and bring my aunt Caryn. She likes tea and cake.'

Ffion smiled. 'Are you close to her, then?'

He nodded. 'She's been like a mum to me.'

A waiter brought their new pot of tea and set it down on the table, then cleared their plates and the cake stand away. Ffion poured tea into their cups. 'Milk?'

'Yes, please.'

'What about your parents?' she asked.

'I lost my mum when I was sixteen.'

'Oh I'm so sorry.' Ffion placed a hand on her chest and her eyes filled with sympathy. 'What happened?'

'Breast cancer.' He hadn't told her this before because it wasn't really the type of thing you threw into conversation during a run. 'She was only thirty-eight. Just three years older than I am now.'

Ffion sat quietly, resting her elbows on the table, her chin on her hands.

'She'd had a lump for a while... but didn't want to make a fuss. Typical Mum.' He sighed. 'I think she was worried about it but didn't want to admit what it was. What do they call it? Denial... When she finally went to the doctor about it, everything happened quickly but the cancer had spread and despite a mastectomy and chemo, it had taken over her body. She fought it as hard as she could but she'd left it too late.'

He shifted in his seat, unfolding his hands and picking at a nail.

'I'm so sorry, Joe. You were very young when you lost her.'

'She was lovely. I miss her, of course, but I've learnt to live with it, I guess. I know how lucky I am that my Aunt Caryn and Uncle Darryl have been so good to me.'

'It's nice that you have family to support you. But... what about your dad?'

'He's fine. Fit as a bull.' Joe laughed. 'He went off to Canada after I graduated from university in Cardiff. He's remarried now to a Canadian woman. She had three young children at the time and so my dad's a very busy stepdad.'

'That's a long way from here.'

'He's a structural engineer so he got a job out there quite easily. I would never have held him back. He stuck around until I graduated then he needed to escape Wales and I completely understand that. Losing Mum broke him but he has made a new life for himself and I'm happy for him. We see each other from time to time, every other year or so. When I can, I go out there, and the rest of the time we talk over FaceTime and Zoom.'

'Do you miss him?'

Joe licked his lips. 'I suppose I do in some ways, but I'm so busy with my own life that I don't give it much thought.' He shrugged. 'Plus, I can still talk to him whenever I want so it's not like I feel I've lost him too. I was always closer to Mum, anyway and my aunt's been there for me since I was born. I used to spend a lot of time with her and my mum because Dad worked long hours, often travelling for work, and after Mum died, Caryn was always there. Even though she was grieving for her sister, she made sure that I was OK.'

'I'm glad you had her.'

Joe met Ffion's gaze and smiled. 'Me too. And so now I live in Cariad Cove with Odin, I teach PE, I run and I coach Ffion Campbell.'

She chuckled. 'That you do.'

'Although I still don't know much about her.'

Ffion took a sip of tea and licked her lips. 'There's not much to tell.'

'I'm sure that's not true.'

She sighed, shifted in her seat, and he worried that he'd made her uncomfortable.

'I'm currently out of work, except for shifts I'm putting in at the hotel. I'm living with my parents after eleven years in Scotland and I'm learning to run and enjoying it. I have a great coach called Joe and I hope to be able to run 5k very soon. I'm not sure what I'm going to do job-wise but I'm sure it will come to me when I'm ready.'

'Why did you come back from Scotland?' Joe asked, hoping it wasn't too intrusive a question.

Ffion visibly stiffened.

'It's OK.' He held up a hand. 'You don't have to tell me.'

She puffed out her cheeks and set her cup down, then rested her chin on her hands.

'I… It's still difficult to talk about. It's not that I don't want to tell you… just…'

'It's complicated.'

She bobbed her head.

'Well, let's park that topic and I'll tell you what I've been thinking about, shall I?'

'Please do.' Ffion looked relieved and Joe was glad he hadn't pushed the matter. If there was something she didn't want to talk about then that was fine with him. He wanted her to be able to relax around him and he knew how it could feel when something was difficult to speak about.

—

'As you know, I volunteer whenever I can at the local animal sanctuary,' Joe told Ffion, and she was relieved that he was moving past the moment of awkwardness and giving her time and space to gather herself.

'I've never been there.' Ffion had heard about the sanctuary from her parents and from Joe, but it had been opened when she was away and she hadn't had a chance to visit yet. Or a reason, really. Not that she didn't like animals, but she hadn't thought of just going there for a visit.

'I know I've said this before, but it's a wonderful place.' Joe smiled and gazed beyond Ffion. 'The owner, Gwyneth Parry, set it up about five years ago and since then she's rescued lots of animals.'

'What animals does she have there now?' Ffion suspected that Joe might have told her this before on one of their runs but sometimes she was so focused on running that she didn't always absorb everything he said.

'Dogs – that's where Odin came from, of course – cats, pigs, donkeys and other small furries.'

'Oh yes… you got Odin from there.'

Joe nodded. 'My life wouldn't be the same without him. Or my aunt's, for that matter. She treats him like a prince and looks after him for me whenever I go to work or out without him.'

'That's lovely,' Ffion said, unable to resist Joe's contagious enthusiasm. 'I'll have to go and visit the sanctuary.'

'Gwyneth does open to the public on certain days, but you could always come with me sometime.'

'Thank you. Maybe we could take my nieces. They're young and they'd probably enjoy seeing the animals.'

'That's a good idea. It's important to teach children to be responsible with animals from an early age.'

'I agree.'

'The thing is though, the sanctuary's always in need of funds and I've been thinking about ways to help out.'

Ffion watched him as he sipped his tea. He clearly cared about this cause and it made her admire him even more. Raising money like this was a selfless act and showed her another side of him that she couldn't help but like. Joe just kept rising higher in her esteem.

'So… seeing as how I like running and animals, I was thinking about doing a sponsored run.'

'That's a brilliant idea!'

'I could raise money by getting sponsors over the next few weeks and do the run in, say, six weeks' time. That would give me plenty of time to raise funds.'

An idea struck Ffion. 'We could have a form in the hotel and create an online version so people can donate that way, too.'

'Thanks! That would be fab.'

'Although…' Ffion paused for a moment as the idea bloomed, 'how about opening the run up to others?'

Joe's tilted his head quizzically, reminding her of Odin. 'What… like a community run?'

Excitement was fizzing in her veins as the plan took hold. 'Yes. That way you'd get more people involved and probably raise more money.'

'I was thinking of making it a ten-kilometre race.'

Ffion winced, her excitement dimming. 'And there was me thinking I could have a go. I have three weeks of Couch to 5k left so if you organised the run for the last Saturday in May, I'd have another three weeks to train on top. I'd love to have a go but ten kilometres would be a bit much for me, I think.'

Joe knitted his brows and rubbed his chin. 'I wouldn't want to cut off people who run shorter distances.'

'Or children and those who can't access the coastal path.'

'I'm really glad I'm speaking to you about it because you're considering all sorts of things I might not have thought of.'

Heat radiated through Ffion's chest. It was nice to feel useful.

'So how about making it a community run day? We could get the people of Cariad Cove involved, as well as whoever else might want to join in, like some of your colleagues and pupils, then we'd have volunteers to man points along the way with drinks and timers and… and we could contact local press too and raise awareness of the sanctuary.'

'Ffion! You're bloody brilliant, do you know that?'

He grabbed her hand where it was resting on the table and squeezed it. His eyes were shining and his cheeks were slightly flushed.

Ffion shrugged off his compliment, trying to ignore the fact that their hands were clasped although her skin was glowing where it met his. 'I have a background in PR. I'm used to thinking about planning and community engagement.'

'Are you sure you have the time to be involved in this?'

Ffion laughed. 'Joe, the one thing I have in abundance is time. Believe me, this would be a project I'd love to be a part of. I'm enjoying running and I can see the benefits of raising money for the sanctuary as well as the benefits for the community. My mam and dad will be glad to help out and get the hotel staff involved too, I'm sure.'

'When you say "the hotel", you're talking about the Cariad Cove Hotel?'

'Yes.'

'The owners, Gwen and Aled, are your parents?'

'They are!'

'I don't know them very well because I've only lived in the cove for a year and I've only been to the hotel a few times for meals and drinks, but they're always very welcoming. I knew they had two daughters but I didn't realise that was you and Mari.'

'Guilty as charged.' She giggled.

'I thought you just worked there.'

'No point telling you everything all at once, is there?' She tapped her nose and gave him an exaggerated wink then bit her lip as she wondered if she'd overdone it a bit. After all, if she was flirting — and she wasn't sure if she was — she was very out of practice and it probably showed. Joe might be thinking she was a complete idiot right now.

Joe looked down at the table where their hands were still touching and gave her hand another squeeze then released her. She scanned his face for clues as to how he was feeling.

'You really are a mysterious one, Ffion, you know that?'

She swallowed with relief that he was smiling as he said it. 'I try.'

'Shall we settle up and head out?' he asked.

'OK.'

'I'll just pop to the loo first then do it on my way back.'

'I can do it,' she said, reaching for her bag.

'No let me. My treat.'

'But I like to pay my way.'

'Perhaps you can pay next time.' He flashed her a mischievous smile that made her knees go weak.

Ffion sat back in her chair and looked around. She really would have to bring Mari and her mam here. It would be nice for the three of them to have some time together and nice for Mari to have some time out. She deserved to be spoilt and seeing as how Bryn didn't make the effort, Ffion would be happy to oblige.

Over at the doorway, she spotted an attractive young woman speaking to a waitress who was checking her iPad.

The woman was the kind of beautiful that drew attention from men of all ages, with her sleek long blonde hair, enviable curves and razor-sharp cheekbones. Ffion watched her in awe, wondering if she was with a local celebrity or sports personality, but when a familiar figure appeared behind her and she turned and touched his arm, Ffion gasped.

What on earth was he doing here in the middle of the day and with a gorgeous woman like that?

Chapter Nineteen

It had been three days since Ffion had met Joe for afternoon tea and three days since she'd seen Bryn with another woman. She'd ducked under the table until Bryn and his companion had been seated, then gathered her things and met Joe as he was returning from settling the bill. After muttering something about needing some air, she'd hurried outside, keen to flee before Bryn spotted her. The thought of confronting him had gone through her mind but that type of behaviour had never been her style and she'd needed to think about it first.

Of course, there could be lots of reasonable explanations why Bryn was at a lovely hotel in the middle of the day with a beautiful woman. She could have been a friend or colleague, a business acquaintance or… something else, and Ffion was torn between wanting to know who the woman was for Mari's sake and wondering if this was any of her business. If Bryn was cheating, then it would be her business because it involved Mari and the children, but if it was all perfectly innocent and something to do with Bryn's job then it was nothing to do with Ffion at all.

Outside the hotel, she had thanked Joe for a lovely afternoon, trying to hide her inner turmoil about Bryn. She had enjoyed her time with Joe and felt sad that Bryn had come along with that woman and cast a shadow over the afternoon; it had been hard to think about anything other than her sister and what might be about to happen to her marriage if Bryn was cheating.

Ffion spent the next two days worrying about what to do. Even running didn't take her mind off it. Should she pretend she hadn't seen anything, or phone her brother-in-law and find out exactly what was going on? Bryn could then clarify if the woman had been a colleague or client and all would be well. She couldn't speak to her parents about it because she didn't want to worry them unnecessarily and because she believed that it was something that Mari should know first anyway. If it had been Ffion and not Mari, and Graeme had been out for afternoon tea with another woman in a possible romantic capacity, then Ffion would have wanted to know. Even the thought brought a sour taste to her mouth. She had trusted Graeme completely, knowing that he would never have hurt her. Mari, however, had been struggling recently with everything she had to deal with and from what she had seen, Ffion didn't think that Bryn was doing all he could. He was meant to be Mari's partner but he'd been acting more like a free man who could go about his life doing what he wanted when he wanted. Including having afternoon tea with beautiful women who were not his wife…

Anger bubbled inside Ffion at the thought. Exactly who did Bryn think he was? Mari deserved better and so did Anwen and Seren. *Poor babies.*

Joe had texted last night and asked if she wanted to go to the sanctuary the next day. The idea of spending time with animals and hopefully escaping her thoughts really appealed, so she'd agreed. Then she'd thought of Mari and the children and asked if they could come too. Joe had said he'd love to meet her nieces and relief had filled her at how easy-going he always was.

And so now, Ffion was on her way to meet them all at the sanctuary. Joe had told her to wear scruffy clothes and wellies as she could end up getting dirty, so she'd put on old jeans, wellies and a T-shirt under a checked shirt. She pulled her hair back into a ponytail and grabbed a baseball cap just in case because the forecast was for a sunny day.

In the car park of the sanctuary, she got out of the car and waved at Mari who was already there. Mari was buckling Seren into a pushchair while Anwen stood at her side, wearing little red wellies, jeans and a hoodie. Her brown hair was in a ponytail like Ffion's and she looked really cute.

'Aunty Ffion!' Anwen ran towards her and Ffion scooped her up and hugged her.

'Hello, beauty.'

Anwen leant back and looked at Ffion. 'We're like twins today.'

'With our hair?'

'Yes! Mammy said I should wear it pulled back to keep it out of my eyes but if there are horses I have to be careful because they might try to eat it.'

'Eat it?'

Anwen tugged at her own ponytail. 'She said sometimes horses will nibble your hair.'

'Oh.' Ffion grimaced. 'Well, we don't want that.'

'No, we don't.'

Anwen's expression was deadly serious and Ffion had to swallow a giggle.

'Are you excited about seeing the animals?'

'Very. I love animals. Mammy won't let us get a dog but I would like one and so would Seren.'

'It's probably because your mammy works long hours and your daddy does too and the dog would end up being alone for too long.'

'Probably.' Anwen frowned. 'It's a sad state of affairs.'

Suppressing a smile, Ffion said, 'I know, sweetheart. But your mammy and daddy work hard so you can have a nice home and a good life. Maybe when you're a grown up you can have a dog.'

'But that's such a long time away. I'm only six and a half.'

'The years will fly, Anwen, believe me.'

She set her niece down and they went over to Mari who was struggling to put a white sun hat on Seren's head. The toddler was wriggling and moaning and kept pulling the hat off.

'Having trouble?' Ffion asked.

Mari turned to her and blew out a breath. 'She won't let me put the hat on because it tickles her… *apparently*.' Mari looked tired.

'Oh dear.' Ffion crouched down next to the pushchair. 'Hello, Seren. Any chance you'll put the hat on for Aunty Ffion?'

Seren pouted her rosebud mouth. She looked furious. Her ginger curls sprung out of her head at all angles making her look like an adorable cherub and Ffion wanted to cover her face in kisses. She knew that the toddler wouldn't appreciate this, though, so she held back and instead, she took the hat from Mari.

'How about if I wear this one then and you can have mine?' She pulled her baseball cap from her bag and offered it to Seren.

When her niece just glared at her, Ffion put Seren's hat on her own head. It was way too small but she managed to balance it there by tugging her ponytail lower.

Seren's lips twitched into a reluctant smile and she took the baseball cap, letting Mari help her put it on. It was big on her small head but Mari tightened it at the back and managed to get it to sit on top of her hair.

'Thank you so much.' Mari smiled tiredly at Ffion. 'I don't have the energy for a fight this morning.'

'Any time.'

'You look funny, Aunty Ffion.' Anwen was grinning at her. 'Seren's hat is too small for you.'

Ffion batted her eyelashes and gave a curtsy. 'I'm sure I look stylish and could wear this on the catwalk.'

Anwen scratched at her forehead. 'What's the catwalk?'

'It's what models walk on when they're modelling fashion.'

'What's fashion?'

'Clothes!' Mari shook her head discreetly at Ffion. It was clear that this conversation could go on and on if it wasn't cut short now. Ffion loved how inquisitive Anwen was but she was also aware that it could get tiring if she lived with it twenty-four seven, as Mari did.

'Good morning, ladies!'

They turned to see Joe standing in a gateway. In faded jeans and black wellies with a fitted navy T-shirt, he looked like he would fit right in working on a farm. Ffion found herself noticing the breadth of his shoulders, the muscles in his arms as he stretched and how blue his eyes were in his lightly tanned face. He'd told her that he'd been helping out at the sanctuary over the holidays and with the nice Easter weather, he'd clearly caught the sun during his time outdoors.

It was good to see him.

That thought made her wobbly as they walked towards him and she was glad of the steadying presence of Anwen's little hand in hers because her head felt light and floaty and her tummy was suddenly filled with butterflies.

Joe led them through the security gate, explaining that the owner took security seriously because there were people out there who'd steal some of the animals if they could. Anwen asked him lots of questions about this and Ffion noticed that he answered them honestly, while leaving out the worst details like the fact that some people would use the dogs for fighting, baiting and coursing. He explained that all dogs that came to the sanctuary were neutered so they couldn't be used for breeding, and Ffion watched with amusement as Anwen processed this information, no doubt storing it for later.

They entered an area with a pretty, old farmhouse and a yard.

'Before I give you the tour, does anyone want a drink or need the toilet?'

'Me!' Seren said from her pushchair.

'And me.' Anwen giggled.

'Never ask young children if they need a drink or the toilet.' Mari shook her head. 'These two will say yes just to have a nose at the toilet and they always want a drink.'

Joe smiled. 'That's fine. You can use the toilets in the house because the ones Gwyneth had put in for the public are being cleaned this morning.'

'Is it open to the public today?' Mari asked.

'Not today,' Joe replied. 'Gwyneth has a few new arrivals coming in so she closes when that happens. But it will be open over the weekend.'

He let them into the farmhouse.

'Are you sure your boss won't mind us coming into her home?' Ffion asked.

'Gwyneth's house is like a bed and breakfast,' he said affectionately. 'She has people staying here all the time, including the staff doing shifts, and she told me to let you use the toilets here anyway.'

They went through to a large kitchen-diner and Joe directed Mari to the toilet, while Ffion braced herself as Odin appeared from another room and charged at her. He bounced around her legs and she rubbed his head, laughing at his effusive welcome.

'He's pleased to see you.'

'I know.' Ffion crouched down and Odin sniffed furiously at her ears, knocking the small hat off her head, then licked her cheek. 'Where was he when we came in?'

'The dogs like the conservatory. It's warm and sunny in there and' – Joe waggled his eyebrows – 'it's where the toys are kept.'

'I see.'

'You dropped your hat.' He picked it up and peered at it before handing it to her.

'It's actually Seren's,' Ffion said as she put the hat back on top of her head where it sat at an angle. 'She wouldn't wear it so I gave her mine and put this one on to show her how nice it is.'

'It suits you.'

'Ha ha.' She poked her tongue out at him then removed the hat and put it in her pocket.

Two other dogs padded into the room. One was a brindle boxer with three legs and the other was fawn with one eye.

'And who are these?'

'This is Bobby the lurcher and Jethro the boxer. Both are rescue dogs.'

'Hello boys,' Ffion addressed the dogs and both wagged their tails but they stayed where they were.

'They're nervous?'

Joe nodded. 'They will be until they get to know you.' He went to the dogs and smoothed their heads. 'It's OK, guys. This is Ffion and she's lovely.'

At the compliment Ffion felt a pleasant warmth infusing her body.

'Well, that was fun.' Mari rolled her eyes as she appeared with Anwen behind her and Seren at her side.

'That doggy has one eye and the other one only has three legs!' Anwen said as she trotted over to Bobby.

'Anwen, slow down!' Mari's tone froze her daughter in her tracks.

'It's OK. Just be gentle.' Joe crouched down and showed Anwen how to hold out her hand for Bobby and Jethro to sniff. 'They're gentle boys but they're a bit nervous so you have to be slow and kind with them.'

'Did somebody hurt them?' Anwen asked, her eyes wide.

'Once upon a time, yes. But they've been happy and safe since they moved here.'

'Poor boys,' Anwen said with a mutinous frown on her small face. 'Some people are mean.'

Ffion glanced at Mari, who was watching her daughter carefully. Mari was right to be cautious and children should never be left alone with strange dogs, but Anwen was listening and learning and being very gentle. Joe really was a good teacher.

He looked up and met her gaze and she smiled. She bet he was good with the pupils he taught, too. He seemed so patient and considerate.

'Right, shall we go for our tour, then?' Joe stood up and the dogs trotted away again, probably off to their sunshine conservatory.

'Yay!' Anwen clapped her hands. 'Can I feed the donkeys?'

'I'm sure we can arrange that.' Joe grinned as Anwen took his hand as easily as if she did so every day.

'Come on, then because they are probably excited about meeting us.' Anwen tugged at his hand and he gamely followed, stooping to hear Anwen's stream of chatter as they set off. It was clear who was in charge today.

–

Joe was impressed with Ffion's nieces. Seren was still very young and had clung to her mother for most of the tour, but Anwen was bright and inquisitive, keen to learn. She'd asked lots of questions and borrowed Mari's phone to take photos of all the animals. She told Joe she was going to write about them for a school project and if he didn't mind, she'd like to write about him too.

Joe had been flattered and Ffion had taken some photos of him and Anwen together as they fed the donkeys, sat in the pen with the rabbits and guinea pigs and raced around the paddock with Odin and some of the other dogs. Odin was a gentle giant with Anwen, sensing that she was young and more vulnerable than the adults, dropping his ball at her feet and waiting for her to throw it then repeating the process over and over again. It was almost as if Odin was teaching Anwen how to play the game with him and Joe wasn't sure who enjoyed it more.

It was also nice to show Ffion around, to let her see another part of his life. She helped out with brushing the donkeys, taking care as she smoothed the brush over their bodies and speaking soothingly to them. When she'd finished, she fed them slices of apple and carrot, keeping her hand flat to avoid getting bitten and giggling as their muzzles tickled her palms.

Next, they went to the cattery, and Ffion sat in a stall and cuddled Beatrix, one of the old cats that had come in the previous week. When it came to moving on, Joe could see that she found it hard to leave the cat behind. Beatrix was a ten-year-old tabby; her elderly owner had passed away and there had been no one to take her on. She was an affectionate cat who liked the company of humans and Joe had thought about homing her himself. People who came to the sanctuary often wanted the younger animals, so older cats and dogs got overlooked. It was sad but the way things were, and Gwyneth did her best to give the animals a good life. She couldn't have any of the cats in the farmhouse because of the lurcher, but she ensured that they all got daily attention, some grooming and a nutritious diet. The sad thing was that cats like Beatrix deserved a loving home and Joe suspected it was what they wanted more than anything else.

As they left the cattery, Mari took the children back to the farmhouse for another toilet break and Joe and Ffion sat at a picnic bench in the yard.

'You like old Beatrix?'

'She's so sweet. I didn't want to leave her. Do you think she gets lonely?' Her eyes filled with sorrow and Joe wondered if she had empathised with the cat's situation in some way.

'She has a good life here and isn't alone for long periods of time because Gwyneth goes in to see her, as do the volunteers… but I'm certain she'd like a home and family of her own.'

'I'm sure she would.' Ffion hugged herself and Joe had to fight the urge to get up and take her in his arms. Sometimes he could see a vulnerability in Ffion that sat just beneath the surface and he wanted to know what it was and if he could help her.

'Ever had cats?' he asked.

'No, but if I had my own place I think I'd like one.'

'Do you think you'll get somewhere soon?'

Ffion sighed. 'I really don't know. I'm drifting a bit at the moment.'

'We all feel like that at times.'

'I guess so. But yes, I do need to get myself in gear. I've decided to see the race through first and after the summer I'll start looking for a job.'

'Locally?' He hoped he didn't sound too keen.

'Probably. I don't think returning to Scotland is a good idea. It's just not the same there now.'

'You said you lived there for eleven years, wasn't it?'

A wistful look came and went in her eyes. 'Eleven years and most of them happy.'

'Did you have a… were you—'

'We're back!' Anwen ran at them and wrapped her arms around Joe. He froze and Ffion laughed. Anwen was such a bubbly, affectionate child and he was still getting used to being one of the objects of her affection. However, he'd had a feeling that Ffion was lowering her guard and about to tell him more about her past, and he'd desperately wanted to hear what she had to say. Not that he minded

Anwen's enthusiasm, but every time he thought Ffion was about to open up, something stopped her.

When Anwen finally released Joe, he looked at his phone. 'What time is it? Ahhh…'

'What?' Anwen asked.

'It's lunch time.'

'What're we having?' Anwen poked her tongue through the gap in her teeth and Joe thought it was one of the cutest things he'd ever seen.

'I've made a picnic.'

'I love picnics!' Anwen grinned.

'Well then, you can help me get it from the farmhouse.'

'Joe, there's no need, honestly.' Mari shook her head. 'I can fix them something at home.'

'It's part of the sanctuary experience. We have fresh eggs, bread that I baked this morning and salad grown on the farm. And I brought plenty of fruit.'

'That sounds amazing. Do you want a hand?' Mari asked.

'No, thanks. I'll take care of it along with my trusty helper. I think Anwen's on the way to securing a job here.'

'I'd like that. Can I work here, Mammy?' Anwen chewed at her lip.

'We'll see.' Mari said as she sank onto the bench and leant against Ffion. Seren was back in her pushchair now, drinking water from a beaker.

As Joe walked away with Anwen skipping at his side, he was filled with admiration for Mari. Anwen had so much energy that she was making Joe tired and he'd only been with her for a few hours. It must be exhausting dealing with two young children day in day out as well as going out to work full-time. Judging by how tired Mari looked today, she'd be grateful for a break, even if it was just for ten minutes.

—

'He's very good with children, isn't he?' Mari said after Joe and Anwen had gone into the farmhouse.

'He is.'

'I wish Bryn had half his patience and energy.' Mari leant her chin on her hands and slumped forwards.

'Are things still difficult?' Ffion asked.

'They're not great. Bryn's either out after work, moping around with a drink in his hand or sleeping.'

'Do you think he's OK?'

Mari turned to face her. 'In what way?'

'Well…' Ffion took a deep breath. How much could she tell her sister? If she did tell her she'd seen Bryn out with a woman, it could make things a lot worse. 'If he's tired and drinking a lot, then perhaps something's wrong.'

Mari's face crumpled. 'What if he's had enough of me?'

'What?' Ffion wrapped her arm around her sister and hugged her. 'Why do you say that?'

'I'm tired all the time. I'm irritable. I use the only spare energy I have on running. I can't be bothered to… you know…'

'Have sex?'

Mari nodded.

'But for that to happen, you need to feel secure and supported. Of course you're not going to be… *in the mood* if you're exhausted all the time. I do think Bryn could be a bit more helpful.'

'I think we're in a rut and we need to get out of it.'

'That's understandable. I'm sure that lots of couples with jobs and young children find themselves feeling the same.'

Mari heaved a sigh. 'We can work through anything… as long as there's no one else.'

Panic shot through Ffion at Mari's words and she looked away, hoping her sister hadn't noticed. Poor Mari. If Bryn was cheating it would break her. And yet, she would survive because people did. Mari had two beautiful children, a good job and a family who loved her. She would make it through this rough patch, whatever way things went.

'Everything will work out.' Ffion kissed Mari's cheek. 'You wait and see.'

There was no way she could tell Mari about seeing Bryn with another woman. Not without knowing the full truth. And for that, she was going to have to speak directly to Bryn and ask him what the hell he was playing at. Perhaps Bryn just needed to know how his behaviour was affecting his wife; perhaps he was struggling in his own way. Until Ffion spoke to him, she wouldn't know.

The farmhouse door opened and Odin bounded out, followed by Anwen and Joe. Anwen was carrying some napkins and cutlery and Joe carried an old-fashioned wicker picnic basket and a jug of what looked like cloudy lemonade. When he reached them, he set the jug and basket down. Ffion met his gaze and something passed between them, something that warmed her to her core.

Whatever she might be thinking about her past, her feelings for Graeme and her sense of guilt at living even though her husband was gone, there was no denying that she had a connection with Joe. Exactly what that connection was had yet to become clear, but she was enjoying spending time with him. Seeing him with her sister and nieces had only impressed her further and she wondered exactly how high he could rise in her esteem.

Joe Thomas was a good man and Ffion knew that she was going to have to try very hard if she didn't want her feelings for him to grow.

Chapter Twenty

The hotel was buzzing with excited staff and guests. It was a sunny April Saturday and a couple were getting married in the large marquee that overlooked the cove.

It was a case of all hands on deck, so Ffion was at the hotel early, laying tables in the gazebo, polishing glasses and tying bows in white ribbons attached to helium balloons.

The hotel regularly hosted weddings though the spring and summer months but it had been years since Ffion had been present for one. Her parents had been up since dawn, rushing around, determined to ensure that the couple had the best day possible and that the guests went away with positive things to say about the Cariad Cove Hotel. Ffion's dad had always said that bad reviews travelled far faster than good ones and that they should always strive to give guests the best experience possible. Ffion had no doubt that today would be wonderful for everyone involved.

The ceremony was at two, so guests were checking in or having brunch if they'd stayed the previous night, while the bride and groom would not be arriving until after twelve. Ffion decided to take a walk along the beach during her break to get some air because she knew that the rest of the day would be just as hectic as the start had been.

On the beach, she removed her shoes and wiggled her toes in the sand, savouring the cool feeling against her skin and the peace and quiet after the hustle and bustle of the hotel. She had been enjoying her shifts there but also knew that she didn't want to spend her life working in hospitality. Her parents loved it but Ffion believed you had to have a certain flair for it, a willingness to surrender your life to the job, and that wasn't for her. Even now, after losing the life she'd loved along with the man she'd adored, Ffion was aware that she wanted a fulfilling career, but she also craved more than that. For her, life outside of work should be more important and the fact that she was thinking that now made her heart swell. After she'd lost Graeme, she hadn't thought she'd ever care about what her future held but slowly, things were shifting inside her like grains of sand on the seabed and she wondered where they'd end up settling. As for her parents, she hoped that when they were ready to retire (if they ever were), someone would come along who'd want to take over the hotel for them. She felt a bit sad that it wouldn't be her or Mari but then, their parents had always told them to follow their dreams and not to feel obliged to work there.

Ffion walked towards the sea. The tide was out and the sand glistened in front of her, its flat, wet surface reflecting the sky. The breeze ruffled her skirt and blouse, finding its way through the buttons at the front and bringing goose-bumps to her skin. It was a mild day but the breeze coming in off the sea was fresh and exactly what she needed.

The couple getting married were the teachers she'd seen with Joe at the Swansea nightclub, who had met at work, loved the area and now wanted to celebrate their love in front of friends and family. Joe would be there. He'd told Ffion that he would have liked to invite her along, but he'd been offered the plus one a long time ago and declined, not having anyone to accompany him. He'd come over shy when he'd told her, making a point of stating that while she wasn't his girlfriend, he'd have liked her to join him as his friend. However, Ffion had told him not to worry and that she'd be there, albeit in a work capacity.

She couldn't help feeling delighted that he'd thought of her. If she'd not been going anyway, she might have felt disappointed, but as it was, she was looking forward to seeing him all dressed up for his friends' wedding. As for the wedding itself, Ffion hadn't been to one since she'd lost Graeme and she had no idea how she'd feel about the whole thing – seeing two people in love, pledging themselves to each other for the rest of their lives, in sickness and in health. She just hoped for their sakes that they had many happy years ahead and that their joy would not be cut short. She wouldn't wish that on anyone. Ever.

She reached the water, shivering a little as it lapped at her toes, soothed her aching feet and her feet sank slightly into the wet sand as she stood there, eyes fixed on the horizon.

You have one life. It's not a practice run…

The words appeared in her head from out of nowhere. Graeme's words to her during his last weeks and days as he tried, repeatedly, to tell her that she had to keep going, had to move on. At the time she had begged him to tell her how. How could she go on without him? How could she enjoy her life without her husband, her life, her love at her side?

'I love you,' she whispered, picturing him how he had been before the illness had raised its ugly head, as he had been when they were innocent of what lay before them, when they'd been wrapped up in the joy of their union. Her words were carried away on the breeze, and she listened carefully, straining to hear him say that he loved her right back.

But all she heard was the soft fizz of foam against the shore, seagulls squawking overhead and the barking of dogs playing farther along the beach.

Graeme was gone but Ffion was still very much alive.

—

'Stay still.' Caryn glared at Joe and he froze, aware that his aunt's glare meant business. 'There. That's how you do up a tie.'

'Thank you.'

Joe stood in front of the mirror in his aunt's hallway and shook his head. 'It doesn't look like me at all,' he whined. 'I hate wearing a tie. Bloody corporate noose.'

Caryn laughed. 'Count yourself lucky, Joe! As a PE teacher you get to wear your sports gear most of the time so you're just not used to dressing smart. However, you look very dishy.'

'Dishy?' He sniggered.

'Yes you do. You scrub up well, Joe.'

'Thanks.'

He'd bought a new navy suit for the wedding, along with a white shirt and silk blue tie with a silver feather print. With a dark brown belt and shoes, he thought he looked all right, even if he felt quite uncomfortable.

'Is that young lady going?' Caryn feigned interest in her nails.

'Young lady?'

'You know who I mean. The one you've been running with.'

'Ffion.'

'That's the one.'

'She's working at the hotel.'

'That's a shame, as it would have been the perfect opportunity for you to ask her to dance. You could have got a few glasses of champagne into you both and who knows what might have happened? Pity she's not your plus one.'

'There's nothing going on between us. We're just friends.' Joe looked away. His words didn't even sound convincing to him.

Caryn raised her eyebrows. 'OK.'

'What?'

'I see how your eyes light up when you say her name. I can tell that you like her even if you won't admit it to yourself.'

He shrugged. 'How I feel doesn't matter. She's not interested in me like that.'

'I can't see why.'

'Something happened in her past. I don't know but I don't want to pry until she's ready to tell me about it.'

Caryn pursed her lips then gave a long sigh. 'Well, if she has reasons for not wanting to get involved, best respect that, otherwise you'll just end up getting hurt. Find yourself a nice woman who is free to date you.'

'Yes, Aunt Caryn.'

'Cheeky.' She nudged him.

'You're sure Odin's all right to stay overnight?'

'Of course he is.'

'I can always stick to soft drinks and drive over for him later.'

'Don't you dare. You have a few drinks and relax. I'll drop him home tomorrow and take a walk along the beach while I'm there.'

'Great. See you tomorrow, Odin.' The dog pawed at his leg and Joe crouched down and rubbed his soft head. 'Be good for Caryn.'

Odin barked, then turned and ran off to the kitchen where Darryl was cooking bacon.

'Have fun,' Caryn said, giving him a hug.

'I'll try.'

Joe left the house and went to his car. As he got in and started the engine, he thought about what Caryn had said about finding someone who was free to date him. But he knew deep down that he didn't want just anyone, and that Ffion had already found a way into his heart. It was all so damned complicated and confusing. He felt like he was skating on thin ice and had to take care that he didn't fall through it by making a wrong move. But he did know one thing for sure now: if he couldn't date Ffion, then he simply wasn't interested in dating anyone at all.

Chapter Twenty-One

After the ceremony, Ffion carried a tray of drinks around the marquee, stopping to ask the guests if they wanted champagne or Pimm's. The sides of the marquee had been rolled up to let in the sunshine and the scent from the roses growing in the surrounding garden. The tide was in and the wedding vows had been made to the sounds of the waves on the shore and birdsong from the trees that framed the hotel gardens.

It was the perfect setting for a wedding and Ffion wondered not for the first time why she and Graeme hadn't got married there. But then he'd wanted the ceremony in Scotland and she'd been so happy to marry him that she hadn't put up any opposition at all. It had been, she'd thought at the time, the perfect way to start her new life in Perth. In a way, she was glad, because it would have been hard to stand in the marquee if she'd got married there herself. It meant that her wedding and her whole married life had happened away from Cariad Cove, and that was probably a good thing.

Ffion had stood at the back of the marquee with the other hotel staff during the ceremony, swallowing hard against the lump of emotion in her throat as the couple said their vows. Weddings were always emotional occasions but for Ffion, the ceremony almost proved too much. She had so many good memories of her own wedding and of her love for Graeme that they nearly overwhelmed her completely. It was, though, another 'first' since she'd lost Graeme and once it was done, she experienced a sense of relief. She had survived it even if it had been a challenge.

And now, it was time for the celebrations to begin.

Ffion moved from one group to the next, collected more drinks when her tray was empty then did the rounds again. Eventually, she came to the group where Joe was standing and he flashed her a lovely smile as he accepted a flute of champagne.

'Hello there.'

'You look very smart.' She admired his suit and the feather print on his tie.

He stuck a finger down his collar. 'Not my natural choice of attire, I have to admit.'

'It suits you, though. You look like a contender for the role of James Bond.' He looked gorgeous, but she wasn't about to tell him that and embarrass them both.

'Uh… thanks.' He glanced down at his drink and small pink spots appeared high on his cheeks. Had she made him feel self-conscious? She was so out of practice in her interactions with men but with Joe she usually felt at ease, so was something changing between them?

'It was a lovely ceremony.'

'They're a lovely couple.'

Ffion could smell his cologne and it was so sexy it was making her light-headed. 'Oh… my tray's empty so I'll have to go and get more.' She needed to pull herself together. A combination of the romance of the occasion, along with Joe looking and smelling so good, was having a funny effect upon her and she was there to work.

'We've got to pose for photos soon.' He pulled a face.

'Let me guess… not your natural choice of fun?'

He laughed. 'Not at all. I hate having photos taken. I didn't mind so much up at the animal sanctuary because I was with Anwen and it felt more natural but when it's all official like this… I get very awkward.'

'I can understand that, but it's for a good cause.'

'That's true.' He drained his glass and set it on the tray. 'I'd better get going and let you smile for the camera.'

'Will I… see you later?'

She met his eyes, having heard the note of hope as his voice rose at the end. His blue eyes seemed darker and more intense because of the navy suit, his face was freshly shaven, his skin smooth and clear. For a moment she wondered what it would be like if she had come as his plus one, to be standing at his side wearing a pretty dress and heels, to have her hand on his arm, to know that she would be going home with him later on.

'You will,' she replied softly. 'I'll be here until the end.'

'Me too. Until the end…'

They gazed at each other, their words filled with meaning, and something inside her trembled as if a tiny earthquake had rocked her. She felt as though something had been imprisoned in her heart like a tiny humming bird and now it was trying to escape. Whatever it was had been firmly locked in place and all it could do was vibrate slightly because it had been locked down for so long. *But it had moved.* Joe was capable of reaching into her and making things shift, even just a fraction. That was more than anyone had been able to do in a very long time.

There might just be hope for her yet.

—

wilight bathed the marquee in a rose-gold light. Joe was sitting at a table with some colleagues as they waited for the bride and groom to take to the dance floor. It had been a lovely day; champagne had flowed, the food had been delicious, and the atmosphere in the marquee had been one of joyous celebration.

He'd been conscious all day of Ffion, watching her work, admiring how professional she was and how nothing seemed to faze her, how nothing was too much trouble. She'd warmed bottles of milk for a wedding guest with young twins, found a clean tie for a male guest who'd spilt gravy down his, taken an elderly guest to the first aider because he'd felt faint and continued serving food and drink without breaking a sweat.

He didn't know how she managed to be on her feet all day like that. And even with her lovely silky hair in a low bun, in a uniform of black skirt and white blouse designed to make her fit in with the rest of the hotel staff, Joe could pick her out across the marquee. He could easily recognise her petite figure, the way she tilted her head and her pretty smile that was now so familiar to him. They had a run scheduled for the next morning and he couldn't wait to go, just so he could have some time with her away from all these people when she wouldn't be working and her time would be her own.

More than once, he'd thought about how he was feeling and behaving. Ffion was occupying a great deal of his mind and if he was a romantic, he might even have thought he was falling for her. Could he be?

The first chords of 'When a Man Loves a Woman' rang out through the marquee and the bride and groom appeared at the entrance then walked along the aisle, passing the tables and beaming at everyone. When they took to the dance floor, everyone rose to their feet and started to clap. Soon, guests headed to join them, and Joe was left alone at the table. He didn't mind at all, happy to sit quietly and watch his friends dancing. There was only one woman he wanted to dance with and she was working.

When darkness fell, thousands of tiny fairy lights came on inside the marquee, while the hotel staff lit candles at the centre of the tables. There was cake, more champagne and speeches, then more dancing.

Full of food and slightly tipsy, Joe decided he needed some air, so he walked out into the garden where the moonlight bathed the water in its silvery glow. Fairy lights twinkled in the darkness and it was like stars had fallen to earth and now glowed where they had landed. He noticed a figure standing near the short wall overlooking the beach and realised it was Ffion.

'Hey,' he said as he approached her. 'You OK?'

She nodded. 'Just having a rest before we clear the tables again.'

'You've been busy.'

'Wedding always are.'

'You still up for a run tomorrow?'

'I think so. Although my feet will be glad when I get to sit down tonight.'

'I bet.'

She pulled her hair from its bun and shook it out, then turned to him. In the light from the moon, she looked ethereal, like a mermaid come straight from the sea or a wood nymph come down from the coastal path.

'You're so beautiful.' His voice wavered as he said the words, knowing he was taking a risk and yet unable to eep his thoughts to himself. The alcohol had loosened his tongue.

'What?' Her eyes were wide as she looked up at him.

From inside the marquee came a new song: Christina Perri's 'A Thousand Years'.

Joe held out his hands. 'Will you dance with me?'

Ffion's lips parted and she pushed her hands back through her hair. 'Joe… I…'

Her hesitation lasted only seconds and when she stepped forwards, Joe felt giddy with relief. She felt so slight and yet so real and warm, fitting into his arms as if she belonged there.

Joe knew right then that she was the one he'd been waiting for, even though he hadn't known he was waiting at all.

–

Ffion's heart raced as Joe held her, their feet moving in time with the music and his heart beating against hers. The intensity of the moment was heightened by the cool dark night and the fact that, although they were only metres away from the marquee, it was like they were completely isolated, their bodies limned by the moonlight.

She rested her cheek against his shoulder and closed her eyes, breathing him in; his woody citrus cologne and beneath it, his own masculine scent, so good that she experienced a yearning to bury her face in his neck and inhale every last molecule.

His one hand held hers while the other rested on the small of her back and their bodies touched. His breath was warm against her hair and she wondered what he was thinking and feeling. As the song changed to Etta James'

'At Last', there was a surge within her and a sob bro
from her lips, making her gasp for air.

Joe released her and tilted her chin, concern etched on
his features as he looked into her eyes. She felt the distance
between them, a cold chasm that she didn't want there.

'What's wrong?'

She shook her head. A tear ran down her cheek. She
swallowed hard against the pain.

Joe gently wiped away the tear with his thumb.

'Please tell me, Ffion. I want to help. I'm worried I've
done something wrong.'

'I… I lost someone.'

'A partner?'

'Yes.' Her voice cracked.

'I'm so sorry.'

He opened his arms and she stepped back into his
embrace and let the tears fall. He held her, not questioning
her further, not asking anything of her, just being there
for her while she cried. It was good to be held, to have
someone to lean on as she grieved for what she'd lost and
for what would never be. And although she felt conflicted
over the feelings she was developing for Joe – feelings
she had not expected to feel – the very fact that she was
experiencing something other than grief and despair was
a glimmer of hope, like a lighthouse on the horizon for a
ship once lost at sea.

Chapter Twenty-Two

Ffion laced her trainers and stood up straight. She'd slept well, which surprised her because after the way she'd cried in Joe's arms, she'd thought she'd be in for a night of bad dreams. However, it seemed that crying had helped to release some of the tension that had been building inside her and in turn, that had cleared her mind.

At first, as Joe had held her, she'd felt bad for crying on him, but once the tears started, there was no holding back. She had sobbed, her body racked by tears, her grief pouring out of her in an unstoppable torrent. Of course, Ffion had cried since she lost Graeme but she often stopped herself, especially if anyone else was around, because her distress made others uncomfortable. Instead, Ffion had resorted to the human tendency to feign bravery, to swallow back the pain and act as if she was OK.

Joe had made it clear last night that he didn't expect that from her. He didn't push her to tell him more once she'd confirmed that she'd lost a partner; he held her and stroked her hair and was there for her while she let go. And she had needed to let go. She knew that now. It was like the morning after a terrible storm when everything is calm again and the air feels fresher, cleaner, renewed. Ffion knew that grief wasn't a straight-road experience, that there would be bumps and troughs and that she wouldn't feel the same way every day, but it was hard when the pain surged again. Being with her family, running and spending time with Joe all helped and she had a sense of optimism now that things might get back to some sort of even keel; that she would be able to live without experiencing constant pain.

Joe was such a good man. He didn't judge her for crying, didn't expect her to act fine, didn't seem to want anything from her other than her company. Their relationship was simple because of that. Ffion didn't want to rely on him or to take advantage of his patience and his compassion, but she did want to spend time with him. He wasn't a game-player; he was straightforward and it was easy being with him.

As for the other feelings she had around him… they were more complicated, but they weren't bad. Apart from the guilt, which had been part of the reason why she'd broken down last night. She felt bad that she was getting on with life while Graeme was no longer here. But she also knew that she would always love him. Graeme would always own a part of her heart. He would live on in her memories, and would forever be a part of her journey.

Shaking off the residual melancholy, Ffion focused on the here and now. She was meeting Joe and Mari for a run this morning and looking forward to the freedom of being outside, feeling the air in her lungs and the sensation as she pushed her body to run farther. Running really was a natural antidepressant and she couldn't believe how much she anticipated each run now.

She zipped up her running fleece, fastened her bum bag around her waist and let herself out of the cottage.

–

Joe threw the ball for Odin again and watched fondly as the dog chased it into the sea. He was waiting on the beach for Ffion and Mari as they had planned to run together this morning. It was like they'd created their own little running club and that was a very positive feeling.

When he'd woken, he'd been afraid that Ffion might cancel. Last night, she'd broken down in his arms and sobbed. They'd been outside where it was quiet and dark and everyone else had been inside the marquee, so he'd been able to hold her as she cried, to try to convey to her that she wasn't alone and that other people could help.

It all made sense now; the way she sometimes seemed lost, how her eyes glazed over as if some internal hurricane was churning her insides in ways that she couldn't explain. Ffion was grieving for a partner, possibly her husband. It might be why she'd returned from Scotland after living there for so long, why she could be strong and yet seem frail, why he'd worried that she was carrying a burden that might prove too heavy for her.

Joe knew grief. Losing his mum when he was so young had left him with his own scars. He knew how it felt to fall asleep with tears on his cheeks and to wake the next morning to experience a moment's respite when he was free of the pain, only to have it all come crashing back down around him. He had seen his dad suffer, his aunt Caryn too, and he'd had days where he coped and others where he'd felt like he wanted to curl up into a ball and close his eyes until everything went away.

He'd been lucky to have his dad and Caryn, as well as friends and supportive teachers at school who were trained to help pupils dealing with grief. He'd come through his loss and yet he would always carry it. There were so many times when he'd want to tell his mum something or when he'd wished she was there to see him: graduation, getting his first teaching post, achieving great times in marathons and more. When he'd moved into his new home, he'd wished his mum was there to walk around with him so he could show her his plans. He had yearned to tell her about adopting Odin, knowing she'd have loved the dog and treated him like a grandchild. And now he wished he could tell her about Ffion, about how he'd met a woman who was special, a woman he'd like her to meet. There would always be milestones that he wanted to share with his mum and each one would twang his grief like a guitar string, loud at first then slowly vibrating to silence.

It meant that he could understand some of what Ffion was going through. But her grief was, he suspected, for the man she had thought she'd spend her life with and so her pain must be beyond measure, beyond words and comprehension.

Joe wanted to help her. His feelings for her were deepening by the day but he recognised that Ffion needed friendship more than anything right now, and so he would give her that.

–

'Are we running with Joe today?' Mari asked.

'We are.' Ffion gave a brief nod.

Mari had met her outside the cottage, looking tired, but dressed in her running gear, ready to train.

'How did the wedding go yesterday?'

'It was lovely. Everyone seemed to have a good time and Mam and Dad were pleased with how it all went.'

'That's good. Hopefully it will drum up more business for their hospitality empire,' Mari said wryly, giving Ffion a nudge to show that she was teasing.

'It is an empire, isn't it? But they deserve success, with all the effort they put in.'

'They do. We're lucky to have such hard-working parents.'

'They're amazing.'

Ffion thought back to last night. The wedding had been a great success and everyone had been smiling. Everyone except for her. She had gone to the toilets after falling apart on Joe, to splash cold water on her face and to cool her hot cheeks. Her eyes still felt a bit swollen this morning but she'd blamed tiredness when her parents had asked about it, and last night, as she'd cleared up with the other staff, she'd blamed pollen, claiming that she'd developed hay fever. The fib had seemed a preferable alternative to admitting that she'd been crying in the arms of a wedding guest.

'Joe was there and he looked very handsome.' She said the words then bit her lip, wondering what Mari would make of them.

'You're spending a lot of time with him,' Mari said.

Ffion stopped walking. 'What's that supposed to mean?'

'Nothing. Nothing at all. I simply meant that you and he are together quite often now.'

Ffion shrugged her defensiveness away. 'He's a friend and we have our fundraising plans to work through.'

'Plans?'

'Yes, remember, we told you at the sanctuary? We're going to set up a race to raise funds for the animals.'

They'd talked about it while tucking into the picnic Joe had set out, and Mari had been keen to participate in the run and help out in any way she could.

'Of course.' Mari shook her head. 'I'm sorry, Ffion, I'm so tired most of the time that I'd forget my own head if it wasn't attached to my body. The running helps, but some days I'm like a zombie.'

'Something needs to change, Mari.' Ffion's thoughts went to Bryn and what she'd seen at the country hotel.

'He's definitely seeing someone.'

'What?' Ffion's eyes widened so much that they nearly popped out of their sockets.

'I saw part of another text flash up on his phone screen, so I tried to check the rest of it and he'd changed his passcode.'

'You don't know what his passcode is?' Ffion's heart began to race so she sucked in a slow, deep breath to try to steady herself.

'Nope. I did… We always had the same one as there was no need to hide anything from each other but for some reason, he's changed his.'

'Do you know when?'

'No idea. It's not like I'm checking his phone every five minutes. I use it sometimes to check the calendar if mine's charging, or to look at photos he's taken of the girls, but apart from that, what reason would I have to check it? So I'm guessing it's something he's done recently.'

Ffion watched her sister's face carefully, trying to work out how she was feeling, but Mari seemed incredibly calm, almost detached.

'Are you all right, Mari?'

'I guess so. I'm not sure what to think, to be honest.'

'This is a difficult thing to deal with and I'm worried about you.'

'We're a right pair, aren't we?' Mari rubbed at her eyes. 'You with your grief, and me with my seemingly errant husband. But what can I do? If I ask him outright, that's accusing him of cheating, and if I don't, am I just the mug who's pretending he's not messing around? The most worrying thing is how I actually feel kind of numb.'

'Could it be shock?'

'I'm worried it could be more than that.'

Ffion waited, knowing that Mari needed to tell her in her own time.

'After I had Seren… when I didn't feel right… it was a bit like this. It's like a numbness settles over me and I just don't feel anything.'

Ffion took Mari's hand. 'You think you're sinking again?'

'I'm not sure. I learnt from being unwell before that there are signs that I'm sinking and that's when I need to take care of myself better. Get more rest, stop dwelling on my inadequacies… more self-care… simple things, like more sleep and less pressure.'

'You're doing so much, Mari. Perhaps you need some time off work.'

'Perhaps. The running has been wonderful, though, you know? Getting my gear on, pounding the pavement, it de-stresses me. But I can't deny that I am tired or that I suspect Bryn is up to something. It's like a vicious circle where my worries make me tired then my tiredness makes my worries worse… if that makes sense.'

Ffion groaned inwardly. She knew now that she had to speak to Bryn as soon as possible. If Mari was feeling this low then something needed to be done.

'It's hard to be calm and rational when you're exhausted. If you want to go to the doctor, I'll come with you.'

'The doctor?'

'Perhaps you need some time off. Even a few weeks.'

'I've just had two weeks off for Easter.'

'But have you rested? Have you been kind to yourself? Have you had any time for you?'

Mari's face crumpled and she shook her head.

'I can be there for you more, you know.'

'I'm just a mum trying to run a home and work full-time and I'm only doing what millions of other people do every day. Most of the women, and some men, I know seem to do it effortlessly and rarely complain. They just get on with it and I feel that I should be doing the same.'

'A lot of people work very hard and juggle work and home. But you should have support and in your case, you do have a husband who needs to step up.'

Mari sniffed, wiped at her eyes then pushed her shoulders back. 'Look… let me speak to the head teacher, see if I can negotiate some of my responsibilities for a bit… possibly ask if I can go part-time after the summer… and if I don't feel any better soon I'll make a GP appointment. Does that sound OK? It's just that I love my job and I don't want to take an extended period of time off unless I really need to.'

'I can't tell you what to do, Mari, all I can do is be here for you. I want to help if I can, as much as I can. As long as you promise you're going to look at making some changes to take the pressure off yourself then that's good enough for me.'

'Thank you.'

'I love you.'

'Love you more.'

They hugged and Ffion squeezed Mari tight. Just last night, she'd been struggling and Joe had supported her and now she was doing the same for Mari. Having people around who cared was so important and could make a crucial difference. Not for the first time since she'd returned to Wales, she was glad that she had come home.

'Anyway… I think we'd better get down to the beach or Joe's going to think we've got lost on the way.' Ffion smiled and took Mari's hand.

'I can't wait to run today.'

'Nor me. I actually look forward to it now because I know that it's going to make me feel better.'

'It's like magic.' Mari laughed. 'If only we'd known how good it made us feel years ago.'

'This was the right time for us to find out,' Ffion said. 'When we needed it most.'

Chapter Twenty-Three

The next week, when Mari was back at school, Ffion sent Bryn a text message asking if she could meet with him. He sent a confused emoji in reply so she said it was about Mari and asked him to therefore please keep their meeting to himself for now.

He said he could meet her at a coffee shop in Swansea as he had a client meeting at ten on Monday morning and could meet with her afterwards. On her way from the car park, Ffion felt conspicuous, like everyone who looked at her would know that she was meeting her brother-in-law behind her sister's back. But, of course, there was nothing illicit about this meeting; Ffion just wanted to speak to Bryn and find out what was going on with him as she was so concerned about Mari.

Outside the cafe, she paused and looked around. It was a dreary day with drizzle in the air and it had made her feel low when she'd woken to see the slate-grey sky above the leaden sea, as if all colour had seeped from the cove overnight. The recent spring sunshine had lifted her, helping her to see the beauty of the world, but rain clouds impacted upon that dramatically. And, she knew, so did what she had to do this morning. She was still torn about whether or not this was the right course of action but if she didn't speak to Bryn and Mari sank even lower then she'd never forgive herself.

She opened the door to the cafe and went inside. Warm, coffee-scented air enveloped her along with the smell of cinnamon and toast. She removed her raincoat and looked around. Bryn was sitting in a booth at the back of the cafe – as if their meeting needed to seem any more clandestine.

She pointed at the counter and he shook his head so she ordered a latte for herself then took it over to join him.

'Morning,' she said, taking the seat opposite him.

'Hello, Ffion.' He attempted a smile but Ffion noted the purple shadows under his eyes, the stubble on his jaw, the yellowy stain on his shirt collar that could have been sweat or egg. 'So… what is it that brings you here today?'

Ffion blew on her latte to buy herself a minute. Around her, Monday morning was happening as usual, as people ordered drinks and breakfast, coffee beans were ground and the espresso machine frothed. Conversation hummed and fingers tapped at phones and laptops. A lot of the customers were young, probably students, as Swansea had a high student population. Life was continuing for them, their futures lay ahead, exciting and filled with possibilities, and that was the way of things; it was how it should be.

'OK, Bryn. Uh… this is difficult. Delicate.'

He nodded and moved his large cup around on its saucer. She noticed the hairs on his fingers, the jagged cuticles around his short nails.

'It's about Mari… as I said in my text.'

'OK.' He stared hard at his cup.

'I'm worried about her.'

'Oh…'

'Are you OK, Bryn?'

She searched his face, the balding head with just a sparse covering of ginger and white hairs remaining, small grey eyes with heavy lids and his pursed mouth beneath patchy stubble. She could see the young man her sister had fallen in love with but only just. Bryn was thirty-five but he could easily have been ten or fifteen years older. His narrow, rounded shoulders and the paunch that strained at the front of his shirt, pushing his tie aside, added to that impression and Ffion wondered for a moment what had attracted her beautiful sister to this man. But then, she admonished herself, that was not for her to judge. Beauty was in the eye of the beholder, was far more than a physical thing, and when Mari and Bryn had got together they'd been very young, marrying when Mari was just twenty-one and Bryn twenty-three. But they'd lasted this long and Ffion hoped they would last much longer as a couple, hopefully forever, but that could only happen if Bryn made some changes.

'I'm…' He sighed. 'I guess so. What is it that's worrying you, specifically?' he asked.

'Mari seems… very tired, overworked and quite low.'

He pressed his lips together until they turned white.

'Bryn… I don't want to overstep here but I'm Mari's sister and I feel that I need to speak to you about this because… I know that she won't. She's a workhorse and she'll keep going until she crashes completely and if that happens, she'll suffer and so will you… and so will the children.'

'I know. I… I have been worried. Mari is very tired but… I'm…' He rubbed a hand over his face and it grated against the stubble. 'I'm just so tired too.'

Ffion swallowed the retort that sprang to mind about golf and not pulling his weight and afternoon tea with attractive women but instead, she held back and said, 'Is there anything I can do to help?'

When his face crumpled, she was thrown. This wasn't what she was expecting.

'What is it, Bryn?'

He pulled a tissue from his coat pocket and blew his nose, dabbed at his eyes.

'Having children is hard. I know you haven't been there…' He held up a hand. 'Not a criticism. I'm sure you and Graeme would have made great parents. But… Mari and I… we love the girls so much but it's hard, you know? In the past six years we've gone from being able to have lazy weekends in bed, going to the cinema whenever we want, heading out to restaurants for meals because we can't be bothered to cook to… being slaves to two tiny people.'

Ffion sipped her coffee, letting what Bryn had just said sink in.

'I wouldn't be without the girls but the adjustment to parenthood has been challenging. Mari is amazing, just incredible but she… doesn't have much time for me any more. And I try… I really do, Ffion, but Mari is so on top of it all. She's a perfectionist and sometimes I feel a bit left out, a bit useless, as whatever I do is often not good enough.'

'Oh.' She took a slow deep breath. She'd heard Mari's side of things, obviously, but had no idea that Bryn would be feeling like this.

'I feel disloyal even talking to you about things.' He drained his coffee. 'I never talk to anyone about Mari or our relationship. I love her so much but I also miss her and how we were.'

'That's… understandable.' Ffion tilted her head. 'If your life is good and you're happy then something comes along that changes everything, it is hard.'

'I'm so sorry, Ffion. After what you've been through… I have no right to complain. Graeme was a good man.'

'He was.' And there was the lump in her throat, threatening to choke her with tears. But this wasn't about her; it was about Mari and Bryn. 'He was the best. But this is about you and my sister… we need to try to help you and Mari.'

'I know I'm at fault,' Bryn said, pushing his hands back over his shiny head as if sweeping back hair. 'I know I could try harder. I just think we've got into a rut and I've sat back and let Mari get on with things.'

'She said she wasn't well after having Seren.'

'She wasn't. She… had some post-natal issues and it was devastating to see her so lost. She was absolutely exhausted all the time but she'd insist on still doing everything, as if she was terrified of being seen as a failure. How she looked after the children as well as she did I have no idea but she's… she's a machine.'

'She's not though, is she?'

'Sorry?'

'Mari is a human being. She's not a machine.'

He shook his head. 'Sorry… I didn't mean it that way. Seren was up half the night and my brain isn't working properly. By machine, I didn't mean without feeling or anything… just that she keeps going.'

'Even machines can break down if they're not properly fuelled or rested.'

'Exactly.' He nodded. 'Which is why I've booked us a—'

'Bryn…' Ffion licked her lips. She had to ask him before she lost her nerve. 'I… I saw you with someone else.'

'What?' His fair eyebrows rose and his eyes widened. 'When?'

'I met a friend for afternoon tea last week and as we were about to leave, you came in.'

He frowned then rubbed at the back of his neck. 'Oh… No…' He laughed. 'That was Patricia. She was helping me organise things for a weekend of pampering for Mari. We've tried to arrange it secretly via text message so that Mari wouldn't know but I had to sign some forms so that was why we met up. That's what I was about to tell you. I've booked us a weekend away.'

'OK.' Ffion watched him carefully, trying to work out whether he was being honest. 'You looked very… pally.'

'I've known Pat a long time. She's the area manager for a chain of luxury hotels and she met me there to finalise details. We were at uni together.'

'Oh.' Perhaps Bryn really did look rough then as Patricia had seemed younger than him.

'Honestly, Ffion, I would never cheat on Mari. She's my world even if I don't always act like it.'

'Bryn… I'm glad to hear that you're arranging something nice for you and Mari but it will take more than a weekend away to make things better. Mari needs more than that. She's exhausted.'

'I know.'

Ffion took a deep breath, determined to get her point across. 'You… seem to go off to golf and to… leave her alone with the children a lot and whether she admits it or not, she needs you there.'

'I know.' He hung his head. 'I've got into the habit of letting her manage everything and it needs to stop.'

'What about work? I don't want to overstep the mark here, Bryn, but I'm worried sick about Mari and if she gets really ill, I'll never be able to forgive myself. Is there any way you and Mari could find some flexibility there?'

'She loves her job, though.' His brows knitted together in confusion.

'She does but she can't continue to do everything right now. The girls will grow up and things will get easier as they become more independent. Hopefully Seren will sleep better soon and then you and Mari might be able to find more time for each other again.'

'I would love that.' Bryn's Adam's apple bobbed. 'I miss her so much.'

'Then help her more. Pull your weight because they're your children too.' Ffion's tone was hard but she wanted Bryn to fully accept what was happening to Mari. He did seem tired and hearing how much he loved Mari was good, but if he didn't do more, then Ffion worried that her sister would become ill. She'd decided not to mention the text messages because he'd already explained that he'd been messaging Patricia secretly to arrange a weekend of pampering for Mari. Ffion felt that if Mari still had any concerns about Bryn's phone, then they were probably best coming from her.

'I'll make some changes,' Bryn said determinedly, sitting up straighter. 'I promise.'

'Tell me more about this weekend away, then.'

Bryn told her about his plans and Ffion agreed to help with the children and the surprise for Mari. It wouldn't cure everything overnight, but it was certainly a step in the right direction.

Chapter Twenty-Four

'Are you sure you'll be OK with them?' Mari was peering out of the car window, her eyes glued to her children.

'We'll all be fine.' Ffion smiled. 'Now Bryn, hurry up and get her away from here or she'll never go.'

'Yes, Ffion!' Bryn gave a small salute from the driver's seat. 'Come on my beloved, let's have some *us* time.'

As he drove away, Ffion kept waving until the car was out of sight, then she turned to her parents who were standing outside the cottage with their grandchildren. Ffion's dad had Anwen's hand and her mam was holding Seren.

'Can we make cakes now?' Anwen asked as she tugged at Aled's hand.

'Absolutely!' he replied.

'And me?' Seren reached out to him so he took her from his wife then went inside with her and Anwen.

'You OK, Mam?' Ffion asked.

'I think so. I just hope those two can work things out. I'm surprised to see them going away, to be honest. Surprised at Bryn for organising it and surprised at Mari for agreeing to go.'

Ffion thought back to the conversation she'd had with Mari earlier that week following her coffee with Bryn. She'd agreed with Bryn that they would be honest with Mari about meeting and about what they'd discussed because she could never keep something like that from her sister. The best way for Bryn and Mari to work things out was to be open and honest. Mari had been shocked then cried then told Ffion she was relieved and grateful.

Mari had admitted that she could see how Bryn might have felt left out and even pushed aside because of her need to have everything under control, which she was sure had stemmed from her fear that she was losing her grip on things when she was ill. And, of course, ever since she was child, Mari had always liked to manage things, as if she didn't think anyone else could do things as well as her. Perhaps it was to do with the fact that she was the older sister and often watched over Ffion while their parents worked. Even though Mari was only a year older than Ffion, the age gap had often seemed wider because of Mari's mature behaviour and attitude.

Mari had also spoken to her head teacher who'd been kind and supportive about Mari going part-time in September – something Ffion felt was a very wise move – and had also said that they could try to sort something else out for the rest of this year. Mari's relief at that brought tears to Ffion's eyes because Mari loved her job and didn't want to lose it but she knew she had to make some changes to regain a healthy balance between work and home.

Mari and Bryn wouldn't be able to wave a magic wand to improve their marriage and their life, but at least now the dialogue was open they could start to move in the right direction.

'They need this,' Ffion said now to her mam. 'It's important for them to have time alone as a couple and time to be themselves.'

Her mam nodded. 'I agree. But in the past they always said they were fine. Mari was terrified of leaving the babies for even a night.'

'Mari has accepted now that she needs a break.'

'I'm glad she's gone. It will do them both good.'

'They'll probably sleep all weekend.' Ffion smiled wryly.

'It won't hurt them.' Her mam laughed. 'Right then… seeing as how I've booked myself and your dad the weekend off – something that is virtually unheard of round here – are you ready to roll up your sleeves and get stuck in? Anwen has a whole itinerary planned for us.'

Ffion made a show of pushing up her sleeves. 'I'm definitely ready.'

'Come on, then.'

Her mam led the way and Ffion closed the door behind them, looking forward to a weekend of fun with her parents and her nieces.

—

'Ta-dah!' Ffion held up the bucket with a flourish.

'That's not right.' Anwen shook her head. 'It's wonky.'

Ffion bit her lip, trying not to laugh. They'd come down to the beach early the next morning with Anwen and Seren to build some sandcastles. Anwen was proving to be a critical boss.

'Bash it down and we can start again,' Ffion's dad winked at her. 'And Ffion, please try harder.'

She nodded dutifully and tapped the bucket to empty it properly. 'I'll go and swill this out then we can try again with a clean bucket.'

After she'd rinsed the bucket in the sea, she turned back to the beach and gazed at her family. Her parents were sitting on the sand in front of their beach tent with Anwen and Seren. Both children wore leggings and T-shirts with small hoodies and sunhats. In spite of this, their exposed skin was white with sunblock because Gwen was terrified that the children might burn while in her care. Neither Anwen or Seren had seemed to mind as Gwen had plastered them with cream, apparently used to having it done by Mari, and Anwen had even started to tell them about a science lesson at school where the teacher had told them how dangerous the sun could be.

The morning was sunny but the breeze was cool so Ffion was wearing a fleecy hoodie that she'd found in her wardrobe, a remnant from her teenaged years spent on the beach. Growing up in the cove she'd spent days and nights sitting on the sand, splashing in the sea and walking the coastal path. She'd been very lucky to grow up in such a beautiful place but knew that she hadn't always appreciated it. Graeme had come to the cove with her while they were at university and stayed there during some of the holidays. They'd shared many kisses in the sand dunes and some more passionate encounters too, although she pushed the thought of those from her mind because some things were too painful to think about.

'Ffion!' She looked across to the cliffs that separated Cariad Cove from Barddoniaeth Bay and saw a tall broad figure, one hand raised in greeting. Bounding along next to him was Odin.

'Hey, Joe!' She waved back and waited for them to reach her. She'd let Joe know that she wouldn't be running this weekend as her nieces were staying over but she'd secretly hoped to bump into him at the beach. With him working and it being a busy week, she hadn't seen him since the previous Sunday and she was surprised to find she'd missed him. Quite a lot.

'I was hoping you'd be down here today.' He was wearing shorts and a hoodie too, his feet bare as he splashed through the tide with Odin, but he had a backpack on so Ffion suspected his shoes were in that.

'The girls wanted to come down to build sandcastles as soon as they woke. Last night, it was too late after we'd baked about a million cakes but before I'd even opened my eyes this morning, Anwen was shaking me awake.'

'Did they sleep in your room?'

'Anwen had Mari's old room and Seren slept in a travel cot in my parents' room. I say *slept* but she had them up and down about six times for drinks and cuddles.'

He grimaced. 'Sounds challenging.'

'It's no wonder my sister and her husband are exhausted.'

'Parenthood is not for the faint-hearted.' He winked at her then frowned. 'Odin!' Joe called to the dog but he'd already approached Anwen and she had her arms wrapped around his thick neck. 'Sorry.'

'It's fine. He must remember her.'

'Remember her? He seems to adore her.' Joe chuckled. 'He's such a big oaf but when it comes to children he's incredibly gentle.'

'I don't suppose, now that you're here, you fancy building some sandcastles, do you?'

Joe's eyebrows rose. 'Sandcastles, eh?'

'I am absolutely rubbish and Anwen is getting more and more annoyed with me. So if you did fancy helping, I'd be very grateful.'

'I'm actually very good with a bucket and spade,' he said with a gleam in his eye. 'So yes, I'd love to help out.'

'Brilliant.'

They walked up the beach together and Ffion's heart pinched when Anwen greeted Joe like a member of the family, giving him a hug then handing him a bucket and immediately started to boss him around. He removed his backpack and pushed his sleeves up then got to work. Ffion sat with them, helping when she could, staying out of the way when she wasn't needed, aware that her parents were watching them all.

When Seren toddled over and sat on Ffion's lap, she held the little girl in her arms and felt the tension she'd carried for so long loosen a little more. Seren's weight in her lap was comforting, her hair smelt sweetly of baby shampoo and when the little girl reached up and patted Ffion's cheek, Ffion's chest expanded with joy.

Things had a way of working out and today was turning out to be a good day.

–

Joe stood back and admired his work.

'How did I do?' he asked Anwen.

She placed her hands on her hips and frowned as she walked around the fortress he'd built in the sand like a mini buildings inspector.

'I like the towers and the pebble drawbridge.' Anwen tapped a finger against her lips, an adult gesture that made Joe want to laugh out loud.

'The shell windows are nice, too.' Ffion pointed at where Joe had stuck shells in the sides of the towers.

'Yes, I like them.' A smile broke across Anwen's face and Joe let loose an internal sigh of relief. 'Thank you, Joe.'

'You're very welcome. I enjoyed myself.'

'You're much better at this than Aunty Ffion.' Anwen rolled her eyes and Joe sniggered while Ffion held her hands up in mock surrender.

'Want to go in the sea.' Seren stood up and pointed at the water.

'Oh, it's too cold for that today,' Gwen said, hugging herself to illustrate her point.

'Not!' Seren stamped a foot.

'It is, darling.' Gwen stood up and reached for Seren's hand but the little girl frowned.

'Going in.'

Seren tottered off down the beach, discarding her hat and hoodie as she went and Gwen ran after her.

'Oh dear,' Joe said. 'Should we help?'

'I'll go,' Aled dusted off his hands. 'Anwen, you stay with Ffion and Joe.'

'Of course, I will.' Anwen tutted. 'I'm not an idiot.'

Aled glanced at his eldest granddaughter and his lips twitched, then he jogged off down the beach.

'Poor Mam.' Ffion grimaced. 'Seren has such a strong mind.'

'She's always like this.' Anwen sighed. 'She's *exosting*. All the time… every day… Seren has the terrible twos tantrums.'

'Gosh that's a mouthful.' Ffion grinned at Joe over Anwen's head and Joe grinned back. Sometimes, Anwen sounded like she was sixty, not six.

There was a shout from farther along the beach and Ffion gasped as Seren ran into the sea, closely followed by her grandparents. But as they splashed through the water, the three of them ran around, laughing.

'Well, I didn't expect that.' Ffion's mouth fell open as she observed them.

'You know what…' Joe rubbed his chin. 'I think we should all go in.'

'Are you mad?' Ffion laughed nervously. 'It'll be freezing.'

'It's not that bad, actually. I was paddling earlier, remember?'

'Yes, but… it's almost lunch time and I feel quite cold today and—'

'It wouldn't be the first time you've gone in recently.' Joe cocked an eyebrow and Ffion's cheeks flushed. 'It's invigorating, right?'

'I don't know.' She looked at Anwen. 'We're watching over my niece, anyway.'

'Anwen?' Joe asked.

'Yes.'

'You feel like a dip?'

'In my clothes?'

'Why not?' Joe said. 'It's not far to the cottage and you can change quickly.'

'It's OK.' She pointed at the beach tent. 'Nanny brought towels and dry clothes just in case.'

'Well, there you are, then.'

Ffion looked around desperately and Joe stifled a laugh. 'Not today.'

'Go on, Aunty Ffion.' Anwen nudged her. 'Get in the sea!'

'No.' Ffion stepped away from them, eyes wide, lips twitching.

'Get her, Joe!' Anwen clapped her hands laughing. 'Make Aunty Ffion swim.'

'Your wish is my command, Lady Anwen!' Joe said, chasing after Ffion. Odin followed them, as they swerved to avoid piles of seaweed and shells, Anwen jogging at Joe's side.

'Faster, Joe!' Anwen was panting now as they ushered Ffion farther along the beach until she was at the water's edge where they cornered her, hands outstretched like goalkeepers.

'I really don't want to go in.' Ffion was holding her hands up in front of her.

'You have to now.' Anwen ran at her aunt and Joe ducked down and scooped Ffion up. She wriggled and giggled and ended up over his shoulder.

'Do it! Do it!' Anwen shouted, clapping her hands excitedly again.

'You want me to take you back to the sand?' Joe asked quietly, wanting to have fun but also not wanting to upset anyone. Perhaps Ffion really didn't want to go in.

'What and disappoint my niece?' Ffion muttered through gritted teeth. 'I can't bear the thought of that even more than I can't bear the thought of being dunked in the freezing cold water.'

'I'll be gentle, I promise,' Joe said, then he lunged forwards and lowered them both into the water, taking care to keep their heads above the waves.

Ffion wrapped her arms around his neck and the cold sea washed over them as they laughed, shivered and bobbed in the water. Odin was swimming around them now, clearly enjoying the game as much as they were.

'Me too!' Anwen waded towards them and held out her arms, so Joe took her hand and brought her to them. He shifted his position to support Ffion and Anwen, and the three of them floated in the shallows.

'Everybody wet,' Seren said as she splashed water at them while Gwen hung on to her other hand, teeth chattering.

'I think we all need some warm drinks and dry clothes, don't you?' Aled asked as he waded out of the sea.

'Sounds good to me,' Gwen said, picking Seren up and carrying her up to the tent.

'What do you think, ladies?' Joe asked. 'Have you had enough, now?'

'Yes.' Anwen nodded. 'I'm cold.'

'Come on then, let's get back.'

He helped Ffion and Anwen back to the sand and they plodded up the beach, water running down their legs, sand clinging to their feet. It was cold coming out of the water but it had been fun and he knew it was a day that the little girls wouldn't forget in a hurry. Odin was with them all the time and when he stopped to shake and covered them all in droplets of water and blobs of wet sand, Anwen screeched with delight.

When they reached Ffion's parents, Gwen wrapped a large towel around Anwen then turned and looked at Joe and Ffion.

'I don't know about you two, but that dip in the sea has made me bloody starving.'

Joe turned to Ffion and they both snorted with laughter.

'I'm pretty bloody starving too,' Ffion said, winking at him.

'Lucky for us that I happened to bring a portable barbecue in my rucksack along with some hotdogs and rolls then, isn't it?' Joe asked as he reached for his rucksack.

'You didn't?' Ffion placed a cool hand on his arm.

'You never know when you might need an emergency barbecue.' When Ffion had texted him to let him know her nieces were spending the weekend, he'd had a suspicion that they'd come to the beach. 'But first, get a towel around you and warm up while I check if I also brought a flask of hot chocolate.'

As the children cheered, Joe opened his rucksack and pulled everything out, silently thanking his aunt for teaching him to always be prepared. He hadn't known for sure if Ffion would be at the beach or if they'd end up spending the day together, but just in case, he'd packed some handy things and now he could do something nice for Ffion and her family. It gave him pleasure to take care of other people and he often took treats in for other staff at school and for his form class at the end of term, but recently he'd found that he wanted to do things for Ffion that would make her happy and bring out her sunshine smile. He hadn't seen it many times, but when it did grace her lovely face, Joe felt like he could look at her all day.

'Thank you, Joe.' Ffion met his eyes and the softening in her gaze made his heart expand.

'It's my pleasure,' he said. And he meant every word.

—

Following their hotdogs and hot chocolate, Ffion's parents had taken the children back to the cottage to shower and change into dry clothes, leaving Ffion and Joe alone. They had both changed into T-shirts and jogging bottoms that Joe had also brought in his rucksack, taking turns to use the cover of the beach tent. She'd said that she bet he'd made a brilliant boy scout back in the day and he'd told her that he had to thank his aunt for teaching him to always be prepared and that he also supervised the Duke of Edinburgh award with the pupils at school. Now they were sitting by the portable barbecue, making the most of the warm glow. Odin lay on the picnic blanket, his head on Joe's leg, his tongue lolling from his mouth, clearly worn out after all the excitement. Ffion knew how he felt.

'Thanks for today,' Ffion said, stretching out her legs in front of her. 'The children really enjoyed themselves.'

'So did I.'

'Me too. Simple things can be so much fun.' She laughed as she pointed at her trousers. They'd had to roll the ankle cuffs up half a dozen times to make up for the height difference between her and Joe. 'How did you know to bring extra clothes as well as the food and drink?'

'Well… If I'm intending on spending much time down here, I always do. Odin often gets me soaked when he's running in and out of the water, and today I just had a feeling that I might need more than one set of clothes.'

Ffion looked down at herself; the clothes he'd given her were soft and they smelt good – like Joe.

The tide was out and the wet sand gleamed like glass under the afternoon sun. Children farther down the beach shouted and laughed and a dog barked, making Odin's ears prick up, though his eyes stayed closed.

'The hot chocolate was delicious. You'll have to let me know how you make it because mine never tastes that good.'

'I can do that.' He paused. 'However… I also have something a bit stronger in my backpack if you fancy it?'

She looked at him and saw the mischief in his eyes. 'How big is that backpack? Are you like Mary Poppins' brother or something?'

He laughed. 'I pack well. I'm quite neat actually and growing up I was an expert at Tetris.'

'I loved that game but could never reach the end. When it got faster, I'd panic. You must be good at keeping your cool.'

'I try.' He waggled his eyebrows. 'So… Do you like rum?'

'I've never drunk much of it so I'm not actually sure.'

He pulled out a hipflask. 'This is Welsh botanical rum. Made locally.'

'Is it nice?'

'Very.'

'I like whisky and have tried lots of single malts but that was because of Graeme being Scottish and…' She stopped, her tongue running away with her.

'Graeme was your partner?'

'Yes.'

Joe unscrewed the top of the flask and handed it to her. She took a sip and blinked hard, expecting it to burn her throat, but while it was warming, it wasn't harsh at all.

'Good?' Joe asked.

'Very smooth.'

'Close your eyes.'

'Why?' She frowned.

'Humour me.'

'OK.'

'What can you taste?'

She took another sip and let it rest on her tongue before she swallowed it.

'Brown sugar… pineapple… cinnamon… ginger.'

'That's right. You're very good at this.'

'It's warming me right through.' She passed the flask to him and he took a sip.

'That's why the sailors used to drink it.' He grinned.

'I always wondered if that was a myth.'

'I don't think so. But this is probably far superior to what would've been consumed years ago. There are lots of different types of rum available now.'

'And gin. There are some fabulous gins out there.'

'Can't say I drink much gin.'

'Well, I'll have to take you out one evening so I can introduce you to some of my favourites.' Ffion realised what she'd said and a flush spread up her neck.

'I'd like that.' He gazed at her from beneath his lashes and her stomach flipped over.

They sat quietly for a bit, passing the flask between them, gazing at the horizon. Ffion felt relaxed and comfortable with Joe, like she could tell him anything. The moment finally felt right.

'Graeme wasn't just my partner, Joe… He was my husband.'

There. She'd said the words. And it hadn't been as awful as she'd anticipated.

'You're a widow?'

She winced. 'I hate that word. The connotations are so sorrowful and gloomy and…' Her eyes stung suddenly and she sucked in a breath, afraid she'd start to cry. 'I… I guess I just wish it wasn't true.'

'I'm so sorry.' Joe reached for her hand. 'I didn't mean to upset you.'

'You haven't. I'm just finding it hard to be a widow and simultaneously, to be me.'

'You don't have to attach any labels to yourself.'

She looked at Joe and saw only kindness in his eyes.

He carried on, looking down at their joined hands. 'In school, we have some pupils who come to PE with the preconception that they'll be rubbish at all sport. It might be because they tried football and couldn't score a goal or because they tried high jump and couldn't leap over the bar or tried swimming and found it exhausting. They label themselves because they tried and failed or because their parents weren't any good when they were at school and told them they wouldn't be. Once they've attached a label to themselves, or had someone else assign it to them, it's hard to break that mental barrier down. But it's not impossible. People can get better at things; sometimes they just need to try something different. One boy I taught hated football but he was a fantastic swimmer. Another, a very small girl in year seven, couldn't throw a basketball anywhere near the net but on the track she was like a grey-hound. The confidence she gained from running meant that she felt better about trying basketball again and by year ten, she was captain of the school team. Everyone has different strengths and that's what I tell the pupils.' His gaze turned back to meet hers, full of compassion and something that was indefinably Joe. 'I think I've digressed a bit... but my point was that at some point in our lives, we all have so-called labels assigned to us that don't have to stick. You might have been widowed, but it's not who you are, not who you're going to be. It's something tragic that happened to you and hurt you and that you'll always carry with you, but it doesn't have to define you.'

Ffion loved listening to him; he was so wise and compassionate and what he'd said made perfect sense. She swallowed another sip of rum, enjoying the gentle heat in her belly and how it seeped into her veins, soothing her, making her feel brave.

'I was afraid to tell you about him.'

'Why?' He blinked slowly.

'I didn't want you to see me that way.'

'What way?'

'As a widow. As someone who's damaged and someone to pity.'

He squeezed her hand and she looked down at his long fingers wrapped around hers, at the fair hairs on his strong forearms and the dusting of freckles on his skin. He was golden, beautiful inside and out, and she was drawn to him. However much she might want to deny it, Joe had got to her and with every moment she spent with him, every conversation, every smile, the connection grew stronger.

'Do you want to tell me about him?'

She swallowed and turned to face Joe properly, adjusting her position so her legs were crossed and her palms were flat on her knees.

'Graeme was my first love. We met at university where we were both studying PR and Media. He'd come all the way from Perthshire in Scotland because he wanted to study away from home and have some different experiences before returning to manage his parents' estate.'

'He came from money, then?'

Her chin dipped slightly. 'You wouldn't have known it because he was so down to earth, but the family estate was huge. *Is* huge. They have holiday cottages, lochs, camping facilities, and run activities like water sports, horse riding, and so on. Some of the land is also dedicated to organic farming so Graeme had a lot to oversee there, plus he still liked to get stuck in with lambing and things. During lambing season I barely saw him because he was so busy.'

'I can imagine.' Joe scratched at his cheek. 'Did you live on the estate?'

'No. But we lived quite close to it so Graeme didn't have far to travel.'

'How big is it?'

'Around 6000 acres.'

'Bloody hell!'

'I know.' She smiled. 'I had no idea until Graeme first took me home to meet his parents.'

'After he… passed away… didn't you want to stay there?'

She shook her head. 'It didn't feel right. Graeme's parents are good people but… we weren't close. They were very… for want of a better word… *proper* about things, and while they kind of tolerated me for his sake, I don't think they ever really liked me.'

'How could they fail to like you? You're incredible, Ffion.'

She could feel herself blushing. 'You're so kind.'

'I'm not flattering you. I'm just telling you the truth.'

Her shoulders dropped as she let Joe's words sink in. He really did like her and she found comfort in knowing that.

'There… there was someone before me… a daughter of a family friend, Scottish born and bred, and I think she was their first choice for daughter-in-law. She was born into money – had grown up riding horses and attended boarding school – and the families had spent a lot of time together over the years. Graeme and Rohanne – that's her name – had a brief relationship before he left for university but it fizzled out. Of course, then he met me and we fell in love and when he told his parents, I don't think they were elated about us at all. I always hoped they would thaw, that they'd grow to like me more when we had children. But it didn't happen and then it was too late. In a way, I'm glad it didn't because I might have been stuck there with a child or children and no husband, and I don't think I could have borne that.'

'I'm so sorry, Ffion. However, I'm sure you could have managed anything.'

'Maybe… but it would have been hard. The thing is… it's not that I didn't want children, because I did… do… someday… And if I had a child then I'd still have a part of Graeme with me now. But the thought of struggling alone without him, trying to be strong for a child… I know it would have been rough. I'm just a walking contradiction because I don't know what would have been better. Anyway, we didn't have a family and that's not going to change now.'

She sucked in a shaky breath then pushed it from her lungs, trying to soothe herself. She couldn't believe she'd told Joe as much as she had already. He was easy to talk to and there was something cathartic about telling him all this. He hadn't known Graeme or his parents, hadn't known Ffion when she was with Graeme, and it was helpful to get it out in the open, like purging herself of sadness.

'How did he… Was he ill?'

'He had a malignant brain tumour. He was poorly for about six months on and off before the diagnosis but you know how it is… you soldier on, putting it down to long hours at work and tiredness. But when the headaches and memory loss kicked in, along with blurred vision and speech problems, he had to have tests. He was stubborn and initially refused to go but by the time he did, the diagnosis was late and we were told that he had a high grade astrocytoma. Graeme weighed up the pros and cons of treatment, had surgery and chemo to try to control the tumour, but they made him low and weak. He'd always been so strong and healthy and hated not being able to do everything he usually could. When the tumour returned aggressively, he declined further treatment.'

'That's very sad.' Joe rubbed at his eyes. 'Words don't express how terribly sad and awful it is. I wish I could say the right thing but I don't know what it is.'

'There are no right or wrong words and the fact that you're listening to me and being so kind is helpful. You know, the strangest thing is that it still doesn't feel real when I talk about it. I don't know if that makes sense but it's like it happened to someone else a long time ago and I'm just telling the story. Obviously, I know it happened to my husband because I have the pain to prove it but somehow, my mind is making it feel like it didn't.'

'It's self-preservation. The only way us humans can keep going when we lose someone is through some sense of detachment.'

'That makes sense.'

'How long ago did you lose Graeme?'

'Sixteen months ago. I tried to stay in Scotland but I struggled and quit my job and realised that I couldn't bear to be there without him. When Graeme was alive, it felt like home, but when he was gone, it felt… empty, alienating. I was at a loss, and knowing how his parents felt about me, staying didn't seem like an option at all so I sold our home, cleared out most of his stuff and the things we'd bought together and returned to Wales.'

Joe held her gaze, his lips slightly parted, his eyes filled with emotion.

'I'm sorry for all you've lost, Ffion, but I'm glad you're here. I don't mean that to sound selfish or cold or anything like that.' He sighed. 'What I meant was, that I'm glad to have met you. I'm glad we're friends.'

'Me too.' And she was.

She wanted to say more, to tell him that her feelings for him were complicated, evolving and growing and that she thought she might actually want more from him than friendship, but something was still holding her back. It had been good to talk to Joe about her situation, and she was relieved that he'd said he didn't see her as being labelled as a widow, but was it fair to expect him to help her with her grief? Just because Joe had a good heart and a compassionate soul, it didn't mean that it was fair to saddle him with her complications. She liked him too much to bring all of that to his life.

'I'm here anytime you want to talk, Ffion. I might not be able to help much but I will listen.'

'Thank you.'

She shifted onto her knees then leant over and kissed his cheek. When their eyes met and his pupils dilated, her resolve to hold back crumbled to dust. There was so much understanding in his gaze, so much more to learn about him and to share with him if her heart could just open up and give them both a chance.

He glanced past her along the beach in the direction of the hotel. 'We have company.'

She turned and saw her parents and nieces rambling over the sand towards them. Her dad was carrying a large cooler and her mam had a tote bag.

'It looks like they've brought dinner,' Ffion said.

Odin sat up and wagged his tail.

'Odin's glad to hear that,' Joe said, laughing.

Ffion reached out and touched his hand, running her fingers over his and wishing she had the time and courage to say more.

'We have all the time in the world,' Joe said, as if reading her thoughts.

She made a silent wish, hoping he was right.

Chapter Twenty-Five

'I can't believe we've reached week eight!' Mari shook her head.

'Last week was tough and this week's going to be even harder,' Ffion said as she bent over to touch her toes.

'I know! Thirty minutes of running. Who'd have thought we could get this far?'

Ffion gulped. She was feeling a bit nervous about running for thirty minutes. Last week, she had done three separate twenty-eight-minute runs and she'd almost given up a few times but running with Joe meant that she'd had constant encouragement. She really wanted to be able to do this today. Some runs were tougher than others though and running for half an hour was going to be a huge challenge. However, the Couch to 5k programme had prepared her and Mari for it and so they should, in theory, be able to do it.

Mari had come over after work as Bryn was looking after the children, so she was able to take some time for herself.

'You had a good weekend, then?' Ffion asked as they walked down to the beach.

'It was wonderful.' Mari smiled. Her skin was glowing and she looked rested.

'How do you feel now?'

'Better.' Mari bobbed her head. 'Things aren't perfect by any means, but we had some time over the weekend to talk and rest and... well... some other stuff too,' she giggled, 'and I do feel more positive.'

'That's wonderful news.'

'Bryn's a good man.' Mari cleared her throat. 'But he and I got a bit lost along the way. It happens to people when they've been together for a long time. Life gets in the way and having children changes everything. I don't know if this new regime that we've planned together will last but I hope with all my heart that it does. We have a history, two beautiful girls and a lovely home and as long as we both compromise... we should be able to find our way through. Marriage is about that, isn't it?'

'About compromise?'

'Yes, and working through the difficult times. No relationship is perfect and no couple has a completely smooth ride. Like everything in life that's worth having, it's about putting the work in.'

'That's very true. There's no reason why it shouldn't get better as long as Bryn does pull his weight.'

'He will. He understands how I've been feeling now, and knows that I can't keep going the way I was.'

'Good.'

'However,' Mari held up a finger. 'I also know that I need to take a step back. I'd got to the point where I was so afraid of failing that I was trying to do everything. Bryn felt pushed out and it's no wonder. And... I couldn't see how he was feeling because I was so wrapped up in my own problems.'

'And you're going to cut down your work hours?'

'Most definitely. A supply teacher is going to cover me for two days a week until the summer term and after that, I'm going to have a job share with a colleague who's returning from maternity leave. I think it will give me a much better work-life balance.'

'Good for you.'

'Something had to give and for now, it's my career.'

'You won't lose your career though, will you? If you're still working, I mean.'

Mari sighed as they reached the sand and stopped walking. She put her hands on her hips and gazed out at the sea.

'Not lose my career altogether, exactly, but I'll lose momentum for a while. As women, we often try to have it all these days but it's not always possible. I was trying to stay on top of work and home and to be flawless at everything, but I simply couldn't do it. Some women do and I take my hat off to them. The guilt for me, though, was horrendous. I felt guilty if I wasn't with the children, if I was marking or doing paperwork on a Sunday afternoon when I could've been playing with them. But if one of them was ill and I took a parental leave day off to be with them, I felt guilty for not being at work. I don't think there's a perfect solution to it at all. Having a partner who pulls their weight is certainly one step in the right direction but being a mum comes with an abundance of love but also a lot of guilt and worry. It doesn't matter how many times people told me that I was only one person and that I could only do so much… I'd still lie in bed at night beating myself up over what I hadn't achieved.'

'How are you hoping to combat that?' It sounded over-whelming to Ffion and she couldn't imagine how Mari would overcome the issue.

Mari shrugged. 'Sadly, there is no magic cure and all I can do is try. Bryn and I are going to create a timetable of chores so everything is written down and there's no shirking duties. Of course, if one of us is tired and the other wants to help out, then we'll compromise but we are aiming to stick to it as closely as we can. I'll allocate certain times to my school work and outside of those times, there will be no school work done. We've also factored in space for ourselves so that we both have some time out. For me, at the moment, that's for running and for spending with you.' She grinned at Ffion. 'Because I'm not about to start neglecting my sister again either.'

Ffion flung her arms open and hugged Mari tight.

'I am also going to write a list of three things I've achieved each day before going to sleep. That way, I'm being more positive in my outlook. It's easier to be mean to yourself than it is to be kind and I need to start framing things more positively otherwise I'm going to turn around in twenty years and see that I've been my own worst enemy.'

Ffion released Mari and stepped back to look at her. 'That sounds like a very good plan.'

'I think so. Perhaps you could try it, too?'

'Me?'

Mari held her gaze. 'You're not always kind to yourself, Ffion. I see it all the time, how you worry about what you should be doing, thinking and feeling. There is no correct way to do this. You just need to accept that what you're feeling is fine. You don't have to run away from life forever, you know?'

'What do you mean by that?' Ffion frowned.

'Graeme is gone and we can't change that but you're here, right now your heart is beating, and you deserve to live.'

Ffion cleared her throat and scuffed the toe of her trainer against the ground.

'I'm trying, Mari. I really am.'

'I know, sweetheart.'

'Are we going to do this, then?' Ffion looked at the beach ahead of them, at the golden expanse of sand and the freedom that awaited. She handed Mari one of her AirPods and set the app on her phone, then tucked it back in her bum bag.

'I'm ready if you are,' Mari replied.

'Then let's go!'

They jogged off along the beach, music and the recorded voice of the coach in their heads, love and laughter in their hearts.

—

'Are you ready yet, Ffion?'

'I'll be down in a minute, Mam!'

Ffion rolled her eyes at her reflection. It felt like being sixteen again, when she'd take ages to get ready for a night out and her parents would end up exasperated at having to wait for her, whether that was because she was going somewhere with them or because one of them was giving her a lift somewhere.

Tonight, she had dressed in a black crinkle tunic and white jeans with a pair of black wedges. She'd curled her hair and even put some make-up on. She was pushing the boat out and why? It was her birthday.

She had hoped it would pass without any fuss – she had even suspected until yesterday that her parents might have forgotten, but then she'd woken to them entering her room with helium balloons and breakfast on a tray.

After her mam and dad had sung 'Happy Birthday' they'd had a Zoom call with Mari, Bryn and the girls and then Ffion had been encouraged to shower and dress ready for a morning walk on the beach with her parents.

It had been lovely, followed by a light lunch at the hotel and an afternoon snooze. Ffion hadn't celebrated her birthday for the past two years, not feeling there was much to feel happy about, and she hadn't planned to celebrate it this year. Her parents, however, had other ideas, and this evening they were off to the hotel again for a bar meal. Ffion was grateful to them for marking the occasion and it seemed like something else she was ticking off the list of things a normal person would do.

Her thoughts turned to the package that was buried in one of the plastic boxes she'd brought from Scotland. It had been the last gift Graeme had given her; he'd bought it and wrapped it when he was ill in case he wasn't there for her next birthday. Last year, she'd been unable to open it. Instead, she had slept with it on his pillow next to her. The thought of opening it had been too painful, too awful, because once she opened it, there would never be another gift from him.

Could she open it now?

Should she?

She shivered with indecision. If she got upset then her parents would be sad too and think they hadn't done enough to make her day special. The last thing she wanted was to upset them, and even though she felt so much stronger than when she'd returned from Scotland, she still didn't feel robust enough to face opening that gift right now. Maybe the day would come, and she sensed that it might be close but she knew deep down that today was not the right day.

Ffion sprayed some perfume on – a lovely bottle that her parents had bought her and that she suspected had been quite expensive – and smiled at her reflection. She had so much to be grateful for. Today was more about being thankful than dwelling on what she'd lost and longing for the one person she could never be with again. She gave her reflection a thumbs-up then pushed her shoulders back and opened her bedroom door, ready to throw herself into the party mood.

Downstairs, her parents were waiting in the hallway, looking a bit shifty.

'What's up with you two?' she asked.

'Nothing.' Her mam smiled and her dad cleared his throat. 'We're just laughing about you taking forever to get ready.'

'Just like when you were a teenager.' Her dad chuckled.

'Sorry,' she said, not feeling sorry at all – just like when she was a teenager.

'It was worth it,' her dad said as he hugged her and kissed her forehead. 'You look, and smell, wonderful.'

'Thanks, Dad. That perfume you got me is lovely.'

'We thought you'd like it,' her mam said. 'It's very you.'

'Shall we go, then?' Aled asked, looking at his watch. 'Don't want to be late, do we?'

Ffion slid her arms into the sleeves of the black cardigan she'd brought down with her and they set off on the short walk to the hotel, but when they got to the side of the building, her dad held up a hand.

'Wait here a moment.'

'Why, Dad?'

'Just wait here with your mam.'

Ffion looked at her mam. 'Is something going on?'

'No idea.'

'Mam?'

Her mam feigned interest in the roses growing in the large stone pots. 'I'm not going to say a word, Ffion.'

Ffion folded her arms across her chest, experiencing a mixture of excitement and nerves.

When her dad reappeared, he was holding something.

'Right, Ffion, I'd like you to put this on.'

'What is it?'

'A blindfold.'

'What? But why?'

'Only for a few minutes.'

'Dad… I don't need a blindfold on.'

'Please, Ffion. Humour us.' Her mam tilted her head to one side and looked at her imploringly.

'All right but don't tie it tight because for once, I've put mascara on, and it'll smudge.'

'No problem.' Her dad tied the blindfold and Ffion felt him take one of her hands, her mam the other.

Ffion's belly fizzed with anticipation. She wasn't used to being looked after like this any more; it made her happy but also a bit nervous about losing control over her emotions. Graeme had always been surprising her with nights out, small gifts like books she'd wanted to read and chocolates she wanted to try, and she had missed being spoiled like that. Had missed seeing his face when he knew that he'd done something to please her because he loved making her smile; he delighted in it, in fact.

'Not far now, Ffion,' her dad said, interrupting her thoughts.

'OK.'

'Just up a few steps,' her mam said, holding her hand tight.

Up steps?

A short walk from the hotel?

The scent of roses and honeysuckle in the air and the sound of the waves breaking on the shore?

The marquee…

'Right then. I'm going to remove the blindfold.' Her dad released her hand and she felt the blindfold loosen, then drop from her eyes. She blinked for a moment, wincing slightly in the twilight, the golds and reds of the horizon making it look like it was on fire.

'Happy Birthday, Ffion,' her mam said as they led her towards the opening of the marquee. The interior was dark after the brightness outside, very quiet and still, and yet Ffion could sense other people there. When the lights came on around them, hundreds of fairy lights twinkling above and in vases on the tables, Ffion gasped.

There were about fifty people in front of her and they all shouted, 'Happy birthday!'

Ffion looked from face to face, recognising old school friends she hadn't seen in years but knew from their photos on social media; lots of the hotel staff and her family. Mari, Bryn and the girls were there and Joe was with them, smiling at her, Odin at his side.

'I don't know what to say.' Ffion's throat was tight and she worried she might cry.

'We just wanted you to have a good time.' Her dad wrapped an arm around her shoulders. 'You deserve to enjoy yourself, love.'

'Is it OK?' her mam asked. 'We did worry it might be too much but we also wanted you to see how many people love and care for you.'

Ffion croaked, 'Thank you. It's wonderful.'

'Now let's get some champagne open and enjoy this party.' Her dad went to get some drinks and Ffion and her mam went over to Mari.

After they'd hugged and Ffion had crouched down to cuddle the girls, she stood up and said hello to Joe and Odin. The dog wagged his tail and sniffed at Ffion's hand and Joe gave her a hug and a kiss on the cheek. She felt drunk although she hadn't yet tasted a drop of alcohol and she was overwhelmed by emotion because her parents had organised the party for her.

Drink in hand, Ffion made the rounds of the marquee, catching up with friends she hadn't seen in years, meeting their partners and hearing about their lives. Some of them asked how she was faring, and some avoided the subject, not knowing what to say or how to broach it, but either way Ffion didn't mind. She understood that it was difficult and as for answering when people asked how she was, she kept her replies brief and positive. What else could she say? How could she convey what it felt like to lose the love of her life, her best friend and the man she'd thought to have a family with? But seeing old friends was lovely and she enjoyed finding out what they'd been doing, listening with interest to the titbits of gossip about former teachers and lecturers, about job vacancies they knew of and thought she might be interested in. After a few hours, her phone was full of numbers, her mind buzzing from all the promises to get together soon. If she took them all up on their offers she'd certainly have a busy few months ahead of her.

She'd ducked outside and was taking a breather at the side of the marquee overlooking the beach when she heard someone come out after her.

'Hello, Joe.' She smiled at him and at Odin who went sniffing around the grass.

'Hi there, birthday girl.' He came to stand next to her. 'Having a good time?'

'Wonderful.'

'Were you surprised?'

'Very. I had no idea my parents had planned this.'

'They mentioned it two weeks ago to Mari and she let me know. They weren't sure it was the right thing to do but wanted to celebrate you being home. They really love you, you know.'

'I'm so lucky to have them.'

'How's the running been this week?'

'Mari and I competed the programme,' Ffion said, a thrill running through her. 'It was such a wonderful feeling.'

'So you can run for thirty minutes now?'

'I can. To think that I could barely run for one minute nine weeks ago is crazy.'

'Well, we've got three weeks until the sponsored run.'

'I can't wait.' Surprisingly, Ffion really was looking forward to the run, even with the pressure of knowing that she'd be running with people other than Mari and Joe for the first time.

'I've raised around two thousand pounds in sponsorship so far.'

'Wow! How did you do that?'

'I have an online form and I've got one in the staffroom at work, plus my aunt is a retired nurse, so she knows a lot of people in the community.'

'That's brilliant, Joe. Well done.' She glanced over at the hotel. 'My form is in the hotel reception and there's one in the bar but I'm not sure how much is on it yet.

Mari has one too though and she's got a few hundred pounds coming from colleagues and parents of pupils at her school.'

'Every penny will help the animals at the sanctuary.'

They gazed at each other, caught up in their thoughts about how the animals would benefit.

'We could even make it an annual thing,' Joe said, looking into his glass then peering up at her shyly. 'If that's not too presumptuous of me. I mean… I know you might not be here this time next year… you could find a job somewhere else or decide to go travelling or… well… anything, really. The world is your oyster now, right?'

Ffion winced. Her oyster? Without Graeme the world seemed big and intimidating, empty and dull.

Or did it?

Their eyes met. A spark shot between them. There was warmth, friendship and understanding between them.

Was there really nothing in the world to look forward to now?

Of course not; look at this evening, at all these people who'd come here to celebrate with her. Joe included. Yes, she missed Graeme but Joe was right; there were things to enjoy and to look forward to.

'Thank you, Joe.'

'What for?'

'For being so kind, patient and supportive.'

He shook his head. 'I don't need to be thanked. I like you, Ffion, and you're a friend now. I…' He licked his lips. 'I…'

'What is it?' She stepped closer to him.

'Nothing.' He looked down at his feet and blushed. 'I'm just glad you're having a good evening.'

'Joe?'

'Yes?'

'Would you like to go back inside and dance?'

'I'd like that very much.'

She hooked her arm though his and they went back into the marquee, Odin trotting after them. Ffion was determined to make the most of the party and to show her parents that she appreciated the effort they'd made for her. She really was lucky to have them, Mari, her nieces and Joe. Every day was a gift when there were precious people in it.

Chapter Twenty-Six

On the Monday before the sponsored run, Ffion paced up and down in the library of the hotel. Joe had phoned her that morning to say that a local newspaper wanted to interview him about the run and its purpose and he'd asked if she'd be with him during the interview. Ffion had hesitated, unsure if she could do it after spending so long away from the world of media and PR, but then her training had kicked in and she'd realised that she was perfectly capable of answering interview questions. Besides which, Joe had admitted that he was a bit nervous about the interview and so she'd decided that she needed to be there to support him too. When she'd told her mam and dad they'd said she could use the library of the hotel for the interview as it was a nice bright room to have photographs taken and there was a lovely view of the beach from the large sash window.

It was just gone four p.m. and Joe was meant to have been there by now but he hadn't arrived and Ffion didn't want to do the interview alone. It was his idea initially and she wanted to support, not lead.

'Ffion?' Her mam's head appeared around the door. 'The journalist and photographer have arrived. Shall I show them in?'

'No sign of Joe?'

'Not yet, love.' Her mam checked her watch. 'But I'm sure he'll be here soon.'

'OK. Show them in and perhaps we can offer them some refreshments and then Joe will get here before the interview starts.'

'No problem.' Her mam left the room.

The door opened again, and a woman entered. She was about Ffion's age, she thought, and looked smart in a dark blazer and navy chinos, her cropped blonde hair accentuating sharp cheekbones and large brown eyes. She was followed by another woman with chestnut-brown hair in a high ponytail, dressed all in black, complete with Doc Martens. The second woman looked tired, as if she hadn't slept well in months, and Ffion wondered briefly if it was work-related pressure.

'Hello!' Ffion held out her hand and shook theirs. 'I'm Ffion Campbell, Joe's friend. It's nice to meet you both.'

The blonde woman gave Ffion a quick once-over as if assessing her, then shot her a bright professional smile, 'I'm Pru Wade, senior reporter at the local rag and this is Liberty Wiltshire, one of our photographers.'

'Yo!' Liberty raised a hand.

Ffion raised her hand in response, thinking now that she could see Liberty up close that she looked like she was in her late thirties, or possibly early forties.

'Is, uh, Joe not here?' Pru asked.

'Not yet. He's on his way. Please take a seat.' Ffion gestured at the four bucket chairs in front of the fireplace. 'Can I get you a drink?'

'Water, please,' Pru replied as she sat down and opened her bag, pulling out a notepad, pen and a large smart-phone. Seeing Ffion look at them, she opened the notepad. 'I know I could use a laptop or tablet but I still prefer to record the interview on my phone and to make notes by hand.'

'Oh…' Ffion was surprised. 'I thought all journalists would use fancy technology these days. At least, that's what I'm used to.'

'I find that aside from the recording, electronics can form a barrier between me and the person being interviewed.'

'That's interesting,' Ffion replied. 'So water for you and Liberty?'

'Nothing for me, thanks.' Liberty was browsing the bookshelves. 'There are some cracking editions of classics on these shelves.'

'My dad collected them over the years.'

'Is he a big reader?'

'Not really but he does like to collect books. I think in part it was to encourage my sister and me to read, and it worked because we both love reading.' Ffion flashed them a smile. 'Back in a moment.'

She left them in the library, and closed the door behind her then leant against it. She wasn't sure why she felt so nervous, as both women had seemed nice enough. Perhaps it was because it had been a while since she'd done anything like this and she needed to get used to it again.

'Ffion.' Joe entered the hotel, shrugging out of his coat. 'Sorry I'm late. We had an emergency staff meeting at the end of the day.'

'Everything all right?' Her relief at seeing him was dampened by her concern at the word 'emergency'.

'Fine. There's talk of school closures in the borough again because there are plans to build a large new learning community campus in Swansea. We've been told that our school is probably not at risk but that if it does become one of the schools they decide to close, all staff will have the option of redundancy or redeployment.'

'Goodness!' Ffion's hand flew to her chest. 'How frightening.'

'It's OK. We've been here before and it comes to nothing but sometimes the LEA likes to remind us how lucky we are to have jobs.' He winked to show he was teasing. 'What will be will be and I'm not about to worry about things I can't control.'

'That's very wise.' Ffion exhaled slowly, trying to push away the tension that had grown with Joe's delayed arrival and then at what he'd just told her.

'Are they here yet?'

'Yes. In the library.'

He tucked his coat over his arm and came to her side. 'Are you all right? You look a bit pale.'

'I'm fine. I was just worried you might not get here.'

'One thing I can assure you of right now, Ffion, is that I am a man of my word. I promise I will never let you down.' He held her gaze and she knew that he meant what he said.

'Somehow I know that, Joe.'

'There you are, Joe!' Ffion's mam bustled towards them, carrying a tray with a jug of water, glasses and a bottle of lime cordial. 'Everything all right?'

Ffion loved how quickly her parents had taken to Joe. They hadn't said anything about him and his friendship with her but she sensed that they were wondering if there was anything between their daughter and the handsome teacher. He'd made such an effort with them and with Mari and her children that Ffion knew her parents already regarded him very highly. Just like she did.

'Let me take that, Gwen.' Joe took the tray from Ffion's mam.

'Thank you, lovely. Right, good luck, you two. Let me know if you need anything else.'

Ffion opened the door and stood back for Joe to enter with the tray. As he passed her, she gently removed his jacket from his arm so he didn't drop it, and he briefly met her gaze, the look in his blue eyes making her legs weaken.

In the library, Liberty was still looking at the books. Pru stood up as they entered the room, her smile broadening when her gaze fell on Joe. He set the tray down on the coffee table between the chairs then held out a hand.

'Joe Thomas.'

'Great to meet you, Joe.' Pru shook his hand effusively, Ffion noticed, seeming far more enthusiastic about meeting him than she had about Ffion. Liberty then shook his hand, barely glancing at his face, before taking a seat and removing her camera from around her neck.

'Great to meet you, too. Both of you.' Joe sat back and rested the foot of one leg on the knee of the other, placing his large hands on the arms of the chair. Ffion thought that he looked completely relaxed as she settled into the chair next to him.

'I'm going to record the interview on my phone but I'll also make some notes. If we could start with your details – names, ages, jobs – then we'll move on to talk about the sponsored run.' Pru placed her phone on the coffee table then raised her pen in anticipation. 'While we talk, Liberty will take some photos in here and afterwards, we can get some more posed ones next to the bookshelves perhaps and down on the beach.'

Joe and Ffion gave her their details then Joe told her about the idea for the sponsored run and how he'd come up with it. Pru's eyes flickered between Joe's face and her notepad. Pru's gaze was intense and Ffion felt a flicker of unease whenever it fixed on Joe as she wondered how interested in him Pru was, and whether her interest was professional or romantic. It could just be in a professional capacity but then it could be more. Ffion tried to imagine how Pru saw him, how she would see him if for the first time. When Ffion had first met Joe, they'd both been bundled up against the cold and Ffion had just been knocked flying by Odin, plus she had been lost in her grief. Pru, however, was cool and professional, attractive and probably driven – the fact that she was senior reporter made that evident. She was looking at Joe for the first time and he was so lovely, so at ease with himself and everyone in the room. As he spoke, his eyes lit up and he leant forwards, gesticulating as he told Pru about the animal sanctuary and what it meant to him, to the animals themselves and to the community. His enthusiasm was infectious and Pru visibly relaxed, leaning forwards too. Joe was handsome but also engaging, a kind, warm-hearted professional who cared about the place where he lived and about making the lives of rescue animals better.

Ffion hugged herself inwardly as it dawned on her that her feelings for him were intensifying. She saw only good things in Joe, and cherished who he was and his outlook on life. She was physically attracted to him but it went deeper than that and while she could appreciate that he was a handsome man, she knew that his heart was the most beautiful thing about him.

'Ffion?' Pru was staring at Ffion and she realised Pru had just asked her a question.

'Uh…'

'Joe told me you've been on board with the idea to do a sponsored run from its conception, then I asked how you started running. Have you always been a runner or is it a more recent thing?'

Pru held her pen poised above her notebook and Ffion blinked.

'I… uh… I've been running for almost three months now. I started the Couch to 5k programme with my sister.'

'And what inspired you to do that?' Pru didn't seem to blink.

Ffion thought of Graeme, of all the pain and the emptiness in her chest, of her loneliness in Scotland and the extreme sense of isolation she'd felt. How could she tell this stranger all of that? Where did she even begin?

Loud ringing started in Ffion's ears and her mind went blank.

The moment seemed to stretch out and sweat prickled in Ffion's armpits. She opened her mouth but words would not come. She felt herself drifting out of her body, her head woozy, her heart pounding so hard she thought it might burst from her chest.

'Ffion has been amazing!' Joe's voice brought her back to the room. He reached for the water and filled a glass, then placed it in Ffion's hands. 'She wasn't unfit before as she's always been a walker but she'd never run until she came back here from Scotland. Isn't that right, Ffi?'

Ffion sipped the water he'd given her and inclined her head. 'That's right, yes. Mari, my sister, and I were talking one day and we both decided it was time to… try to get fitter. It's a funny story actually…' She glanced at Joe, hoping he'd take over because she felt exhausted.

'It is!' Joe picked up her cue. 'I came across Ffion and Mari on the beach after they'd tried to start running without building up to it. To put it lightly, they were suffering so I suggested the Couch to 5k as a way to build up gradually. The rest, as they say, is history. They completed the programme recently and are both now devoted runners.'

'That's right. Running has become part of my life now,' Ffion agreed. 'I run with Joe and I run with Mari. I can't imagine not running.'

'Was there a reason why you came back from Scotland?' Pru asked.

'I… needed my family.' Ffion pressed her lips together to indicate that she didn't want to say any more about her reasons for returning.

'Don't we all at some time in our lives.' Liberty was grinning as she knelt down and pointed her camera at Ffion and Joe. 'I'd be lost without mine. I went to uni in Exeter but I've come back to Wales. Missed my mam too much to stay away.'

'Me too.' Ffion smiled gratefully at Liberty.

'So what's next? After the sponsored run, I mean?' Pru asked.

'As far as the running goes…' Joe shifted position on the chair and reached over and took Ffion's hand. Pru's eyes widened slightly as she watched him and Ffion's heart swelled. 'We've been thinking about starting up a community running club.'

Ffion looked at him and he squeezed her hand.

'We enjoy running so much that we want to share our love of it with the locals.'

'Kind of like a local fitness drive.' Pru pursed her lips as she scribbled on her pad. 'This is gold for the paper. Everyone's so into wellness these days that I'm certain your run will become popular very quickly.'

'We've had a lot of help with organising the event from people within the community... in fact, the response has been overwhelming. For example, locals have helped with spreading the word about the sponsored run, some have signed up for it themselves and volunteered to run stalls at points along the coastal path and the beach so that there are refreshments and support available. Some of businesses around Cariad Cove and in Swansea have offered to sponsor the event and there's also talk of holding a summer festival this year to maintain momentum in terms of fundraising and celebrating what the area has to offer. There will be a sponsored run as part of that as well, so there will be more opportunities to raise funds for the sanctuary. Therefore, I have to agree with you, Pru. I believe that we could set up a Cariad Cove community running club and that it would go down well with locals.' Joe was glowing with enthusiasm.

'That sounds fabulous.' Pru tapped her pen on the notepad thoughtfully then wrote something on the paper.

'If you charged people a joining fee, you could donate that to the sanctuary too.' Liberty lowered her camera. 'I'd join. I'm a lapsed runner but I do love running and I miss it. The thing is that I don't like going out alone, though. For one, I worry about the risks as a lone woman; two, I feel self-conscious; and three, it's nice to have some encouragement.'

'Exactly!' Ffion slapped her hand on the arm of the chair. 'That is exactly how I've felt. Joe and Mari have helped me keep going. And running is such great therapy. Whatever you've been through… and I've been through some tough times… running can help you to get through them. Building a strong body can help build a strong mind.'

'What a quote!' Pru grinned. 'Loving this interview, guys. Ffion… I don't suppose you'd like to share what you've been through, would you? Human interest angle and all that?'

Ffion glanced at Joe and he rubbed his thumb over her knuckles. This wasn't his decision to make.

'Not at the moment. Perhaps in the future but for now I don't want it to overshadow the sponsored run and why we're doing it. Maybe one day I'll be ready to tell my story but not just yet… I'm still coming to terms with things and I don't want to cloud that by seeing it in print.'

'I completely respect that, Ffion.' Pru's eyes were warmer now. 'I'm not some hard journo who'll use your pain to sell papers. And I can see now that you've been through a difficult time. However… if you decide to tell your story – perhaps at the next sponsored run – will you share it with me first?'

'Most definitely,' Ffion promised. 'And one day, I think I will be ready.'

'Well, thank you both for being fabulous. I'll pack up and head off but Liberty here will take some more photos. Good luck to you both. And… off the record because I'm not sure how deep your friendship goes… I have to say that you make, or would make, a lovely couple.'

Ffion opened her mouth to reply but Joe was laughing and she found herself joining in. What had started as a tense experience for Ffion had turned into a pleasant one and that had been mainly because Joe had been at her side, supporting her, encouraging her and helping her to believe in herself, just as he had done with running.

With Joe at her side, Ffion felt capable of doing just about anything.

Chapter Twenty-Seven

The day of the sponsored run had arrived. Ffion was up bright and early to eat a good breakfast and to psychologically prepare. She knew she could manage the distance, as she had done it in training, but the pressure was on because she needed to complete the run in order to be paid by the people who'd sponsored her.

She'd continued to train over the previous three weeks since her birthday, running with Joe and with Mari, and sometimes alone. It had seemed that there were more people out running too, or perhaps she just noticed it more now, kind of like when you bought a car, you'd see more of that model around. She wondered if any of them would join the running club Joe wanted to set up and hoped it would be a success because it would be a great thing for the community. In the four days since the newspaper interview, lots of people from Cariad Cove had helped out with posting fliers advertising the event, handing out fliers in Swansea city centre, walking the coastal path to check for potential hazards that might have sprung up recently, and placing temporary signs and distance markers around the course to mark the route for the runners. Several local businesses had agreed to provide refreshments, as well as to sponsor future events.

Over the past few weeks, Ffion had also been to the sanctuary a few more times with Joe, helping out with cleaning kennels and stables, exercising the dogs and feeding the donkeys. Spending time with the animals was grounding. They lived in the moment, not worrying about yesterday or tomorrow, simply existing in the present. Ffion found time in their company comforting. Racing around the paddock with the dogs, witnessing their joy as they chased after a ball or Frisbee; brushing the donkeys and feeding them treats, feeling their soft muzzles tickling her palm; making the stables and kennels clean and fresh: all were simple activities with a purpose that made her feel useful, as if she was making a difference to the animals' lives. Sometimes she went into the cattery and sat with the cats, sweet Beatrix in particular, smoothing the cat from her head to her tail and listening to her calming purring. Why no one had applied to adopt her yet she couldn't understand, but Ffion was always glad to see her and it seemed that the feeling was mutual because the cat always rushed to greet Ffion and curled around her legs. Ffion wanted to know that Beatrix had a home to go to but she also knew she'd miss her when she was adopted.

And something else had happened; Ffion had run out of the antidepressants she'd brought with her from Scotland and decided not to renew her prescription. The dosage had been small anyway and her doctor had confirmed on the phone that it would be fine to stop taking them. She no longer felt that she needed the medication to cope; she had her family, running and she also had Joe.

When she'd dressed in her running gear, Ffion headed down to the kitchen where her parents were having coffee. They'd helped out with arrangements for the day and were putting on refreshments at a main stand on the beach just in front of the hotel. Ffion was so proud of them for getting involved and for being so generous with their donation.

'You ready?' her mam asked as she handed Ffion a coffee.

'I'm ready.' Ffion smiled but her whole body felt twitchy. 'I'm a bit nervous, though.'

Her mam stroked her cheek, her brown eyes filled with love.

'You'll smash this, Ffion. You and Mari have worked hard to prepare and your dad and I are very proud of you both.'

'Thanks, Mam.'

'You know, your mam has even talked about us giving it a go.' Her dad chuckled.

'Really?'

Her mam blushed. 'Well… briefly… and after a glass of wine, Aled, when I was waxing lyrical about my youth. I mean… I'm not sure I'd last thirty seconds.'

'Nonsense, Gwenny girl, you have incredible stamina.'

Ffion cringed as her dad winked knowingly at her mam and gave a throaty chuckle. There were certain things she'd rather not think about.

'Oh Mam, honestly,' she said, keen to move the conversation on from her parents' bedroom antics, 'the Couch to 5k programme is amazing. I was the least fit person in the world until I started doing it and now I can run for thirty minutes. It's an intense nine weeks but I feel better for it.'

Her mam's eyes glistened. 'You look so much better too, Ffion. When you came home, we were so worried about you. I said to your dad that you looked so thin and exhausted, like you didn't have an ounce of energy left in your whole body.' A tear trickled down Gwen's cheek and she wiped it away. 'We didn't know how to help you, sweetheart.' Her voice broke.

'Mam! It's OK.' Ffion closed the space between them and hugged her mam tight. Her dad joined them, arms around them both, and the three of them stood that way until Gwen stopped crying.

'I'm so sorry.' Gwen sniffed. 'I've been trying very hard to hold it together because the last thing you need is me sobbing.'

Ffion leant back to meet her mam's eyes. 'It's understandable that you'd feel sad and worried. I know it's because you love me. I've come a long way since I came home to Cariad Cove. I felt broken, like I'd never enjoy anything ever again. I was taking medication and struggling to sleep and feeling tired all the time. After I left Scotland behind, I didn't think Wales would be any better but I was wrong. Being surrounded by my family and friends, being near the sea and running have all helped me enormously. I feel… like me again.'

'Ffion love, we're so glad.' Her dad's voice was husky with emotion and she gazed up him, realising that he'd been holding it together for her sake, too. Her dad always seemed so strong and reliable and she often forgot that he had a soft underbelly when it came to his family.

'Mam, Dad… I'm not over Graeme… and I don't think that's the right choice of words anyway, but I feel more equipped to deal with things now. He was my world and I'll always love him but he's gone and I have no control over that. What I do have though, is you, Mari and the girls, running and the sanctuary and… a good friend in Joe. I'm stronger, possibly, than I've ever been because I've been to rock bottom and risen again. I still have a way to go, I know that, but I'll get there.'

She smiled at them, hoping that she was alleviating some of their concern, smoothing away some of their grief, because she could see that like Graeme's parents, in a way her mam and dad had lost a child too. Ffion had been floundering as she tried to navigate her way through her grief, and only time and small steps taken one at a time were ever going to help with that. She wanted to embrace life again, for her parents' sakes, for her sister and her nieces, for herself and, of course, for Graeme.

'Anyway… we'd better get down to the beach and ensure that everything's ready for today.' Ffion stood up straight, pushed her shoulders back and took a slow deep breath, readying herself for the challenge ahead.

'Mari's meeting us down there,' Gwen said. 'Bryn's bringing the girls and he's going to wait on the beach with them.'

'That will be nice for Mari.' Ffion thought of her sister and how important having Bryn's support was to her. 'Come on then, Mam and Dad. Some of us have running to do.'

—

Joe walked down to the beach, holding Odin's lead. He waved when he spotted Caryn and Darryl who'd come to support him and to look after Odin while Joe ran. He could've taken Odin but because it would be busy, he didn't want the dog getting in people's way or getting lost in the crowd. Odin would no doubt enjoy himself, but for today, it was best that he stayed on the beach.

The last Saturday in May had brought glorious sunshine to Cariad Cove. It was mild but breezy and thankfully dry, because while running in the rain was actually quite enjoyable, it wouldn't have been nice for the supporters who'd come to cheer the runners on.

'Hello, Joe.' Caryn hugged him when he reached them, then crouched down and did the same to Odin. The dog's tail swept in wide arcs of joy.

Joe smiled. 'Thanks again for coming.'

'Of course we'd come. We're here to cheer for you.' Caryn gazed at him, her blue eyes sharp behind her glasses. 'You're like a son to us, Joe. In all honesty, love, you are the son of our hearts.'

'Don't get all soppy on me now.' Joe rolled his eyes teasingly then swept her into his arms and squeezed her. 'I love you, Aunty Caryn.'

She laughed. 'Less of the *Aunty*. I know you only call me that when you want something.'

Joe shot her a cheeky grin. 'You know me so well. But today, all I want is for you to look after Odin and to hang around for the post-run barbecue so I can introduce you to everyone that you'll be running with in the club.'

'We're looking forward to it.' Caryn's eyes widened as she realised what he'd said. 'But not that last bit! I'm still not convinced that I'm a good candidate for this running club malarkey.' She giggled.

'We shall see! Right, then.' Joe looked over at the tables near the concrete ramp that led down to the beach. There were three tables surrounded by a small gazebo to provide shade, and around the posts of the gazebo, colourful red and green bunting flapped in the breeze. The people sitting at the tables were taking names and handing out running numbers. It all looked very official and Joe felt excited to be a part of it. Ffion's parents had played a big part in organising the run, had funded the refreshments and admin, and their reach in the community, along with that of others keen to help, had meant that more people had got involved and volunteered to help out.

He did a quick scan of the people already wearing numbers. There were about fifty so far and at the last count, there had been seventy runners applying to take part. Some were sponsored and some were keen to participate in the event because they liked running and saw it as a competition. For him, it wouldn't be a race against anyone except himself. His sponsor form stated that he'd run 10k but didn't have a target time on it because he wanted to ensure that he raised money for the sanctuary no matter what. He knew that his time might be affected by a variety of elements, like if he had to stop to help anyone out, but as long as he completed the run, he could still raise essential funds.

'You get on, Joe, and we'll see you later.' Caryn patted his shoulder. 'Odin will be fine with us and, of course, we'll watch your things, too.'

'Thanks.' Joe handed his aunt his rucksack. 'See you later.'

Joe jogged over to the gazebo and waited to collect his number. Two familiar voices caught his attention and he looked up to see Ffion and Mari standing off at the side of the gazebo. Ffion was wearing bright blue running tights with a fitted vest top and she had a number pinned to the back and the front. She wore a matching headband along with a pair of sunglasses and her hair was scraped back into a high ponytail. She looked professional, fit and healthy, and happy as she chatted with her sister.

Once he'd been given his number, he went over to the sisters.

'Morning.'

'Hey, Joe.' Ffion smiled at him and his spirits lifted higher than they were already. 'Are you looking forward to this?'

'I am. You?'

'Definitely.' Ffion and Mari nodded together. 'We were just saying that we're a little bit anxious because there's a lot riding on this… you know, with it being sponsored… but we are looking forward to running.'

'You'll be fine,' he said. 'Both of you. You're more than capable of running this today.'

'The 10k is starting soon, isn't it?' Ffion asked.

'Yes. They'll start us off first, then when we're ahead, they'll start the 5k.'

'I wish I could run that far but not yet, I guess.'

'There will be next year and possibly the summer festival run too. We'll get plenty of practice in with the running club and get you running farther.' Joe held her gaze, wishing he could have a moment alone with her to reassure her with a hug.

'Maybe,' she said playfully.

'Hopefully,' Mari added. 'We need to keep pushing ourselves, Ffion. Imagine the sense of achievement at running 10k. I'll be super proud of myself if I can do that – and just think about the cake I can eat afterwards to reward myself!'

'5k is a huge achievement at the moment, thanks, Mari.' Ffion laughed and shook her head at Joe.

Joe fixed his number to the front of his T-shirt then tried to twist around and do the same with the number for his back but Ffion batted his hands away and did it for him. When she'd finished, she rested her hands on his shoulders for just a moment and his heart beat faster at her proximity.

'Catch you later?' he said, turning, his voice husky.

'You will.'

He headed to the starting line where others were already warming up. The run would take them up the ramp and around the front of the hotel to the road that led up to the cliffs and along the coastal path. Once they reached the 2.5k mark there, they'd turn right and cut through a field that took them to the village. They'd follow the road from the village down to the beach, run to the cliffs at the far end, then turn and run back to the Cariad Cove Hotel, thereby completing the 10k. Initially, the plan had been to run along the coastal path to a 5k marker then back the same way, but someone had pointed out that there would be congestion on the path and so permission to run through one of the fields had been granted by a local farmer. The shorter run would be along the beach to the cliffs that separated Barddoniaeth Bay from Cariad Cove and back. Depending on timing, those doing the 5 and 10k could end up running at the same time. Joe wished he would be running all the way with Ffion but hoped he'd have the chance to train her to run it another time.

If she stayed around. Which he really hoped she would because the thought of not seeing her regularly made his chest ache.

–

Ffion watched as Joe set off, his strong legs carrying him easily towards the hotel and up to the coastal path. She wished she was going with him but knew that it would be too far for her at this point and that she had to be content with running the 5k. However, it would give her something to strive for and who knew, this time next year she might be able to manage more.

The beach was busy, with runners and supporters bustling about as well as tourists who'd come to Cariad Cove for the day and had their interest piqued by the event. Ffion had seen her dad encouraging people to sign sponsorship forms as well as handing them his business card in the hopes of drumming up future custom. Not that the hotel needed it; from what Ffion had seen since she'd come back, there always seemed to be plenty of guests at the hotel and bookings at the restaurant. Her parents worked hard and had built up a successful business together and they continually strove to give back to the community, whether that meant funding repairs to the old village hall, raising money to equip the children's park on the village green or, as now, helping with the first ever Cariad Cove community run.

'Looks like it's time for us to get ready.' Mari nudged her.

Ffion's stomach fluttered. 'Oh my.'

'We can do this.'

'We absolutely can.'

They linked arms and made their way to the starting line and began to warm up, stretching their limbs and jogging on the spot. When they were lined up ready to go, Ffion felt like a coiled spring, her whole body tense, every fibre of her being prepared to launch.

And then they were off…

–

Joe accepted a paper cup of water from the elderly man running the refreshments stand on the coastal path.

He swilled it around his mouth, dropped the cup in a recycling bag then turned and made his way across the field. His body felt strong, his limbs warmed up and he knew he had plenty left to give. It helped that there were groups of people along the way cheering and waving Welsh flags, including Gwyneth, who'd come to support the fundraiser that would help the animals in her care.

His legs moved with an easy rhythm, carrying him along the field and then back through the village. Car windscreens glinted in the morning sunshine, the sky was a flawless blue and the breeze caressed his skin, cool and fresh with the promise of summer ahead.

As he ran, thoughts of the time he'd spent with Ffion over the past three and a half months – like their runs, their visits to the sanctuary, their time at the beach – made him feel like something had been happening without him being fully aware, like an underground mountain spring that was on the verge of bubbling to the surface.

He pushed himself to run faster, wanting to get back down to the beach and to see how Ffion was faring. Would she be running effortlessly or struggling? Some runs were wonderful but some were hard. That was part of being a runner; you never knew when you'd have the best run of the week or the hardest one for months. Simple things like a cramp, a stiff muscle from not warming up properly or not eating enough to fuel your body could impact upon how you felt. He hoped with all his heart that Ffion was doing well and that she was enjoying this, her first community run.

–

Ffion glanced at Mari.

'You OK?'

'Yuh!' Mari was puffing a bit. They'd only been running for around ten minutes, taking it nice and steady as they headed for the cliffs of Barddoniaeth Bay. Around them, other runners passed, heading in the same direction or running back to the finish line. The sand gleamed under their feet and tiny droplets of water flicked up, landing on Ffion's blue trousers and blotting the material like ink. The breeze had died down and she felt warm, glad she'd gone with a vest top and worn the headband. As for the sunglasses, they were a lifesaver because the glare from the sun on the water would be eye-watering now.

'You've got this, Mari.'

'I know.' Mari panted. 'Not sure why… but I'm struggling… today.'

'Well, keep going… because you're strong enough… and fit enough… to make it.'

'Yes!' Mari gave a brief nod and they kept moving.

When they reached the table that marked the turning point, they accepted small cups of water that they downed then dropped into a recycling bag, before turning back the way they'd come. The hotel seemed such a long distance from the cliffs and Ffion suppressed a sigh. She'd walked this hundreds of times over the years and had run it over recent weeks, and she'd always made it. She could make it again.

Then she saw him. Striding towards them.

'Joe!' she gasped as he did a quick turn and fell into stride with them.

'Ladies.' He flashed her a grin. 'Everything OK?'

'I'm struggling,' Mari said as she hung her head, clearly trying to keep going.

'You've got this, Mari,' he said. 'Slow down a bit and lift your head, relax your shoulders and breathe in slowly. You're not filling your lungs properly because you're panicking.'

Mari did as Joe told her and Ffion saw the difference it made.

'You only need to get back to the ramp and you can do this. I'm with you and Ffion's with you.' Joe's voice was low and reassuring, his confidence in their ability inspiring. Ffion took one of Mari's hands and Joe took the other and they kept going, digging deep and pushing themselves as hard as they could.

Ffion laughed out loud as the rush came, driving itself up from her feet like a hot spring, rising through her legs and tingling through her body. This was it. This was what it was all about. This felt so good!

'Why are you laughing?' Joe asked.

'Runners' high,' Ffion replied.

'Lucky… you!' Mari muttered. 'Still waiting… for mine.'

When the cheering started, goosebumps rose on Ffion's skin, and she looked towards the finish line where a large crowd had gathered.

'Look Mari, they're waiting for us.'

Every runner that finished received whoops and applause, the sounds drifting along the beach, filling the air with a jubilant community spirit that seemed to fill Mari with a burst of energy.

'I can bloody well… do this!' Mari shouted.

'Yes, you bloody well can!' Ffion replied, and they ran faster, linked to each other and to Joe like an unbreakable chain, and soon they were at the finish line. Bryn and the girls rushed at Mari, covering her in kisses and hugging her tight.

Ffion could barely see for tears as her mam and dad hugged. It was an incredible moment and a sense of achievement flooded through her as she realised that she had done it. She had run the 5k without stopping, without struggling, without hesitation. She was stronger than she had known she could be, more resilient than she had believed possible. Ffion was alive and she was a runner.

She was alive…

She turned, her eyes searching for him.

He was there. Waiting.

'Joe.'

His Adam's apple bobbed. 'You did it.'

She swallowed. '*We* did it.'

She stepped towards him, their eyes locked, everything around them fading away as they accepted that this moment was theirs; they had created something new, a memory to add to the ones they already shared.

Life was moving on and Ffion was going with it.

Chapter Twenty-Eight

The party at the beach went on all afternoon and well into the evening. Ffion's parents had their large commercial barbecue brought down to the beach along with coolers of beer and cider. The sponsored run had raised over six thousand pounds for the sanctuary – a substantial donation had come from a local celebrity who'd asked to remain anonymous – and Gwyneth Parry had come down to the beach to thank everyone for taking part.

As darkness fell, the beach was lit by the fires people had built in circles of stones and by the moonlight that fell across the sand and made the sea shimmer like melted platinum. Mari and Bryn had taken the girls home over an hour ago but Ffion's parents were still busy on the beach, offering people food and drink, their hospitality so inherent that they didn't want to see anyone go without.

Ffion sank onto a checked blanket in front of a sand dune and hugged her knees to her chest. Her legs were a bit achy and she was tired but it had been wonderful day. She felt a variety of emotions settling over her, but one dominated. She let it rest there for a moment, recognising it as a sense of contentment. Afraid of disturbing it, she sat quietly, gazing into the fire in front of her, allowing herself to just be in the moment.

'Are you cold?'

It was Joe, his long tanned legs shown off by his surf shorts. He sat next to her and she turned to him, taking in his oversized surf brand hoodie and dark beanie.

'If you are, it's probably because you're wearing shorts.'

He laughed. 'In spite of the fact that I'm usually prepared, in my excitement about the race, I forgot to bring joggers but I did remember my hat and hoodie so I'm fine. However, you look cold so I brought you this.'

He slid a fleece blanket around her shoulders and she snuggled into it, enjoying the softness against her skin.

'Thank you.'

'How're you feeling?' he asked.

'Good.'

'Aching?'

'A bit but nothing major.' She yawned. 'Although I am tired now.'

'You'll sleep tonight.'

She looked down at where his hand rested on his knee and entwined her fingers with his.

'Thank you, Joe.'

'What for?'

'For being you.'

The firelight played over his features, making his short hair shine like gold, his eyes appear lit from within.

'I just try to be a good person, Ffion. A good friend.'

When he looked up there was something in his gaze that hadn't been there before and it made her breath catch in her throat.

'Joe?' she whispered.

'Ffion.' His voice was gruff, his breath shaky as he exhaled. He moved closer, gently cupped her cheek and lowered his head.

When he kissed her, everything else disappeared; the sea lapping at the shore, the laughter and low murmur of the people chatting on the beach, the crackling of the logs in the fire.

The kiss seemed to go on and on, and something inside Ffion felt like it was thawing – giving way, giving in to need, warmth and desire.

When Joe gently broke away, Ffion was breathless.

'I'm sorry,' he said. 'I shouldn't have done that.'

'I'm glad you did.'

'Are you? I don't want to overstep the mark or put any pressure on you. I know what you've been through and… I…' He sighed long and low and rubbed at the back of his neck.

Ffion placed a hand on his arm. 'The last thing you do is put pressure on me, Joe. You're one of the kindest, sweetest men I've ever met.'

He slowly raised his eyes. 'What do you want, Ffion?'

'I don't want to spend tonight alone.'

He stood up and held out his hand. Ffion took it, knowing that if she went home with him, it would change everything, but she felt perfectly OK with that.

–

When Joe woke the next morning, he did so with a smile. Ffion had come back to his home and stayed the night. He hadn't expected it or even anticipated it, because as far as he'd been concerned, they were friends and that was all Ffion wanted right now. He'd asked her several times through the course of the night if she was sure that this was what she wanted and she'd reassured him, kissing his fears away.

He had been afraid because he liked Ffion, had feelings that ran far deeper, but knew what she'd been through. The last thing he wanted to do was to complicate things further for her. But she had told him she was sure, that she wanted to hold him and be held, and so they had kissed for hours then finally fallen into bed and made slow, sensual love.

Waking with her in his arms was the best feeling in the world and yet he was afraid to disturb her in case he broke the spell. Her skin was velvety smooth, her hair smelt of coconuts and spread out like a fan around her head. The contrast between the hard planes of his body and her soft curves had stirred him many times throughout the night, rousing him to caress and kiss her, and creating a yearning in him to be inside her again and again.

Those same feelings flooded back now and he tried to think of something else, to ignore the way her leg rested over his, how her hand felt on his chest and how her hair felt as she moved her head and it slid over his skin.

She was beautiful inside and out… she was everything.

–

Ffion blinked hard. The light coming through the bedroom curtains was bright and her eyes stung. She moved, then realised that she was naked in Joe's arms.

He was naked too and so handsome that he took her breath away. His broad shoulders looked tanned against the white pillow case, there was a shadow of stubble on his jaw and his eyes were such an intense blue that they made her think of summer skies and happy days.

'Morning, Fi.'

'Hi.' She sat up, holding the sheet against her chest, feeling suddenly self-conscious as she recalled their nocturnal activities, how brazen she had been as they'd rolled around in each other's arms, their limbs entwined, their bodies joined, moving together as one.

And the way he was gazing at her… Only one man had ever gazed at her that way before and a boulder of guilt settled in her stomach.

'You OK?' He sat up too, concern distorting his features. 'You look… sad.'

'I'm fine.'

Wasn't she?

'You don't regret… last night?'

She put out a hand. It met the warm skin of his chest with its dusting of golden hair. She pulled her hand back.

'No. Of course not. It was… wonderful.'

But I need to go!

'Do you want some tea? Coffee? Breakfast?'

'Uhhh…' She scanned the room, looking for her clothes. 'What time is it?'

What have you done?

He reached for his phone on the bedside table.

'Just after seven.'

'I'd better go.'

His face fell and Ffion's heart fractured. He was so lovely, so alive, so beautiful, so sweet. Last night he had made love to her tenderly and passionately; he had brought her body back to life after a long time of inertia and she had felt whole again. Her desire for him had broken down the final barriers of her grief and she had revelled in their union.

But what right did she have to feel that way when Graeme was cold, his body buried deep in the ground of a Scottish cemetery?

No right. No right. No right.

She hadn't been with another man since before university and from then on it had only been Graeme. Her body had been his and his alone. They had loved each other. Deeply. Found joy in each other and their physical and emotional bonds.

And now she had betrayed him.

'I'm sorry.' She slid out of bed and searched for her clothes, picked up a T-shirt and pulled it on, then a pair of shorts and some socks.

'Ffion...'

'I'll call you.'

She hurried out of the bedroom and down the stairs, almost falling over Odin who was lying in the shadowy hallway. She found her trainers and slid them on, rubbed Odin's head by way of apology then let herself out of the house before Joe could follow her.

And then... she ran.

—

Joe stood at the top of the stairs completely naked. Ffion had pulled the sheet from the bed as she'd got up to search for clothes then she'd grabbed Joe's T-shirt and shorts in her panic and run downstairs. Joe had looked for something to put on but been worried that she'd leave before he could speak to her, so he'd hurried after her but she was already letting herself out of the house when he reached the stairs.

Then she was gone.

And Joe was left alone; naked, hurt and confused. Vulnerable.

How could something so wonderful go so wrong?

Odin was sitting at the bottom of the stairs and he looked up at Joe, his ears pricked as he let out a low whine.

'I know, boy. I don't understand what happened either.'

Joe padded back to bed, pulled the sheet over himself and lay on his side, his hand resting on the imprint from Ffion's body. It was still warm. He could taste her on his lips, smell her on his skin. She really had been there.

He suspected that he knew what might be wrong. Ffion had let herself be happy after a long time of grieving for her husband and now she was feeling guilty. It was something he had worried about because she was a thoughtful and compassionate human being. She had clearly loved her husband and losing him had broken her, but Joe had watched as she'd pieced herself back together over the past few months, had watched her blossom as she found ways to live with herself again.

Ffion was the most beautiful woman he'd ever met and the most precious. He knew that he'd fallen in love with her; last night had sealed the deal for him, but he didn't know if she felt the same. If she could let herself feel the same.

He wanted to follow her, to take her in his arms and let her cry, rant and do whatever she needed to do to get past this, but he also knew that right now, the best thing he could do for her was to give her space.

Only Ffion could work out if this was right for her, if this was what she wanted and needed. Joe would be here waiting to see if she decided that being with him was right.

But the wait would be hard...

–

Ffion had gone home to her parents' cottage, stripped off the clothes she'd realised were actually Joe's and gone straight to bed. Her parents hadn't been there so she assumed that they were working and was glad that they wouldn't see her coming home like this after spending the night with Joe.

In her old bed, she pulled the covers up to her chin and closed her eyes but images from the previous night haunted her. Joe was a good man and he didn't deserve this. It wasn't his fault that Graeme had died. She had told him she wanted to be with him last night and then she'd run away. He must be feeling truly dreadful now and the thought that she'd caused him pain was awful.

Restless and antsy, she got out of bed and pulled on some pyjamas, then opened the curtains and let the brightness of the morning in. She threw open the window and the sea air filled the room, briny, cool and fresh.

What was she going to do?

She looked around the room and her eyes fell on the plastic boxes she'd brought with her. Perhaps it was time to go through them, to finally sort them out. She had to do something because lying there wasn't going to work and there was suddenly a burning need inside her to find a certain thing that she'd brought with her.

She dragged the boxes towards the bed, sat on the edge and opened the first one, pulling out some of her clothes and setting them aside before reaching Graeme's things.

She lifted out his grey and white checked shirt and pressed it to her face. He'd loved this shirt and worn it until the material had gone bobbly. After he'd decided to throw it out, Ffion had slipped it into the airing cupboard, wanting to keep it as it reminded her of many happy times. When she'd been packing to move out of their home, she'd found the shirt there, buried beneath piles of blankets and towels they'd received as wedding gifts and never got round to using, and it had been an emotional moment. She'd been unable to give the shirt away to charity or to recycle it, needing to keep it with her.

Their wedding photo album and the photo books they'd made over the years were also in the box. The majority of their pictures were on phones and iPads, but now and then they'd surprised each other with some of their photos in printed form. She spent a while flicking through them, letting the tears fall, but also smiling at their happy faces, at how much fun they'd had, how in love they'd been.

Finally, she put the photo albums on her bed and came to the gift Graeme had given her, telling her to open it on her next birthday or when she needed it most. It was wrapped in innocuous brown paper but for Ffion there was nothing innocuous about its contents. Graeme had been passionate about recycling and using brown paper had been one of his ways of helping the environment. The paper on this gift was wrinkled, having probably been used more than once, and the tape holding it together was also made of paper.

Once she opened this, there would be no going back. It was Graeme's last gift and there would be no more.

She ran a finger over the tape, trying to decide what to do.

But until she opened it, she'd never truly move on because she'd always know that there was something left to hold on to.

She thought of Joe, of their runs, the way he made her smile and the way she felt in his arms. How could something so good be wrong?

It wasn't wrong. And that was probably the hardest thing to admit.

She slipped her fingernail under the tape and peeled it back, then opened the paper, revealing a beautiful notebook. The cover was hardback, decorated with a woodland scene featuring trees, plants, animals and a sunset. As she moved it from side to side, the light caught the colours, making it seem to glow. It was beautiful, thoughtful and typically Graeme.

She opened the book and an envelope fell out. Her name was on the front in her husband's looped handwriting. It was time.

She opened the envelope, pulled out a letter, and started to read. Graeme's deep voice and thick Scottish accent enveloped her with every word.

> *My darling Ffion,*
>
> *If you're reading this then I am gone. That sounds really strange. Who can imagine the world without them in it, right? But the whole purpose of this letter is to tell you some things that I've already said to you but that you might have forgotten. Your mind has been all over the place lately and no wonder...*
>
> *I don't know how long it is since I died, but knowing you, it's probably been a while. You always liked to keep surprises, to delay opening gifts because you said you liked the anticipation more. Savouring the moment, you called it. Just one of the things I love about you... However, I expect you've delayed this moment because you're afraid of opening this last gift from me. You'll open it when the time is right, though. I know that to be true.*
>
> *Ffion, my darling, you need to know that you have been my world. I loved you from our first*

date. Your smile, your laugh, the way you brighten a room just by being in it. The thought of leaving you behind breaks my heart, but what can I do? I've fought as hard as I can but it's got to the point where I have nothing left to give. I could keep trying, keep having operations and more chemo but what will remain? I'm already losing my strength, my memory, my masculinity. I'm no longer the man I was, can no longer scoop you up and take you to bed, make love to you all night long like I used to. I can't drive, can't make a cup of tea without getting tired. I'm so sick of being sick.

You've been incredible, Ffion. You're so brave and strong. The way you've been by my side, fighting with me, caring for me and supporting me has been amazing. Do not ever feel that you let me down or didn't do enough because you have been everything. I know what you're like, I know that you'll pick faults with yourself, look for your weaknesses and flaws but you DO NOT HAVE ANY!!!! You have been my reason for carrying on through the pain and the sickness and the darkness. Without you, I'd have surrendered to this damned disease a long time ago.

I'm not giving up now because I don't want to be here any more; I'm accepting my fate, that my time has come. I want to rage against cancer for taking me away but I don't think either of us will cope with much more. I'm disappearing by the day and so are you, and I don't want that. I want you to remember me as me. I'm depleted now but I wasn't always like that, so please, when you think of me, let it be Graeme your friend, lover and husband. The man I was before all this.

I could go on and on but my eyes hurt and my hand aches and I've had to take a few breaks anyway just to try to remember the words I want to use.

Just, please, don't ever forget that I love you. We had something special, Ffi, but it doesn't mean that you won't find that again. Part of me hates the idea of you with someone else but the biggest part of me is desperate to know that you will go on, that you will be happy again and that you will love. You have a big heart, you are a wonderful woman and you deserve to live a full life.

For everything you have given me, I thank you. For the laughter, the tears, the happy home, the passion, the time, the friendship, the love.

I am holding peace in my heart now, letting go as I need to do, and when you are ready to move on, you will too.

The notebook is for you to fill with good things about your life after me. We have thousands of memories but you will forge new ones. Make them good, my love, and write them down so you don't forget. Every day, even just one line about something that made you smile will be a positive step. It will help you, I hope, to see that there is life after us, that you can be happy without me around.

Please find joy, my beautiful wife. Honour what we had by living. Make me proud.

Love you forever.

Your Graeme XXX

Ffion picked up the book, placed the note inside it, then she lay down on the bed and cried.

Chapter Twenty-Nine

The next day, Ffion dressed in her running gear, packed the notebook and a pen in a small rucksack and set off along the coastal path. She warmed up then started to run, feeling her limbs loosen and her heart beat faster, enjoying the sensations for what they were: proof of life.

Before leaving the cottage she had sent a text to Joe, letting him know that she was going for a Monday morning run along the path and that she'd be at the picnic spot – hopefully seagull-free by now – at ten if he wanted to talk.

When she got there, she stretched for a bit then sat on the bench and pulled out her notebook. The letter was folded safely inside the back cover where there was a pocket, almost as if it was made for holding Graeme's letter.

She pulled the lid off the pen she'd packed and chewed on the end. Graeme wanted her to live, had asked her to be happy. The guilt she'd felt for so long about surviving him was pointless – disrespectful, even – when her husband had asked her to go on, to live a full life, to be happy as he wanted her to be.

Every day, she would write about something that gave her joy until the book was full. She would do that for Graeme and for herself, too.

What made her happy?

Looking down at her blue running tights and the sparkly trainers Mari had got her for her birthday, at the fancy watch her parents had bought her that tracked her heartbeat and daily steps, her heart squeezed.

Running!

Today's entry would be about running and everything it had come to mean to her.

Ffion started to write, filling the blank page with words about how good running made her feel, what she liked about it and how far she had come. So lost was she in writing that she didn't hear the footsteps approaching until Joe and Odin had joined her.

Joe sat opposite her on the picnic bench and Odin plonked himself at Joe's feet. Joe smiled but his eyes were wary, as if he wasn't sure what to expect. As if he was worried that this was the end even though they'd barely begun.

She closed the notebook and put the lid on the pen. 'Hi.'

'Hi.'

'Joe, I'm so sorry—'

He held up a hand. 'It's OK, Ffion. You told me early on that things were complicated and now I know the full story, I understand.'

'Oh…' She swallowed. 'Actually, I wanted to say sorry for leaving yesterday morning. I panicked, felt the need to flee, but I just needed some time to think. Then I found this…' She gestured at the notebook. 'And a letter from Graeme. This was his last gift for me and I couldn't bear to open it before, so it's been buried in a plastic storage box under some of my things.'

'What made you open it now?' he asked, his brow furrowing.

'What do you think?' She got up and walked around the bench to sit next to him. 'I had reached a turning point where I had to choose between life and no life, between love and emptiness.'

She took his face in her hands, felt the heat of his skin, his pulse beneath her fingertips. He gazed at her, his eyes filled with emotion, with affection, with her.

'What did you choose?' he whispered.

'I choose to live and to love.'

'To love?'

'Yes.'

He stood up, taking her hands in his.

'I love you, Joe. I want everything we can have together. I want to be me, Ffion, with you by my side. If you want me, too. I mean… I would understand if you didn't after how I left.'

He stared at her, chewed at his bottom lip, sighed.

'Ffion… I love you too. Of course I do.'

He wrapped his arms around her and kissed her until she was dizzy with desire and love, then she rested her head against his chest, feeling the reassuring beat of his heart. Something nudged her leg and she looked down to find Odin pawing her, wanting to be part of the moment too.

Ffion had lost the man she'd loved but he would always have a place in her heart.

However, there was room in her heart for Joe too, and she was ready now to embrace that love and all the joy it would bring.

'I wish there was a way to get you home quickly,' Joe said, his blue eyes filled with mischief. 'I think we have some unfinished business to attend to.'

'I think we do.' Ffion grinned. 'Fancy a run?'

Epilogue

'Hey you,' Ffion said, as Joe opened his front door.

'Good afternoon, gorgeous. I missed you.'

'I've only been gone four hours.'

He laughed and reached for her, pulling her into a hug.

'Anyway, what was so urgent?' Ffion asked. 'I barely managed to finish my Bakewell tart and latte at the cafe. Mari was still tucking into her toastie.' She'd left Joe that morning to meet Mari and catch up as she hadn't seen her that week.

Joe gave her a crooked smile. 'I have a surprise for you.'

Ffion's stomach flipped. 'A surprise? You know I love surprises.'

And she did. In the five weeks since the sponsored run, Joe had surprised her many times with picnics on the beautiful beaches around Cariad Cove, with meals at fancy restaurants in Swansea city centre, with new designer running gear that he told her he'd seen and couldn't not get for her and with how wonderful he was in so many ways. They had continued to run together and with the Cariad Cove running club that met on Sunday mornings. They had just over thirty members now and received more applications by the day. It was great fun running with other people and they'd already been able to start putting money aside from the membership fees ready to donate to the sanctuary, just as Liberty the photographer had suggested. Ffion hadn't seen her again but hoped that she would.

'I was going to wait until the summer holidays to share this surprise with you, but the longer time went on, the more I couldn't wait.'

Ffion placed a hand on her chest. 'I'm nervous now, Joe.'

'Don't be.' He tipped her chin and kissed her, sliding his hands through her hair and making goosebumps rise all over her skin.

'Is it that kind of surprise?' she asked huskily and he chuckled.

'Not yet. Later for that.'

'Spoilsport.' She pulled his head down and kissed him hard.

'OK, not that much later but not quite yet.'

'I'll hold you to that.'

'Come on then, I have to show you and see what you think.'

'Is it inside?' She tried to peer around him but he blocked the doorway.

'Yes, in the lounge.'

Joe had worked hard in the evenings and at weekends to finish decorating his lounge and Ffion had helped him to pick colours and soft furnishings. He'd picked up a sofa and two chairs from an upcycling shop that had opened nearby and Ffion loved how colourful they were, both decorated with bright patchwork material, their legs carved from polished mahogany, their cushions large and comfy. Joe had also asked her to help him choose other items for the cottage and together they'd made it into a home. There were a few things still to finish but most of the rooms were done and Ffion loved staying there with Joe and Odin where she felt relaxed at and home.

'Is it a new lamp?' Ffion asked as they entered the cool hallway and she kicked off her shoes before following Joe to the lounge.

'Nope.'

'A new... rug?'

'Nope.' He flashed her a mischievous grin.

'A new TV?'

'Nope. You know I only recently bought a TV.'

'Yes but the amount of drool on it from Odin means it's like watching movies through a smoke screen.'

Joe laughed. 'That's a bit of an exaggeration and I do clean it daily.'

Ffion grabbed his hand. 'I'm just teasing you.'

'I know and I like it.'

He placed a finger on his lips then pushed the door to the lounge open. He entered the room slowly, so she did the same.

'Ffion,' he whispered. 'I'd like you to meet our new family member.'

Ffion's mouth fell open and her vision blurred, and not just because Joe had said *our* family member. She blinked to clear her eyes and gazed at the scene before her.

On the sofa, snuggled up together like lifelong companions, were Odin and Beatrix. The cat was purring loudly and Odin was snoring like a steam train.

'Beatrix... has come to stay?'

'For good.'

'You've adopted her?'

'Yes. Well... I was hoping that could be *we*. I know how fond you and Beatrix are of each other.'

'I love her.' Ffion sucked in a shaky breath. 'I just…
I didn't think I could adopt her because I don't have
my own home yet and can't have her at Mam and Dad's
because Dad is allergic and… now she's here.'

She turned to Joe and buried her face in his T-shirt.
Then a thought came to her. 'But how are they already
such good friends?'

'Well… I've been planning this for a while and so I've
been letting Odin and Beatrix get to know each other up
at the sanctuary. We spent time with her almost every day
and the soppy pair get on really well.'

'This is just amazing, Joe. Thank you so much. I was
hoping that she'd find a home and yet worried that she'd
be adopted by someone else and I'd never see her again.'

'That's not going to happen now. Go and say hello.'

'Yes.' Ffion gave him a quick kiss then approached the
sofa and sat down carefully next to Beatrix. Odin peered
up at her, not halting his snoring but his tail thumped
against the cushion. Ffion ran a hand over the cat's fur
and Beatrix stretched, got up and rubbed her head against
Ffion's hand, turning so Ffion could stroke her from head
to tail. 'Hello Beatrix. You're finally home.'

Beatrix flopped onto her side against Odin and Ffion
continued to stroke her, love filling her heart for the cat,
the dog and most of all, for Joe. She had a feeling that
there was nothing he wouldn't do to make her happy and
wondered how she'd got so lucky.

'Well, I'm feeling pretty pleased with myself.' Joe sat on
one of the chairs and folded his hands in his lap. 'Looks
like that was a good move.'

'You have no idea how happy this makes me.'

'I think I have an inkling.' He winked at her then leant forwards and rested his arms on his knees. 'How was Mari?'

Ffion hugged herself. 'She's so much happier. I know it's early days for her and Bryn but they're getting on much better and have started couples' counselling. Bryn made a lot of promises but Mari wanted them to become better at communicating and so they're seeing a professional to help them to work things through.'

'That's probably a good move.' Joe rubbed at his chin. 'At least the chance of things slipping again will be reduced by setting some ground rules.'

'I feel for them because no one wants to end up in couples' counselling but if there's a problem and they want to save their marriage, then that's what they need to do.'

Joe got up and came over to the sofa, kneeling down in front of Ffion. He took her hand. 'I would go to counselling with you if we ever needed to sort something out.'

Ffion caressed his face, gazing into his blue eyes. Joe was an open book and she knew that what he said was true. 'So would I. What we have is worth fighting for.'

'I'm grateful every day that you came into my life.'

'And all because of Odin and running.' Ffion laughed.

'I love hearing you laugh.'

'I love you.'

Joe wrapped his arms around Ffion and they kissed, then she rested her head on his shoulder, treasuring the security she felt in his arms when she could lose herself in his scent and feel the steady beat of his heart.

'I was going to ask if you fancied going for a run but I think that can wait until tomorrow.' Joe stood up and pulled Ffion up by her hand. 'These two are very ontented there together and I don't think they'll notice if we slip away for a while, do you?'

'I don't think they'll notice at all.'

Joe led her to the doorway and she paused to look back at Odin and Beatrix, two creatures she would once have considered an unlikely pair. But then, she never would have imagined herself as a keen runner, falling in love with a teacher from Wales or deciding to settle back in Cariad Cove. She still hadn't made a decision about what she would do workwise but she had time for that and she was growing stronger by the day, becoming the woman she now knew she could be. Life had dealt her some blows but she was still standing, happy and healthy, and rebuilding her life.

There was much to be thankful for. She truly believed she had a future ahead of her and it was all because she'd decided to come home to Cariad Cove.

Acknowledgements

My thanks go to:

My husband and children, for your love, support and encouragement. You – and the dogs, of course – are my everything. Special thanks to my darling girl, Molly, for being my running buddy – it's always more fun with you at my side – and to my amazing son, Dylan, for encouraging me to keep going!

My wonderful agent, Amanda Preston, and the LBA team.

The fabulous team at Canelo – with special thanks to my lovely editor, Emily Bedford, for your encouragement, enthusiasm and insightful suggestions, and also Fran Riccardi, Louise Cullen and Iain Millar. It's always a pleasure to work with you all.

My dear friends for your love and support over the years – and in no particular order – Sarah, Dawn, Deb, Ann, Sam, Clare, Yvonne, Emma, Kelly and Caryn for always being there.

A lovely lady I've known for many years – Sally-anne Atkinson. Huge thanks for helping me with English/Welsh translations for Cariad Cove (Cildraeth Cariad) and Barddoniaeth Bay (Bae Barddoniaeth). I know how busy you are and I'm very grateful for your time and help.

My very supportive author and blogger friends. You are all amazing!

The wonderful charities Greyhound Rescue Wales and Hope Rescue for the incredible work they do every single day.

All the readers who take the time to read, write reviews and share the book love. I hope you enjoy this story.

And finally, huge thanks to the NHS – for many reasons, but especially for the Couch to 5K app. This app helped me start running, and the running, in turn, helped me through a difficult time.

Right, time to put my trainers on and get out there… ☺